PASSIONATE PROTECTION

Jonah arched to remove bullets from his belt, and his body ground against her. She caught her breath as he loaded the pistol, suddenly feeling the heat of his body. She felt the wall she had erected around her feelings begin to crack and crumble. She moved her head the merest bit to rest her cheek against the roughness of his jacket. "I've never had anyone shoot at me before," she managed to say.

"I have." Jonah released the hammer of his gun and rested his chin on the top of her head, his arms going around her. "Don't be frightened. I won't let anyone hurt you."

When she tilted her head and looked into his eyes, the rifleman was forgotten, and all she could think of was the male body pressed against hers. Sweetness, raw and deep, wound its way through her, and she wanted to hold on to the moment forever.

MOON RACER

CONSTANCE O'BANYON

LEISURE BOOKS NEW YORK CITY

A LEISURE BOOK®

August 2003

Published by

Dorchester Publishing Co., Inc.
276 Fifth Avenue
New York, NY 10001

ISBN 0-8439-5188-5

The name "Leisure Books" and the stylized "L" with design are
trademarks of Dorchester Publishing Co., Inc.

Printed in the United States of America.

Cameron Melton, this is your book, my sweet granddaughter. You may have had to wait longer than the others because you are the youngest, but last is not least, and you are so much in my heart. This proud grandmother cherishes you every day.

Randal Henderson, has anyone ever told you how wonderful you are? If they should want to know, let them ask your Aunt Constance.

To the real Navidad, Christmas, who touched my family's life in ways he can't imagine. You are an angel who came along when we needed you the most. Your kindness could not be captured on the pages of this book, but I had to give you a voice, and my family's deep gratitude.

MOON
RACER

Prologue

Texas, 1870

The wind was cold and damp as it whipped Abigail Hunter's tangled hair across her face. Her body was still and her small hands were twisted into tight knots at her sides until her brother Brent took them and held them firmly in his strong grip.

For eight-year-old Abby the last two days had been confusing and devastating. Tragedy had struck their family at its very heart, and she wondered how it was possible to hurt so badly and still live.

Through blinding tears she stared at the simple pine box that held her mother's remains. Since there were no flowers to be had this time of year, Abby had woven her pink hair ribbons through a branch of live oak, and Quince had placed it on the coffin for her—a pitiful tribute to a woman who had so dearly loved flowers.

The men who worked for the Half-Moon Ranch were gathered near the family, their hats removed, their heads bowed. The foreman, Buck, met Abby's eyes sadly and nodded slightly. Charley Herbert, the barber and undertaker, was there, standing off to the side, but still a grim reminder to the young girl that he was the one who had brought the coffin to the ranch.

Reverend Crawford was praising Beth Hunter's virtues. Although the preacher was sincere, his words meant nothing to Abby. He didn't know how gentle their mother's touch had been, or how it had comforted Abby through so many illnesses—he couldn't tell the mourners how soothing her mother's voice had been, or the patience she had used when Abby had needed guidance—and Abby was always needing guidance. All that was her mother was gone forever, stilled by death's hateful hand.

The reverend was assuring Abby and her brothers that their mother had gone to a better place. But wouldn't it have been better for all of them if she had remained with the family on the Half-Moon Ranch? So many dilemmas tore at her mind, and questions nagged at her that only her mother could answer.

The young girl glanced, in turn, at each of her three older brothers and saw the same grief she felt reflected in their eyes. Brent was now gripping her hand so tightly it hurt, but the discomfort helped her think about something other than the anguish that tore at her heart. She watched her brother Quince's hand tremble from the effort he was making not to cry. Her brother Matt stood alone, stoic and silent, solitary in his grief. She knew he had cut himself off from the rest of them so he could better control his sorrow.

Conspicuously absent from the grieving family grouped around the grave site was Abby's father, Jack Hunter. Abby glanced slowly up at Brent to find him watching her with concern. At twenty, he was the eldest, and it would probably fall to him to keep the family together. A sob escaped her throat, and Quince touched her on the shoulder and patted it several times. She suddenly felt her stomach churn; she was sickened and shaken to the very core of her being.

It was difficult to understand the horror of what her father had done. How could he shoot and kill her mother, when to Abby's knowledge he had never even raised his hand to her in anger? Brent said it was because he was drunk, but Abby couldn't imagine that drinking would make a man want to kill someone he loved.

Reluctantly her eyes strayed back to the coffin. Then she glanced at the crowd of people that stretched all the way to the road. Matt had earlier declared that they had come only to stare at a murderer's family, but Abby was sure they were there to pay their respects to her mother.

She met Iona Montgomery's gaze and saw the sadness and compassion in the older woman's eyes.

Mrs. Montgomery had been her mother's best friend, and it was comforting to have her there. Her daughter, Juliana, gave Abby a sympathetic smile, and Abby managed to smile slightly in return. Then her attention was drawn to Edmund Montgomery, Juliana's stepfather, who owned the only bank in Diablo. He nodded at Abby and held her gaze for a moment. She stepped closer to Brent and lowered her head. She always felt uneasy around Mr. Montgomery, even though she didn't understand why.

The reverend had finished the eulogy and was talking in a quiet voice with Brent, but Abby wasn't listening. She was watching their friends and neighbors walking to their buggies, some of them already leaving without speaking to the family. The wind kicked up more, and Abby shivered.

Matt knelt down beside her and wrapped his coat about her shoulders, then held her close to his body to get her warm. Finally he took one of Abby's hands, and Quince took the other.

Abby was unaware that people were whispering and gossiping about her family, their heads nodding, their mouths pursed in disapproval. She was too young to realize that, in the years to come, the cruelty of those same people would surround her and exclude her from their inner circles. She saw only the three men with shovels standing off to the side, and she shuddered with dread as Charley Herbert gave them instructions. She shook her head in horror—those men were going to lower her mother's body into the ground and cover it with dirt!

She felt desperate. Jerking free of her brothers, she ran toward her mother's coffin, determined to stop the men. It was Quince who caught up with her and went down on his knees, holding her close.

"You have to let her go, darlin'." There were tears in his green eyes, eyes that looked so much like their mother's. "We all have to let her go."

Quince held her, speaking comforting words until she stopped trembling. Finally she wiped her tears on the back of her hand, and he led her back to the others.

Matt pulled her aside and bent down to her. "Abby, I won't be going back to the house with you. I've already told Brent and Quince, and I wanted you to know, too—I'm leaving. It'll be a long time before I come back."

Her eyes filled with fresh tears. "Mama's gone, and now you're leaving, too? Please don't go away!"

There was incredible sadness in his eyes. "You are so young and may not understand this, but if I stay, I'll probably do something I'll regret."

She touched his face, then slid her arms around his neck. "I understand better than you think—you're afraid you'd do something to hurt Papa for what he did to Mama, aren't you?"

He hesitated for a moment, then nodded.

"Will you write me?"

He eased her arms from around his neck and stood. "I'm not much for letters, Abby."

When she would have given him back his coat, he shook his head and buttoned it at her throat. "Take care of yourself, sweetheart. I know it seems like your world has turned upside down. Time passes, and wounds heal. Trust me."

She watched Matt walk away and mount his horse; she didn't take her gaze off him until he disappeared from sight. She already missed him, and she wondered if she would ever see him again.

Brent put his arm around Abby while Quince walked beside them toward the ranch house, their grief too deep, their hurt too new to put into words. The day was gray, and her heart was empty . . . cold . . . broken.

Her attention was drawn to the ranch hands ambling toward the house. The Montgomerys and a few other friends walked behind them. She wiped her eyes and closed them, but tears still seeped between her lids and ran down her cheeks. She wanted the comfort that only her mother could give her.

Matt had told her to give it time, but time would not bring her mother back, and time would never wash the blood off her father's hands.

Chapter One

Hill Country of Texas, 1880

"Abigail Hunter, where are you?"

The housekeeper's high-pitched voice reached Abby just as she opened the front door, so she quickly stepped outside, taking pains not to let the screen door slam behind her. Although she tried to move silently, her boots clomped across the wooden planks of the porch, and she groaned.

"I'm out here," she answered in a fatalistic tone, knowing nothing short of death would stop Frances from having her say.

While waiting for the housekeeper, Abby braced her hands on the railing and breathed in the heat of the early-morning air. There wasn't enough breeze to stir the leaves on the oak tree near the barn. The

7

thin, ragged clouds showed no evidence of the rainstorm that had struck with such force around midnight.

Thinking about the troubles that faced her family, she gripped the railing until her fingernails dug into the wood. Matt was still in England, and no one knew when he would come home, or if he ever would. Brent and Quince were married and had moved out of the house, leaving her alone to contend with their father, now that he'd come home from prison.

She had tried to forgive him for what he had done to her mother, but it was hard. Abby wanted to love him, but Jack Hunter was not an easy man to love. And in truth, she resented the way he had moved back into their lives, demanding that they do things his way. While he had been in prison they had managed to scrape by just fine without him. Recently he had borrowed money from the bank to buy land they didn't need and horses that they couldn't afford. None of them knew what their father would do next to throw their lives into chaos.

She drew in a cleansing breath, her mind moving on to other matters—the tension between Brent and Quince had lessened a bit, and she was glad of that. Both of them worked hard to keep the bank from foreclosing on the Half-Moon, but they had different opinions on how that should be accomplished.

Abby looked toward the paddock, where two blooded foals sired by her stallion, Moon Racer, frolicked through the high grass along with the cow ponies that were Brent's dream for the future. Wild mustangs grazed in the pasture just beyond the barn, Quince's contribution to the ranch.

She sighed. Stubbornness ran deep in the Hunter family—she had a wide streak of it herself. As a result of Brent's dedicated management and the army contract Quince had acquired because of his friendship with one of the officers at Fort Griffin, they had been able to make the last two bank payments. She glanced down at her trousers with a pragmatic frown. Even if she was a girl, there were a few things she could do to help her brothers. Without the encumbrance of modesty, she knew that she could train cutting horses as well as any man, probably better than most. She had broken her first of many horses at the age of twelve, and she was about to break another.

The screen door whooshed open, jarred against the house, then slammed shut, and Frances appeared. Aggressively wiping her hands on her stained apron, the middle-aged, sturdily built woman looked formidable until Abby saw the concern reflected in her faded blue eyes. The housekeeper never failed to speak her mind and to give the family her opinion on any given subject. And from the frown of disapproval Abby saw on Frances's face, she knew she was about to receive the benefit of that advice.

"I see where your mind's taking you, young lady. I knew when I told you about Nate Johnson's horse, you was gonna try and break him. Were you listening when I told you he'd already throwed Curly and Red? Brent says the animal can't be broke, and he's sending him back to the Circle J with his regrets."

"Brent also says that I shouldn't argue with a mule, a skunk, or with you, Frances."

"Abby!"

She had never been able to get around Frances with flattery, but she always made the attempt. Cunningly, she tried to smile, but the best she could manage was a slight curve of her lower lip. "Your biscuits were delicious, as usual, and your grape preserves were the best I ever tasted. Is that the same recipe you used last year?"

Frances's hands went immediately to her hips. "Don't think I don't know your tactics by now, Abigail! Never you mind about my preserves—you aren't gonna ride that horse if I have any say about it."

Abby's mouth settled into a firm line before she said, "Mr. Johnson will pay good money if we break that horse. Brent gave up too easily."

"Lord have mercy, Abby, you're eighteen years old! You've gotta quit strutting 'round in britches and acting like you could stand toe-to-toe with the menfolk. Don't you think it's time to start acting like a lady?"

Abby had a vague memory of her mother's gentle instructions. Mama had urged her to sit straight with her hands folded in her lap, to stand tall and not allow her shoulders to slump. She remembered her mother saying how important it was for a lady to always have a lace handkerchief with her. There were other instructions her mother had given her on proper behavior, but Abby just could not remember them all, and she certainly had no use for a lace handkerchief. Her brothers needed her help around the ranch, and she had no time for such niceties anyway.

"You'll never catch a husband behaving the way you do. When a man's looking for a wife, he wants someone who is soft and sweet and kinda humble."

Abby raised her chin stubbornly. "I wouldn't give you that," she declared, snapping her fingers, "for a man who would require me to be sweet and witless." She smiled guilefully. "Besides, why would I need a husband telling me what to do when I have you for that, Frances?"

"Harrumph. I blame Brent for the way you turned out. He let you run wild, doing whatever pleased you. He used a light hand with you 'cause you lost your ma."

"I didn't lose my mama; Papa killed her," she said bleakly.

Frances shook her head. "Have a care what you say, miss—your pa's done his time."

"Papa may have served his time according to the law, but how can I forgive him for what he did?"

The housekeeper's eyes softened when she reflected on all Abby had endured during her young life. Although Frances had not worked for the family until after Beth Hunter's death, she knew the way people hereabouts treated the young girl—they refused to let their daughters befriend her, and they certainly wouldn't allow their sons anywhere near her. Frances had watched Abby pull further into herself each time someone in town snubbed her. She had buried her anguish deep so her brothers wouldn't notice how hurt she was by the rejections of their neighbors. Now, as if Abby's life hadn't been complicated enough, her father had been released from prison, giving their neighbors another reason to turn their backs on her. Frances suspected that Abby chose to wear trousers to play down the fact that she was a woman. It was no wonder she didn't realize that she was on the verge of being beautiful; there was no one around to admire her. But Frances was determined to guide the young, motherless woman, if she could get through to her.

"Look at how happy Brent and Quince are now that they're married, and Brent about to be a father. Don't you want that same kind of life for yourself, Abby?"

"I'd rather be like my brother Matt, who has no responsibilities and will probably never come home, and why should he? At least he doesn't have to worry about foreclosures in England."

Frances touched Abby's shoulder. "Someday a man will come along who'll be worthy of you, and you'll want to change to please him."

"I like horses better than men—you feed them, water them, give them a good rubdown, and in return they give you all their affection."

"That's not far off from what a husband would do for you if you rubbed him down."

"I don't want to talk about this anymore," Abby said crisply.

The housekeeper looked at her suspiciously. "You aren't gonna try and ride that horse, are you?"

Abby stepped off the porch, adjusting her battered hat at just the right angle to protect her eyes from the sun. "I haven't made up my mind yet. But if I do, he won't throw me like he did Curly and Red."

She didn't need to see Frances's face to know she was scowling at her. She did hear the loud huff as the housekeeper stomped back into the house, letting the screen door snap shut behind her.

The high-pitched cry of a hawk penetrated the silence of the land as the winged predator rode the wind currents on a quest for small game. Moments later the hawk's cry was muffled by the thundering hooves of three horses, ridden by uniformed soldiers who wore the insignia of the Sixth Cavalry.

The eldest of the trio, Sergeant MacDougall, was a man of medium height who had a shock of white hair that had once been as red as a rooster's comb. He tugged his cap low over his forehead; much to his disgust, he knew his skin would still burn if exposed to the punishing Texas sun. For twenty years he had lived the nomadic life of a cavalryman, had fought in many fierce campaigns, and was thankful he had lived to tell about them—which he did often, in glowing and exaggerated terms. His hitch would be up in another two months, and he'd decided that he was too old to reenlist this time. There was a small stretch of land back in Tennessee he wanted to buy so he could spend the rest of his years sitting on the front porch swapping tales with his neighbors.

His bushy brows came together across his nose and formed a frown when he glanced at Private Davies, who was one of his newest recruits. The lad was not yet accustomed to the discipline of army life. He was straight off a Georgia farm and as raw as they came. It was always the same with the new ones, but MacDougall knew he would either make a cavalry-man out of the lad or break him completely.

The sergeant's gaze moved to the commanding officer, who rode between them. Maj. Jonah Tremain sat high in the saddle, his blue eyes squinting against the brightness of the sun. There was a restlessness in the major that didn't fit with the usual West Point polish, and he carried himself with an aloofness that intimidated most men—but not the sergeant.

MacDougall didn't generally like officers, but this one was different. He was tough when he had to be and set strict standards of discipline for his men to follow. MacDougall had fought in three campaigns with Major Tremain. He knew the officer never asked a soldier under his command to do anything he wasn't willing to do himself. He always stood shoulder-to-shoulder with his men and went right into the thick of battle with them. Oh, he was a strictly by-the-book officer, all right, but he didn't mind getting a little dirt on himself. MacDougall had asked for, and been granted, a transfer from Fort Griffin to Fort Fannin when the major had been given the command there.

At the moment Major Tremain had a lot of problems on his young shoulders. Fort Fannin was a post needing a strong man at its head. The previous commander, Captain Gregory, had been cashiered out of the army and was now doing prison time for corruption. The real trouble was that three of the payrolls destined for Fort Fannin had been stolen, and Major Tremain was determined to find out who was behind the robberies. So far the investigation had not turned up any of Captain Gregory's accomplices, and the captain wasn't talking from his prison cell.

Sweat rolled down MacDougall's face, and he cursed silently. He wished the major, who kept his coat buttoned to regulations, would begin to feel the heat and allow them to shed theirs.

As if Jonah had read MacDougall's mind, he held up his gloved hand for them to halt. "Let's get comfortable for now. However, I'll expect the two of you to be in full uniform when you ride into Diablo."

Jonah unfastened the brass buttons and slipped out of his blue uniform coat. Folding it neatly, he secured it to the back of his saddle. He watched as the other two men did the same.

"Major, sir," the private stated, loosening the top button of his shirt as well, "I never knew Texas was this green till I saw Fort Fannin."

Jonah dismounted at the edge of the cliff and propped a polished black boot on a limestone boulder. He glanced at the hills that seemed to roll one into another for as far as he could see. "I know what you mean, Private—this part of Texas took me by surprise when I first saw it."

"I don't like it much here," Davies stated. "It's too hot, and nothing like back home."

MacDougall scowled as he wiped his mouth after taking a drink from his canteen. "You aren't here to like or dislike anything, soldier—you're here to do just what the major wants you to do and nothing more."

"Yes, sir." The young recruit's glance went nervously to his commanding officer. "Major, sir, can I ask how far it is to this town we're going to?"

"Diablo should be no more than a few miles ahead, Private." Jonah rested his arm on the saddle, then leaned closer to MacDougall so the younger man couldn't overhear. "This is where we part company. I'll meet you in Diablo in two or three days. Meantime, poke around town in an unofficial capacity. I still have a gut feeling the payroll robberies are somehow connected to someone in Diablo."

MacDougall nodded. "I wonder how many more men besides Captain Gregory are involved? It sure seems that the information about the shipment is coming out of Diablo."

"I have come to that same conclusion. I can't tell you any more than that—not yet, anyway. I *can* tell you that I want your uniforms visible in Diablo. Let's see if we can shake the trees and make someone nervous."

"I'll make sure we're noticed, all right, sir. You can depend on it."

MacDougall watched Jonah hoist himself into the saddle, then met his piercing blue eyes. "When you see Quince Hunter, would you mind giving him my regards, sir? And tell him since he quit scouting for us, I hardly ever lose at poker."

Jonah gave him a brief nod. "Should you need me for any reason, I'll be at the Half-Moon Ranch. Ask around; anyone can give you directions."

MacDougall and Davies saluted as they watched the major ride away.

"I'm glad he's gone. It makes me nervous when he's 'round," Davies admitted, dabbing the sweat from his brow. "It seems to me he thinks mighty highly of himself."

MacDougall whipped around and glared at the private, his voice cracking like a whip. "You have a lot more to be nervous about with me, trooper. If I ever hear you speak ill of Major Tremain again, you'll be looking through the bars of a guardhouse from the inside out."

"Sir, I didn't mean no disrespect," Davies said quickly, glancing down at the ground. He knew that the major had brought Sergeant MacDougall with him when he was transferred from Fort Griffin, and he should have realized that the sergeant would defend their commander.

"That gentleman," MacDougall said as he watched Jonah disappear behind an oak grove, "is one of the finest officers you'll ever serve under. If you weren't such an undisciplined, misguided chawbacon, you'd know that. When we get back to the fort, I'll see that you have extra duty so you can think about your attitude."

Davies lapsed into silence and mounted his horse. He'd have to be on his best behavior during the rest of this assignment so he could convince the sergeant that he was worthy of the Sixth Cavalry.

Jonah slowed his horse to a canter. It was only midmorning and already as hot as hell. He had a momentary reprieve from the heat when a high-flying cloud lingered between him and the sun. He took in the scenery, appreciating the wild, untamed beauty of the land that was infused with the brilliant colors of an artist's palette.

A feeling of unease had been stirring within him all morning, and he felt as if something was about to happen—something he would have no control over—something that would change his life forever. He had experienced this same sensation only one other time—the day he'd almost lost his life in an Indian battle. He suddenly nudged his horse into a gallop and prayed that another cloud would pass between him and the sweltering sun.

By nature Jonah was not superstitious, but he could feel his life hurtling toward something. The feeling lingered, troubling his mind.

Chapter Two

Abby dismounted beneath the sturdy live oak and dropped Moon Racer's reins, knowing her horse would graze contentedly until she was ready to leave. She grasped a low-hanging branch and hoisted herself upward into the dense growth of prickly leaves, as she had done many times before. She climbed until she came to her favorite spot. It had always been her refuge when she needed to shut out the rest of the world—a place to gather her thoughts or just to ponder her day-to-day life, undisturbed.

She settled comfortably where two branches arched together, creating a secluded space among the dense foliage. She held her breath when a white-winged dove landed on the branch just above her, and she remained perfectly still to observe the extraordinary phenomenon. She became fascinated when the bird gracefully fanned its elegant feathers and tucked its head amid the softness. Abby shifted her weight only slightly, but it was enough to startle the dove, and it took flight. She shook her head and sighed with regret.

The storm the night before had made the air smell fresh and clean, but it had done little to cool the temperature. If anything it had elevated the humidity considerably, and her shirt was plastered to her body with sweat.

She allowed her gaze to wander. As far as the eye could see was Hunter land, she thought with pride. She was a part of this land; it was in her blood.

Her horse whinnied, drawing her attention. No one seeing Moon Racer today would guess that the stallion had almost died when he was a colt. His mother had been attacked and killed by a wolf pack, but somehow Moon Racer had escaped with only minor wounds. The owner had given the foal to Brent, thinking it wouldn't live, and Brent hadn't thought so either when he had given it to Abby.

At that time she had practically lived in the stable, unwaveringly determined to keep the colt alive. She had bottle-fed him and rubbed him down several times a day. She had even slept beside him at night and covered them both with a blanket.

Today the beautiful roan stood sixteen hands high—he had a white blaze on his forehead and four white stocking feet. His bloodline was flawless: his dam had been the famous Calliope, who had never lost a race; his sire, Tucan Runner, had a lineage that went all the way back to champion Spanish stock.

Moon Racer could outrun any horse in their stable, but Brent didn't want him entered in any races, and neither did Abby. The stallion was too valuable to the Half-Moon as a stud.

The stallion moved down the hill in search of sweeter grass, so Abby continued her musing. This place no longer offered her the emotional comfort it once had. She was lonely and really had no one to confide in. There were times when she wanted someone to share her thoughts and ideas with, but she was totally alone.

With an exasperated sigh, she came to the conclusion that Frances was right: she was getting too old to hide from her troubles like a child. She was a woman now, and she needed to face her problems straight on.

She leaned back for a moment and closed her eyes, freeing herself of her need for this solitary hideaway. After today she would not come there again.

Moon Racer whinnied and stomped his feet, letting Abby know he was ready to return to the stable. She slid downward, caught a branch, and swung toward the ground.

Abby saw a horse just below her, then a flash of blue, but it was too late to stop her descent. Her sudden appearance had startled the animal, and it reared on its hind legs, sending the rider tumbling backward to the ground.

With her heart thundering inside her, she ran forward and bent down beside the man. His eyes were closed, and she was afraid she had killed him. "Sir, are you hurt? Can you hear my voice?" she asked frantically. "Sir, sir!"

He did not move or answer, so she darted to her horse, grabbed her canteen, and ran back to him. When she knelt down beside him, she noticed for the first time that he was a soldier. Placing her hand on his shoulder, she shook him gently, but still he did not respond. In desperation, she unscrewed the cap of her canteen and dashed water in his face. She was overcome with relief when he blinked and slowly opened his eyes.

Staring up at her were a pair of the bluest, angriest eyes Abby had ever seen.

Maj. Jonah Tremain sat up slowly and shook his head to clear it. "Why in the hell did you douse me with water?" he demanded, wiping his sleeve across his wet face.

"I'm sorry, sir," she said. "I thought you were unconscious."

"I wasn't unconscious—I was merely trying to stop the world from spinning and catch my breath."

"I wouldn't wonder." She bit her lower lip. "I didn't see you until it was too late."

Jonah muttered an oath as he rolled to his feet with as much dignity as he could muster. "Dammit, boy—"

"I'm not a boy," she stated with growing irritation. She was beginning to dislike the soldier.

"Well, even so, what did you think you were doing scampering about in that tree? Do you make it a practice to drop down on every unsuspecting traveler who happens by?"

Abby was about to answer him in anger when she saw him limp as he took a step. Guilt-ridden, she reached out and touched his arm. "You're hurt. Lean on me, and I'll help you to your horse—I'll get you to a doctor."

He shook her hand off and studied her warily. "The limp is from an old wound," he clarified. "But if it makes you feel any better, my shoulder will probably be bruised by tomorrow."

She clamped her lips together while she dusted dried grass from her trousers and stared into those cold blue eyes. "I'm so very sorry, sir. It was just an unfortunate mishap."

He gave her his sternest glare as he rubbed his shoulder. "Is there something wrong with your hearing that kept you from picking up the sound of my horse?"

She stared at him grimly. "My mind was on other matters at that time."

"Is that so? What could be so interesting up in that tree to hold the attention of a mere child?"

She raised her gaze to his, anger flushing her face and tightening her throat. "I'm not a boy or a child." Her chin went up higher. "And what I think about or don't think about is none of your concern."

"It is when you involve me in it," he replied, flexing his shoulders and wincing in pain.

"I said I was sorry, sir." But she didn't sound sorry—she sounded impatient and irritated.

She gathered Moon Racer's reins, shoved her booted foot into the stirrup, and swung into the saddle.

Jonah suddenly noticed her mount and reached out to touch the horse's shoulder, allowing his hand to slide up the smooth neck. "This is what I call mighty fine horseflesh."

"Yes," she answered stiffly. "You aren't telling me anything I don't already know."

Jonah suddenly noticed the way the damp shirt revealed the swell of her breasts. How could he have mistaken her for a boy when there was so much evidence to the contrary? It was an honest mistake, he admitted to himself—he had never expected to find a female wearing trousers.

A single long braid hung down her back, and she definitely had the delicate features of a girl. She spoke well enough, but in appearance she resembled a poor sodbuster's daughter. "How did you come by such an animal?"

His question surprised her, and she answered with more civility than she had intended. "He was a gift from my brother."

Jonah knew superior horseflesh when he saw it, and this animal was definitely exceptional. "Would you consider selling him?"

She was looking down at him, her spine straight. "Not at *any* price."

He ran his hand along Moon Racer's shoulder. "Everything has a price."

She had never met a more arrogant man. "No, some things are priceless."

She spun Moon Racer out of his grasp and started to ride away when she saw the man's horse in the distance. It gave her momentary pleasure to think of him limping to catch his mount. But her sense of fairness would not allow her to leave him stranded; after all, she had been responsible for his mishap. She rode up to his horse, stretched forward, gathered up the reins, and led the animal back to the soldier.

Jonah was further irritated because he had landed on his slouch hat and squashed the crease out of it. He was scowling when he recreased it and then adjusted it on his head. He pulled on his jacket and made an attempt to dust the grass off, while ignoring the girl as she tried to hand him the reins of his horse.

Abby's gaze fell on the two gold bars on his shoulders. He wasn't just an ordinary soldier. "I thought officers were supposed to be gentlemen," she blurted out before she could think.

He arched a dark brow and said mockingly, "And so they are . . . if there is a lady about." He swept off his hat with an exaggerated bow that infuriated her even more.

She dropped the reins at his feet. "Good day to you, sir."

Now he was grinning. "*Good-bye* to you, ma'am."

He was standing with his back to the sun, and it suddenly seemed to Abby that he was surrounded by light. The blue of his uniform enhanced the blue of his eyes, and she felt a strange tightening inside her. Bewildered by the new sensation, she wanted only to get away from him.

"If I never see you again, it'll be too soon for me."

His gaze was arrogant, his shoulders tense and straight, when he said, "Amen to that!"

Abby whirled Moon Racer around and galloped toward the house. She frowned when the full impact of what she had done hit her; that officer could have been badly hurt, and it would have been her fault. Then she remembered blue eyes that had gone from angry to mocking, and hoped his shoulder would pain him for some time to come.

She gave a toss of her head. He should have been watching where he was going. And after all, he had been trespassing on Hunter land.

A short time later Abby entered the barn, and she was certainly not in a good mood. With her jaw set firmly, she was more determined than ever that she was going to ride the Johnson horse.

When she heard movement overhead, she glanced up at the loft and saw Navidad pitching hay. When he noticed her he paused at his work, and with a worried look on his dark face, descended the ladder to stand before her.

"Señorita Abby, say to me that you have not come here to ride that bay horse."

Most of the hands that worked on the Half-Moon Ranch were loyal and usually stayed with the family for a long time. Some of them, like Red and Curly, had been there since before Abby was born. She felt affection for them all, but her favorite was Navidad.

The Mexican man had come to work for them five years earlier, and he had an exceptional gift for handling horses. His dark mustache was brushed with gray, and the leathery texture of his skin gave testament to the fact that he spent a lot of time in the sun. The most extraordinary thing about him was the

26

kindness of his nature and the compassion reflected in his dark eyes. He was one of those rare human beings who really cared about people and was always doing good deeds for someone.

He and Abby had forged a special bond from the very beginning, when she had teasingly called him by the English translation of his name. It had pleased him at the time, and the name had stuck, as far as she was concerned.

"Christmas, I had this same argument with Frances this morning, and I don't intend to have it with you. I'm going to ride that bay, and neither you nor anyone else is going to stop me!"

Curly had walked into the barn in time to overhear their conversation. He was tall and muscular, and Abby watched him scratch his head, then shake it before he spoke. "Don't guess it would do any good for me to try and talk you out of ridin' that horse if Frances couldn't. That woman is so cantankerous she could curdle cream."

"I would not think to argue with you, Señorita Abby. I am only asking you, do not do this," Navidad implored, the worry lines deepening in his forehead. "Señor Brent will not be glad with me if you ride that horse."

"Yep," Curly added. "Brent's already told me to take the gelding back to the Circle J this very day." He gave Abby a guarded look, and then he went even farther. "Brent gets plumb mad when you put yourself in danger. You know how he is."

Yes, she knew how Brent was. He had taken care of her when everyone else had gone away—he was the one person who had remained constant in her life, until he had moved to the cabin by the creek so he wouldn't have to be near their father. When he had first departed the family home, she had felt betrayed and deserted but had finally come to understand why Brent had left. Although she herself could never leave, she had discovered that by keeping busy, she could avoid being in her father's company for days at a time.

Her thoughts went back to the Johnson horse. "Neither of you has anything to worry about; I'll take the blame if Brent gets mad. Besides, I don't think that horse can throw me." With a determined resolve, she shoved her hat more firmly on her head and poked her thick, dark braid underneath the brim so it would stay in place. "Do either of you have any more objections?"

Navidad seemed to want to say more, but instead he looked away from her.

Curly, however, threw his hands in the air as if surrendering and shook his head. He knew that when a Hunter got set on something, there was no point arguing, and Abby was the most stubborn of them all. "No, ma'am! No, sirree. Not me. I just work here."

She stalked to the tack room, where she found her well-worn tan chaps hanging on a peg. With expert ease she fastened the belt around her waist and hooked the buckles about her trouser-clad legs. When she reappeared, Navidad was leaning against the pitchfork. He watched as she grabbed the bit and bridle from a hook.

"Christmas, will you help me saddle him?"

Resigned, the Mexican nodded and followed her out into the sunlight while Curly ambled along behind them.

Abby paused at the fence to admire the reddish-colored gelding as he defiantly tossed his black mane. She placed her folded arms on the top rung and rested her chin on her sleeve, studying the bay's movements in an attempt to take his measure. He had a wild look in his eyes and a proud tilt to his head as he went on a quest to find an opening in the fence. She considered his stride and even the twitch of his muscles.

"Why did Brent decide the horse can't be broken?" she asked.

Curly scratched his head ponderously, a habit he had developed over the years. " 'Cause he throwed me and Red afore we could even settle in the saddle. I gave up on the third try; Red stayed for four."

"So," she observed, her eyes never leaving the horse, "he is a spinner."

"You got that right—ain't no one gonna get in the saddle, much less break that devil." Curly nodded at her. "Not even you."

Abby watched the horse for a few moments more, then climbed over the fence and dropped down on the other side. "I'll just see if I can take some of the fight out of him."

Navidad hoisted her saddle on his shoulder and followed her over the fence. "I will be sorry when Señor Brent hears of this."

"I told you not to worry."

Abby approached the horse cautiously, but he still flared his ears and backed away from her. After several tries she finally managed to slip the bit between his teeth and loop the bridle over his head. The horse kicked his hind legs when Navidad attempted to throw the saddle blanket across his back. Abby grabbed and held the animal's ears so Navidad could land the saddle and fasten the cinch.

She nodded, and Navidad covered the horse's eyes with his battered hat, giving her time to slide her boot into the stirrup. Just as the gelding had done with Curly and Red, he started spinning before she had a chance to settle into the saddle. But she slid her legs around his belly and tugged on the reins.

Navidad wisely ran for the fence and found a safe seat on the top rung beside Curly.

"I've watched her grow up," Curly said. "I've seen her ride many a wild horse, but this one might be too strong for her to handle. There's gonna be hell to pay when Brent finds out."

"*Sí*. That is so."

"I've always admired that little gal's grit, but I worry 'bout her high spirit. One day she's gonna come up against a situation she cain't handle."

The Mexican frowned. He was afraid Curly might be right.

Chapter Three

Quince Hunter greeted Jonah Tremain with a warm handshake. "Now, this is an unexpected pleasure, Major. What brings you out my way?"

"I had business in Diablo and thought this would be a good time to visit an old friend."

Even though Jonah stood six-foot-one, Quince Hunter still had a good two inches on him. Quince liked the man in spite of the fact that he was a Yankee and an officer.

"Welcome to the Half-Moon Ranch." Quince grinned and shook his head. "You're still at Fort Griffin, aren't you?"

Jonah raised an eyebrow. "No, thank God. I didn't sit comfortably in that command chair. Of course, as it stands, I may be worse off now." Jonah frowned. "I was given command of Fort Fannin."

"I would congratulate you, but I heard about the corruption involving Captain Gregory. Has that all been straightened out?"

Jonah worked his hands out of his gauntlet gloves and tucked them into his belt. "Not yet." He looked at his friend. "Of course, if you would agree to scout for me again, you could help find the men I'm searching for. I'd like to have you with me."

"Not a chance, Jonah. I like it just where I am."

"I thought that would be the way of it, but I had to ask. Don't think I have forgotten that you saved my life. I am here now to repay that debt."

"You owe me nothing, Major. I was just doing what the cavalry paid me to do."

Jonah shook his head. "You warned me that Geronimo was leading us into a trap, but I was more interested in capturing him than in watching for an ambush."

Quince nodded, indicating Jonah's leg. "It looks like you still carry a little souvenir from the encounter."

"The limp, yes. I can usually tell when it's going to rain by the ache. The doctor assures me that the limp will probably go away in time, but I should be able to forecast the weather from now on."

Quince looked puzzled. "Next week we'll be driving twenty head to Fort Griffin." He smiled. "Have you come to check up on the cavalry's investment?"

"Not at all. Your word has always been good with me." Jonah's expression became serious. "Other than wanting to see the Half-Moon, I have an altogether different motive for being here."

Quince clapped Jonah on the back. "You can't know what that army contract has meant for me and my family. Everyone has been wanting to meet you and thank you personally."

Jonah's mouth curved into a smile. "I am here to offer you a new contract." He patted his front pocket. "I had it drawn up before I left. I need you to supply horses for Fort Fannin, and I need them fast."

Quince looked stunned. "I don't know what to say besides thank you. You have already done so much for us, and now this. . . ."

Jonah shook his head. "Dammit, will you quit complimenting me and let me get on to the other reason I'm here?"

"All right—shoot."

"I know how well you train horses for the cavalry, but I wonder if you can also train one suitable for a delicate lady?"

Quince raised his brow. "And who would the lady be?"

"Miss Patricia Van Dere."

"Sidesaddle trained?"

"Yes, of course. I did say lady."

Quince didn't need to think before he answered. "Sure. We can do that for you."

Jonah glanced about him. Quince had once told him that the Half-Moon was run-down. But the house had a new coat of paint, and the barn and stable looked like they were in good repair. "You have quite a place here."

"Actually, I don't live here anymore. My wife has a nice spread, the Diamond C, and I moved there after we were married." Quince watched his friend's face. "You did know I'm married, didn't you?"

"Yes. I had heard that. Congratulations!"

"I'll tell you about my wife later. Right now I want to hear about this lady you mentioned."

"I don't think I ever told you about Patricia. She is my fiancée."

"That's what I thought you were saying." In a teasing tone Quince said, "If you've ridden all the way out here to invite me to your wedding, a written invitation would have sufficed, but it would have denied me the pleasure of seeing you again."

"The wedding isn't until next June, but you'll get an invitation."

"I'm sure we can find your lady a suitable mount. All you have to do is decide if you want a gentle horse or one with spirit."

"Gentle, I should think." Jonah thought about the times Patricia had dutifully ridden beside him, until one day he realized she was not enjoying herself. After some tactful prodding, she had admitted that she was not fond of horses. "Yes, definitely gentle."

"We have two that might be suitable. When do you need it?"

"The general will be accompanying Patricia to Fort Fannin for a visit next month. I had hoped to present her with the horse at that time."

"Your father is coming west?"

"So it would seem."

Quince knew that Jonah always referred to his father as "the general," and he had often wondered why, but was too polite to ask. "It's too late to ride to the north pasture today. Of course, you'll be staying here at the ranch for a few days."

"If it wouldn't be an imposition."

"Major, no one is more welcome on the Half-Moon than you are. When my family learns that you have awarded us the contract for Fort Fannin, they'll be even happier to see you."

"Nonsense. Don't mention it. I chose you for the contract because I need someone I can depend on—you have already proven that you can deliver saddle-ready horseflesh on time."

"Thank you anyway. Now, what would you like to see first?"

Jonah could almost feel life pulsing around him: he heard the whinny of a horse, the wind in the branches of a tree, and it stirred a strange excitement within him. "Actually, I want to observe the operations of a working ranch. I want to see everything."

Quince laughed. "Now, that will take some showing, but I think we can manage it."

Jonah looked up at the sun to gauge the time of day and judged it to be midafternoon. "Who trains your horses for the sidesaddle?"

"My sister, Abby. She's one of the best trainers on the ranch."

Jonah watched Quince for a moment before he spoke. "I heard your father is out of prison."

"Looks like bad news travels fast."

"I wonder if you remember telling me about your family that night we got roaring drunk in Tucson?"

Quince remembered the incident all too well because it was the first time he had ever seen Jonah drink. They had been tracking a band of *banditos* for two grueling weeks across the Arizona desert. It had been about dusk when they came upon a small ranch situated a few miles from the Mexican border, where they were met with a gruesome sight. The *banditos* had murdered a whole family, including three children. After burying the bodies, the soldiers had ridden back to the fort, where Jonah had demanded permission to track the raiders into Mexico. He had been incensed when the commanding officer had forbidden him to pursue them across the border.

"It's funny what a man will talk about when he's drunk," Quince said. "As I recall, we drank for three days. Otherwise I would never have shared my family secrets with you or anyone."

Jonah expressed indifference with a shrug. "Why not? I told you about my family."

"Oh, yeah," Quince said with irony. "As I remember it—correct me if I'm wrong—your great-grandfather served under General Washington and distinguished himself at Yorktown. Your grandfather graduated from West Point with the highest honors ever achieved and went on to serve in Congress. Oh, yes, I almost forgot—your father was one of General Grant's officers and was decorated by Abe Lincoln himself and is now a retired general."

"As *I* recall," Jonah said, "I bared my soul to you, somewhere between the good brandy we started out with and the foul-tasting swill we ended up buying from the trading post. I have a vague memory of confessing that the general had my life all planned out for me before I had even taken my first step." He imitated his father's voice, " 'All Tremain men go to West Point and pursue a military career.' "

"Until that night I thought you liked being in the cavalry. You're certainly good at it—look how high you've risen in rank in just the last two years."

"I might have chosen to join the cavalry on my own, but I'd have liked to have been given the choice."

Quince nodded in agreement. "I know what you mean; life sometimes has a way of choosing for us."

Jonah decided to move on to another subject. "You look fit and hearty for a man who's just become a husband."

"Jonah, my friend, you are looking at a happy man. But then, you've already met my Glory, so you know how fortunate I am that she chose a saddle bum like me."

"Wild, untamable Quince, his wings clipped by a woman." Humor twinkled in Jonah's eyes. "I'll venture to guess you haven't told her everything about your past, such as how the women at the post always gave you . . . the eye."

"Sometimes, when you're dealing with women, the past is better left to the past." Quince leaned against a fence and crossed his arms. "I'm anxious to meet the woman who's about to clip your wings."

Jonah didn't want to talk about Patricia today. Sometimes, like now, he had difficulty even remembering her face. But she was the woman he would marry . . . because it was expected of him, just as he had been expected to go to West Point. He had no objections to Patricia; she would make an admirable officer's wife. "I suppose we all surrender to the inevitable in the end. Look at you, choosing marriage over scouting."

Quince shook his head and held his hand out at shoulder level. "The reason is about this tall, and has red hair and dark eyes." Then Quince motioned, indicating that Jonah should follow him. "No offense, Major, but I don't miss eating dust and spoiled food, and fighting heat, renegades, and snakes."

"I feel a calmness in you that only a good woman can bring out in a man. You are fortunate, my friend," Jonah told him.

Quince knew there was certainly no calmness in Jonah. It had always mystified him why the major never spoke of the woman he was to marry when everyone down to the newest recruit knew he was soon to marry. "What is your business in Diablo?" he asked curiously.

"It has to do with the missing payrolls meant for Fort Fannin. Both times our payrolls were hit, the shipment originated in Diablo. It could be a coincidence, but I am looking into every aspect of the robberies, no matter how small the lead."

"You don't have much to go on, do you?"

Jonah unbuttoned the top button on his uniform jacket. "The trail gets colder with each passing day."

"What about Victorio? I know you were tracking him up in New Mexico territory."

"Colonel Grierson is on his trail at the moment. At last report he had driven him back into Mexico. But we all know you can't keep Victorio where he doesn't want to be. He has sworn that he will fight to the death, and I believe him."

Quince was glad he didn't have to go chasing after the Apache chief. "Such is the life of a soldier."

Jonah nodded in agreement. "You sign up for the glory; you stay for the fight."

"Yeah. That's one reason I quit. There was no glory, and there was always a fight."

"Quince," Jonah asked, changing the subject, "have you heard of a man named Norman Williamson?"

Quince frowned thoughtfully. "I have heard that name . . . somewhere. Isn't he the Indian agent at Fort Fannin?"

"Yes, that's him. The word whispered about the state is that he gives tainted meat to the Comanche, although no one has caught him at it. I only encountered the man once, but he wouldn't meet my eyes when we spoke. It irritates the hell out of me when someone does that."

"I've heard nothing good about him. If I were you, I'd certainly keep an eye on him."

"I intend to delve into his background, and I have someone watching him."

"Do you think you'll be called on to go after Victorio?"

"It's almost a certainty. As far as he is concerned, the die has been cast, and there is no turning back for the army. Victorio and his band recently killed eight soldiers of the Ninth Cavalry and took their horses. If I encounter him, my orders are to either capture him, kill him, or force him back into Mexico so the Mexican government can deal with him. I can assure you that if I have a choice, I'll drive him back into Mexico. It doesn't sit well with me that I have to fight a man who is only trying to preserve his way of life."

"I don't envy you." Quince understood very well the turmoil brewing inside Jonah, whose main concern was to protect the settlers in the area. "You may not have a choice in the matter."

Jonah removed his hat and blotted his forehead with his sleeve. "Show me your horses, and then you can feed me."

"Come on; I'll show you a bit of horseflesh that'll rival any you've ever seen. But this horse is meaner than hell, and I won't be recommending him for your lady."

Chapter Four

Abby's entire attention was centered on the horse beneath her, so she was unaware that Quince and his visitor had joined Navidad and Curly at the fence to watch.

Jonah propped a booted foot on the rail, his gaze touching for a moment on the rider before his attention was drawn to the horse. The gelding was spirited, with an untamed streak of rebellion—its muscles contracted and rolled with each lunge it made.

By now several other cowhands had ridden in from the range and quickly gathered along the fence, some whistling and others calling out encouraging remarks to the rider.

Quince's body went rigid, and he clamped his jaw in a firm line while he gripped the fence. If the horse threw Abby, he wanted to be able to jump the fence and get to her before she was trampled. He should have anticipated that his sister would do something like this. Dammit, she always had to test fate and take everything just a little farther than anyone else!

Abby was completely focused on the horse, anticipating which way it would move so she could move with it. She could feel the animal's intake of breath—she could even feel its skin twitching.

Suddenly the horse was airborne, and she was almost unseated. Her legs tightened on its belly, and her gloved hand yanked on the reins. The gelding came down with such force that the impact jarred her whole body.

She was going to be sore tomorrow.

By now Abby had a good idea why this horse had thrown the other riders; he had stores of reserve strength beyond those of any animal she had ever ridden. Even now he wasn't tiring. He turned and spun; he kicked and reared; but Abby stayed with him, moving as he moved.

It was some time later that she felt the animal's anguish—she knew the very moment the gelding started to tire, and she almost wished the splendid creature could be allowed to run wild and free. But her resolve hardened—they needed the money Mr. Johnson would pay them for breaking the gelding.

Jonah's gaze went to the slight figure mounted on the horse. It was inconceivable that a man of such small stature could handle a horse with such boundless fury. One would be the conquered, the other the

42

victor. At that moment he knew that the rider would be victorious. He stopped breathing as he watched the rider's final mastery over the beast.

"If he is an example of your trainers, it's no wonder the Half-Moon has such a good reputation. Is that your brother?"

Quince felt his heartbeat ease, and he relaxed. "No," he said, shaking his head and drawing in a relieved breath. He watched the gelding give a final defiant kick and then lower its head. "Not my brother," he said softly and with pride. "That's my sister, Abby. Damn if she didn't do it!"

Jonah stared in stunned disbelief as the rider galloped the horse around the paddock. He was further amazed when she removed her hat and threw it into the air, allowing one long black braid to tumble down her back. Paying closer attention to detail, he could now see the evidence of her gender—each movement the gelding made caused the girl's breasts to bounce gently. He was both astonished and irritated when he recognized the girl who had spooked his horse that very morning.

"By damn, Quince, she's gone and done it!" Curly said, laughing and jumping over the fence to help Abby with the now exhausted animal.

Navidad ran alongside the horse. "You did it, Señorita Abby! I should not have had the doubt."

Abby stood in the stirrups, bowing and flourishing her hands while the cowhands applauded and whistled, and her brother grinned with pride.

She slid out of the saddle and handed the reins to Curly. "He was a tough one, but I think even your little granddaughter could ride him now."

"Come, Jonah," Quince said, laughing. "I'll introduce you to the jewel of the Hunter family."

Jonah had already met the hellion, and he had a bruised shoulder to prove it. He could almost sympathize with the unfortunate animal that had become her latest victim.

Abby placed her hands on the fence and hurtled over with ease to be caught in her brother's arms.

"I should be mad at you for what you did—but I'm just too damned proud, darlin'!" Quince said.

She always brightened under his praise, and she did so now. "He was as tough a challenge as I've ever faced."

Her brother, remembering his manners, turned her to face his visitor. "You remember I told you about Major Jonah Tremain? Jonah, my sister, Abby."

She had always wanted to meet and thank the major who had awarded her family the contract for the mustangs. But the smile froze on her face when she recognized the officer she had encountered earlier in the day. Her chin went up to a higher level as he stared back at her, his head dipping in greeting, his blue gaze boring into her. Seeing him in full uniform, his saber and gun belt in place, his silver spurs reflecting the sunlight, she thought he was the most overpowering man she had ever met. He seemed to take up all the air, leaving none for her to breathe.

"Major Tremain," she said at last. "Quince has told me so much about you." She watched him guardedly, not extending her hand to him but clamping them both behind her back and lacing her fingers tightly together. She waited for him to tell her brother that they had already met. She glanced from him to Quince, wondering what her brother's reaction would be when he learned what she had done.

Jonah was examining a pair of emerald eyes sparkling from a face covered with dust. "I've heard about you as well, Miss Hunter. Although Quince omitted telling me the extent of your many talents."

She felt relief flow through her—he hadn't told her brother that she had knocked him off his horse. But she had detected the hidden meaning that laced his every word. Quince, however, seemed oblivious to the major's barb. Her voice held no warmth when she said, "My brother should have warned you about me, Major. I can imagine I am something of a shock to you."

He watched her unfasten her chaps and unbuckle them from about her waist while casting him a prideful glance. With a flourish, she tossed the chaps carelessly over her shoulder. She had a flamboyant nature that Jonah found surprising in a woman, yet he could not look away from those glorious emerald eyes. He wondered why he hadn't noticed their color that morning. Of course, he had been occupied with other matters at the time.

"Quince told me you could break a horse to sidesaddle, but he failed to elaborate on the full extent of your horsemanship."

She removed her gloves and tossed them and her chaps to Curly. "For those women of faint heart, I can provide a fainthearted nag." She wiped her sleeve across her face. "How is your shoulder, Major?" With that as her parting shot, she turned away and walked toward the house, her head high, her spine straight.

Quince looked bemused. "She must have meant to ask about your leg. I told her you were wounded." With a lift of an eyebrow, he watched Abby hurry toward the house. "She has always shown an interest in meeting you. But if I didn't know better, I'd think she didn't like you at all."

Jonah was also staring at Abby's retreating back. He finally said in a voice laced with humor, "I don't know her well enough to judge, but I don't believe our first meeting went very well."

Quince shrugged as if it were of no importance. "You can never tell with Abby. She's like a high-strung filly—she either likes you or she doesn't."

Jonah didn't know what to think about Abby Hunter. She had managed to shock him twice in one day with her unconventional behavior. "Why did you allow your sister to ride such a dangerous animal?"

Quince looked pensive a moment. "You saw her—have you ever seen anyone more capable of handling a horse than she is? I never questioned her right to help out around here. If you were her brother, you would have learned long ago not to try to keep her from anything she has her mind set on."

Jonah thought of his own two sisters and counted himself fortunate that neither one of them would have gone near that horse.

"Come with me," Quince said. "I have just enough time to show you the stable before supper."

* * *

Abby was still seething as she climbed the steps to the porch. She should have been proud of her accomplishment, but seeing herself through that officer's eyes had somehow dampened her joy—especially since he seemed critical of her actions. She had heard about him so often, and she had wanted to meet him. But Maj. Jonah Tremain was nothing like the man Quince spoke of with such respect.

She had decided to go directly to the kitchen to tell Frances what had happened between herself and the major when she heard a rider approaching from the direction of town. With a feeling of dread, Abby watched Edmund Montgomery dismount and walk toward her.

Although her father considered the banker a friend, Abby didn't trust him at all. He was a deacon in the church, and the people of Diablo commended him for how devotedly he had tended his wife before she died, but Abby always felt apprehensive around him. She could never forget that he had once pulled a gun on Brent, or that he was sometimes too familiar with her. She was disgusted by her own subterfuge—she did not like him, and yet, because of their father's friendship with the man, she was forced to be polite to him.

"Mr. Montgomery, if you have come to see Papa, you made the trip for nothing—he isn't here."

Edmund climbed the steps and stopped so near her that she had to step back a pace to avoid colliding with him. "What if I told you that I came to see you?"

Abby stepped back another pace as he advanced toward her. "I wouldn't believe you."

He spoke with a slow Southern accent rather than the clipped drawl of a Texan, and his tone was too soft to suit her.

"It always brightens my life to see you, Abby."

Many people thought him charming, and to be sure he was tall and distinguished-looking, with blond hair that was slightly graying at the temples. But his eyes disturbed Abby—they were a hard, marble blue with no warmth in them at all.

Reluctantly remembering her duties as hostess, she asked, "May I offer you something cool to drink? I'm sure you're thirsty after your long ride from town."

He dabbed at the back of his neck with a snow-white handkerchief. "It is hotter than usual for this time of year." Shoving his handkerchief back in his pocket, he took her arm and led her toward the door. "Where is everyone?" He looked toward the barn. "Is anyone else around?"

"Yes," she said quickly, not wanting him to think she was alone. "Quince is in the stable with an army officer. I don't know where Brent is, and I suppose Frances must be somewhere in the house, probably in the kitchen."

Edmund reached for the door and held it open for Abby to pass through. "It seems a bit strange that an army officer would visit the Half-Moon." A deep frown creased his brow. "I noticed a couple of soldiers hanging around town this afternoon—I wonder if they are with him."

"I wouldn't know."

He stared down at her, his hand touching and sliding up her arm, his gaze stabbing at her. "You are damp and warm with perspiration."

"No," she said, prickling, "I'm dusty, tired, and sweating." She moved quickly away from him, leading him into the parlor. She offered him a chair, but he went to the picture of her mother that hung over the fireplace; it seemed to be a ritual that Edmund performed every time he came to the ranch. He always stood beneath the portrait and stared at it.

"Did you know," he asked after a long silence, "that I was with your mother when she posed for this?"

"My father never told me that."

"The artist was so taken with Beth's beauty that he gave the painting to her when he had finished it. If any of you ever want to sell the portrait, I'll pay handsomely for it."

Her head snapped up, and she stared at him. "Why would we want to sell my mother's portrait to you?"

Edmund shrugged. "Maybe you'll need the money someday. And she was a beautiful woman; I'd like to have this likeness of her . . . if you ever do decide to sell it."

"I believe my family would sell the Half-Moon before letting Mama's portrait go. I know I would."

"You never know what you'll do when you're desperate." His eyes turned cold, and his voice dropped in tone. "I want you to remember that we had this conversation."

Abby glanced away from him, wishing she could just leave. Where was everyone, and why did she have to entertain Mr. Montgomery? Swallowing her feeling of uneasiness, she turned toward her mother's likeness. "I wish I could remember more about her," she said, striving to make conversation.

Edmund came up to her, touching her hair and allowing his finger to trail down her cheek. "You are very like her, you know. If you want to remember her, just look in the mirror. Underneath that smudged face you have Beth's features, and you are a temptress just like she was."

Abby knew she certainly wasn't trying to tempt him! She stepped quickly away from his grasping hands. "I need to change before supper. If you want to talk to Quince, I'll get him for you."

He smiled, showing a perfect row of white teeth. "I don't want him. I'd rather talk to you."

She edged toward the door, knowing she had to get away from him. "If you will excuse me, I'll have Frances bring you a cool drink."

He reached for her hand, drawing her back into the room. "No, don't go yet. I have something to tell you."

Abby stiffened; her mind was screaming that this was not right. His hand glided from her shoulder to her arm, brushing against her breast on its way to her hand. The movement was just subtle enough that she could not accuse him of fondling her—she was not sure if he had done it on purpose, or if it had been accidental.

"Why are you here?" she asked, drawing away from him and feeling as though she wanted to wash everywhere he had touched.

"I came to tell you about your father."

He eased her closer to him again, and she wedged her elbow between them. "What about Papa?"

He stepped away from her as if he sensed he was making her nervous.

"Your father bought a new horse yesterday morning, and by afternoon he had already entered it in the two-mile race. I told him it was rash to suppose he could win the race when he wasn't familiar with the horse, but he wouldn't listen to me."

Abby felt her heart plummet. "Papa didn't have the money to buy a racehorse. Please tell me you didn't loan him money again, Mr. Montgomery."

"Sure I did." His eyes hardened. "Jack Hunter is my friend."

"Brent and Quince aren't going to like it when they find out you loaned Papa money. You know very well Brent has asked you not to extend Papa any more credit."

Edmund waved his hand dismissively. "Brent is too cautious, and he's too hard on your father, for that matter." He shook his head as if in disbelief. "Anyway, I was happy for your father when his horse won the race, and you should be, too."

She watched his face, afraid to hear the truth, and yet needing to know. "Did he win much money?"

He liked playing mind games with her—first raising her hopes, only to dash them. "Not anything to brag about. It was the starting race of the day—the teaser."

"But there was some money?"

"Yes, there was."

"Enough to pay you back for the horse?"

"Not anywhere near that." His mouth smoothed into a straight line as he smiled. "He had just enough winnings to invite all the men to accompany him to the Lone Star so he could buy drinks all around."

Abby's hopes were dashed, and she had a sick feeling in the pit of her stomach. It was always the same with her father—horse racing was in his blood, and he had no head for business. It was all Brent and Quince could do just to keep the ranch going from day to day, while their father made it harder for them with his gambling and wild buying sprees.

Edmund smiled slightly when he saw the misery in Abby's eyes. "Your father was in no condition to come home last night, so I put him up at my place," he said in a pretense of sorrow.

"Thank you for giving Papa a place to sleep," she said, forcing herself to be polite. "But please don't loan him any more money."

"You have to understand, when a friend asks me for help, I give it when I can. That's what a banker does."

"Papa doesn't seem to know what to do with himself since he returned from prison. And he isn't making good decisions. If you were his friend, you would see that."

"Poor Abby." His hand ran up her arm while he stared over her shoulder at the likeness of her mother. "Sweet Abby. I am not only your father's friend; I'm yours, too. I want you to know that you can come to me for anything."

She twisted away from him as she got a whiff of the too-sweet scent of his cologne. She hated the touch of his hand on her, and she could hardly resist the urge to bat it away. "I—"

He pulled her back to him, holding her so she could not escape this time.

"Please let me go, Mr. Montgomery."

His hot breath touched her ear. "Call me Edmund—I have waited a long time to hear you say my name."

Abby was about to shove him away when she heard footsteps on the front porch. "That'll be Quince." She was glad when Edmund's hands dropped to his sides. "You can ask him what to do about Papa."

Before he could say anything further, she hurried out of the room, relieved to get out of his reach. She would make certain that she was never alone with him again.

Quince had seen Edmund's horse, so he was not surprised to find him in the parlor. After introducing Jonah to the banker, Quince excused himself so he could let Frances know about their guest and that the family would all be gathering for supper.

Edmund eyed Jonah warily. "Do the two soldiers I saw in town belong to you, Major?"

"Yes, they do." He gave no more information.

"Do they have any special reason to be in Diablo? I heard the troopers were asking a lot of questions," Edmund pressed. "I saw by their insignias that they were with the Sixth Cavalry out of Fort Griffin."

Jonah took an immediate dislike to the man. "No. We are from Fort Fannin."

Edmund's eyes dilated just the merest flicker as he absorbed that bit of information. He watched the young major closely when he asked the next question. "Perhaps you're here to call on Abby," he implied glibly.

"No. I'm not." Jonah moved to the painting; at first he thought it might be Miss Hunter, but the nose wasn't quite right, and the dress was from another era. There was a serenity about the green-eyed woman that Miss Hunter certainly didn't possess.

"Beautiful, wasn't she?" Edmund asked, nodding at the portrait.

"Yes. Is that the mother?"

"That's right—she was." Edmund stared into the green eyes that would haunt him for the rest of his life, even from her grave. "Abby's very like her, don't you think?"

"Perhaps, a little."

Edmund's gaze bored into the young officer. "How long will you be staying at the Half-Moon?"

The man's persistence made Jonah suspicious, so he continued to make his responses vague. "I haven't yet decided."

"I had heard a rumor that a young officer was given temporary command at Fort Griffin until Captain Irving returns from Washington. Could you be that officer?"

Jonah's eyes narrowed, and he stepped away from the banker and settled onto a straight-backed chair on the opposite side of the room. "Captain Irving has returned by now."

Edmund was having a hard time controlling his temper. No one had ever treated him with such disrespect. The officer was much too imperious to suit him. As always, though, the banker managed to hide his true feelings behind a smooth smile. "I have a friend who is the Indian agent at Fort Fannin. He said something to me about a young officer who was taking over command there. Could you be that officer?"

"Yes."

"Are you acquainted with Norman Williamson?"

Jonah's eyelids closed halfway. "I have met the Indian agent, but I wouldn't say I was acquainted with him."

An uneasy silence fell across the room as Jonah speculated on the relevancy of a friendship between the Diablo banker and the unscrupulous Indian agent.

At last Edmund spoke. "Nothing can turn a young girl's heart to romance quicker than the sight of a man in uniform." Rage smoldered just below the surface, but Edmund struck a perfectly serene pose. "I'm sure Abby has noticed you."

The banker's rude probing was become entirely too personal for Jonah. "I don't know Miss Hunter very well, but I don't believe she is interested in me one way or another."

"I wager you find her fascinating."

Jonah was on the verge of losing his temper. He had no intention of discussing Quince's sister with this man, so he turned the conversation and threw a question at Edmund. "Why don't you tell me about your friendship with Norman Williamson?"

"Norman and I have known each other for a long time. He is an easy man to do business with, don't you think?"

"I can't speak on that point, since I've had so few dealings with him."

Much to Jonah's relief, Quince reentered the room, and the probing questions stopped.

Edmund had already decided he would have his hired man, Kane, keep an eye on Major Tremain while he was in the area.

Chapter Five

After bathing and dressing in clean clothing, Abby went to the kitchen to help Frances with the evening meal. She found the housekeeper mixing a bowl of frosting to ice the cinnamon cake that cooled on the windowsill. When Abby saw the scowl on the older woman's face, she knew there was going to be trouble.

"Well, missy, I heard that you made a complete spectacle of yourself today."

Abby dipped her finger in the frosting and licked it. "You can't be very mad at me if you made my favorite cake." Then she carefully lifted the cast-iron lid on the pot that was bubbling on the stove. "Umm, this stew smells wonderful! That's my favorite, too."

Frances gave a disapproving grunt. "You could

57

have worn a dress, since we're having company to supper."

She hoped it wasn't Mr. Montgomery. "Who?"

"That fine major will be staying with us for a few days. I got him settled in Matt's old room. By the way, Brent and Crystal will be here for supper, and so will Quince and Glory."

Abby dropped the heavy lid back in place, reached for a stack of plates, and began arranging them around the table. "As you know, I have only two gowns; one is too tight across the bodice, and the other one is at least three inches too short. And they are both hopelessly out of style."

"That's your fault, Abby. I know your brother Matt sends you money so you can buy clothing, and don't say he doesn't."

For all Frances's gruffness, she was the watchdog of the family. She knew everything that went on, and she tried to take care of all of them. Abby wished she would just give up on trying to make a proper lady out of her.

"It seems more important to pay the bill at the feed store, so that's mostly how I use the money."

It finally dawned on the housekeeper that Abby was setting the kitchen table. "Since we're having such important company, I thought we'd use the dining room."

"The major can eat in here like the rest of us. Although I doubt he's ever seen the inside of a kitchen."

"Why do you say such things? You know Quince will want you to be polite to his friend."

After Abby had finished setting the plates around the table, she went to Frances and smiled teasingly, putting her arm around the older woman. "So you want to change my ways just to get rid of me, do you?"

Frances smiled sadly. "No, it's not that. I just want to see you happy before I die."

Abby had heard all this before, and she knew the lecture by heart. At the moment, though, she had other matters to worry about. She certainly didn't relish the thought of sitting down at the table with Major Tremain and making polite conversation after all that had transpired between them. She stared at the dinner plates as if seeing them for the first time. Some of them were chipped; others were actually cracked. "Do you think he'll notice that the dishes aren't a matched set?"

"If you mean the major, he'd be too polite to mention it even if he did notice."

"From the way Quince spoke about Major Tremain, I thought he would be someone I could really like and respect. But when I met him, he wasn't anything like the man my brother described."

Frances swirled her knife around the cake, making the frosting peak on top. "You're too critical, Abigail. The major is my notion of what a real gentleman should be like."

"If he's considered a gentleman, there is no hope for the rest of the men of the world," she replied haughtily. "Major Jonah Tremain is pompous and arrogant, and I don't—"

"Good evening, ladies," came a clipped voice just behind Abby. "Something sure smells good in here."

Abby turned to find Jonah just behind her. He must have overheard her unflattering remarks about him, but his cool gaze gave nothing away. He might be a gentleman to Frances, but he wasn't to her. "I would venture a guess that you don't have anyone in the cavalry who can cook as well as Frances."

He continued to look down at her until his dark lashes swept over his eyes. "I'm sure you are right—I can't wait to taste those biscuits I smell, Mrs. Reilly."

Frances colored with pleasure and nodded. "We'll eat as soon as the others get here."

Abby turned abruptly away to place frayed napkins beside each plate. "I don't know if Papa will be home in time to eat with us." She hoped he wouldn't come home drunk, as he had on so many occasions.

Jonah's gaze followed Abby as she placed knives and forks at each plate. She was tall for a woman—he would guess somewhere around five-seven or -eight. It was hard to tell her shape because of the baggy trousers she wore. Her skin had a healthy golden glow to it. He could not imagine her bothering to follow the regimented ritual most women practiced to maintain a pale complexion. When she moved past him to set more utensils on the table, he caught a whiff of sweet honey—probably the soap she used; he could not imagine her taking the time to dab perfume behind her ears either.

The single black braid that hung down her back swayed with every movement she made. He found himself fantasizing about how she would look if her hair were unbraided and fell loosely about her face.

His gaze lingered on the swell of her breasts, then settled on the top button of her shirt as he imagined himself unbuttoning it to explore the delights that lay beneath.

His carnal thoughts rocked him a bit, yet still he went on assessing her other features. Dark brows arched above those wonderful eyes—her lashes were long and curled against her cheek. Her pert nose could have made her almost cute, but her fragile bone structure made her beautiful.

He mentally compared the perfection of Patricia's porcelain, milk-white complexion to Abby's golden hue. He had never seen Patricia when she wasn't well-groomed; she never had a hair out of place, while Miss Hunter threw convention to the wind with her unsuitable apparel. Still, he would never forget the sight of Abby breaking that gelding. Much to his surprise, he was finding that she was taking up a great deal of his thoughts. In fact, the memory of her unusual green eyes had remained with him throughout the day.

When Abby turned back to find him watching her, he quickly focused his attention on the housekeeper. "That cake looks mighty good."

"It tastes good, too," Frances said with certainty. "My grandma brought the recipe with her all the way from Pennsylvania—she was Dutch, you know."

"Then Reilly must be your husband's name."

"It was; may he rest in peace. He came out here

from Ireland and didn't last the second winter. But that was thirty years ago."

"I am from Philadelphia myself."

The housekeeper paused with frosting dripping from her knife. "I recall my grandma telling me when I was young that not a day went by that she didn't miss the countryside back east." She quickly wiped up the frosting that had spilled on the stove and smiled at him. "She never got to go back."

Abby was disgusted by the way that man had charmed Frances into making a fool out of herself—the housekeeper was practically purring like a barn cat.

Quince's voice broke into her thoughts, and he came trailing into the kitchen, accompanied by Glory, Brent, and Crystal. Abby stood off to the side, observing how graciously the major acknowledged both her sisters-in-law. He certainly had not shown her the same kind of courtesy. She began to dislike him even more . . . if that were possible.

She noticed Brent staring at her with hazel eyes so like their father's. As he approached her, he bestowed a look on her that she had come to know only too well.

Disapproval.

"Here it comes," she said quietly. "Go ahead, tell me how you think I shouldn't have ridden the Johnson horse."

Brent shook his head. "Dammit, Abby, that horse—"

Quince appeared beside Abby and slid his arm around her shoulders, quietly conveying his support.

"That horse," he finished for his brother, "is saddle broken, and I have the money from Mr. Johnson right in my pocket. Leave her alone, Brent."

The two brothers glared at each other until Glory cleared her throat. "Isn't anyone but me hungry?" she asked, causing everyone to talk at once.

The huge oak table could easily seat twenty, and had on many occasions when Abby's mother had been alive, and the sheer number of guests had spilled over from the dining room into the kitchen. Of course, the neighbors never came around anymore, and since her father had returned, mealtime was usually a silent and painful event.

Abby watched Brent and his wife. Crystal's blond hair was pulled away from her face with a blue ribbon, and she seemed to be blooming with health—her stomach was rounded from the child she carried. Abby observed the soft glances that passed between the two of them and wondered what it would feel like to have someone look at her that way. She glanced at the major and found him watching her so intently it made her squirm in her chair.

Quince was also watching Abby, but his gaze was questioning; no doubt he was wondering why she was not joining in the happy banter. "You'd better eat, little sister, or you are going to get even skinnier than you are, and no man will want you until we can fatten you up."

She glared at her brother. "As if I cared."

Glory patted Abby's hand. "Don't let him tease you. He's just as proud of you as he can be."

Glory matched her name in sweetness and appearance, although Quince claimed his wife had a temper to match her flame-colored hair. She was wearing her hair up tonight with wispy curls about her lovely face. When she turned her winsome smile on Quince, he looked as if he would practically melt at her feet.

Abby glanced across the table to find Major Tremain still staring at her.

"Major," she said, determined to show him that she wasn't intimidated by him. "I understand Quince saved your life."

"That's right; he did."

"I suppose when Yankees come out here they think they know the lay of the land and are surprised to find themselves in trouble."

She heard Quince's intake of breath and saw the disapproving frown on his face.

"Yankee?" Jonah's mouth eased into a smile. "Now, that's a term I haven't often had applied to myself. My father fought in the Civil War, but I was only sixteen when Lee surrendered to Grant."

She bristled. "Surely you are referring to the War Between the States, Major. That's what we call it here in Texas."

He paused with his fork halfway to his mouth and said in a tone one might use with an unruly child, "If you prefer, Miss Hunter. It actually comes down to a matter of semantics, doesn't it?"

Knowing his sister and how far she would go to make a point, Brent intervened. "I am happy to have this chance to thank you." He stared pointedly at Abby. "Major, I know it's because of your friendship with Quince that we have the army contract. And my brother has told me that you want us to supply horses for Fort Fannin as well. How can our family ever thank you for still another contract?"

Abby's face flushed at the news. The major *had* helped her family in the past, and he was helping them again. She stared down at her plate, remembering how discourteous she had been to him that morning, and tonight also, for that matter. But she just didn't like him.

"As I told Quince today," Jonah was saying, "we have all benefited from the contract. And Brent, I wish you would drop the 'Major' part—just call me Jonah."

"Major"—Abby stressed his title—"with your sworn duty to protect the people of Texas, how do you plan to tackle the Indian problem?"

"Miss Hunter," he replied, his lips almost curving into a smile, as if he knew she was taunting him, "I learned quickly that the Indians are much better horsemen than my troopers, but we still have the advantage over them."

He had more charm that anyone had a right to, and a male beauty that could not be matched by any man she had ever seen. He probably had enough women paying homage to his handsomeness; she certainly wasn't going to be one of them. She fastened her gaze on the gold bars of his wide-shouldered uniform, determined not to look into those hypnotic blue eyes. "And what would that advantage be?" she asked in a breathy voice that took the sting out of her words.

He laid his fork across his plate and gave her his full attention. "What we lack in horsemanship we make up in firepower. We have superior weapons, Miss Hunter."

She made the mistake of looking into his eyes and found them flaming with the passion of life, and she tingled all over. It took her a moment to speak. "Is that right?"

Now his words were stilted, as if he wearied of their conversation. "I can assure you it is, Miss Hunter."

Abby became aware that her family was watching her, and she could feel their uneasiness. Even Crystal and Glory were frowning at her. Undaunted, she charged forward. "We have driven the Indians from their lands and left them nowhere to go, haven't we?" She expected him to argue the point; in fact, she depended on it.

He wiped his mouth on a napkin before he spoke. "I see you and I share the same view on that. But sadly the conflict is almost over for them. The plight of those who haven't been shipped off to reservations is extremely dire."

"Yet you helped bring about their downfall," she insisted.

"It is the way of life," Jonah replied. "The strong have always held sway over the weak. For myself, I followed orders—but I think . . . I hope I have never killed any man except in duty to my country."

She bit into a biscuit, feeling everyone's eyes on her. Most of all, she could feel both her brothers' disapproval mounting. It was hard to chew and downright impossible to swallow. There was an unspoken rule in this house—they were never to be rude to guests. Abby didn't understand why she had felt the need to challenge the major at every turn. He had proven to be a worthy and gracious opponent—he had left her nothing to debate.

After a moment Jonah turned his attention to Glory, who was speaking to him. "My husband tells me you were in the New Mexico territory searching for Victorio."

"I never got close enough to take him on in battle. He's good at avoiding capture."

"Isn't he dangerous?" Crystal asked.

"Yes, ma'am, he is," Jonah said. His gaze went to Abby. "I doubt any of us would react any differently than he has if we had been driven from our land."

Abby heard someone enter the front door, and an uneasy feeling enveloped her. "That will be Papa." Her gaze met Quince's, and she could see they shared the same thought—they hoped that Jack Hunter would not be drunk.

Moments later her father appeared in the doorway, smiling and sober. "It's always nice to see my family partaking of a meal together." His gaze went around the table and stopped at the man in uniform. A broad grin lit his face, and he extended a hand while walking toward Jonah. "I don't need to be told who you are—you have to be Major Tremain."

Jonah stood, shaking hands with Jack. "Mr. Hunter. I am grateful for your hospitality. And I have never dined better."

Frances must have heard Jack's voice, because she returned and set a plate before him. It did her heart good to see the family together like this. It didn't happen very often.

The talk turned to horses, and Abby was relieved when the meal was finally over. The men migrated to the porch where it was cooler, while Glory and Crystal stayed to help her with the dishes, giving Frances a rest.

"You two go on and join the men," Abby said. "I'll finish in here."

Glory shook her head. "That won't do, Abby. That gorgeous man out there couldn't take his eyes off you all during supper. Crystal and I will finish here and *you* can join your brothers."

Abby draped the dish cloth over her shoulder and lifted a stack of saucers into the cupboard. "I can assure you that if the major *was* looking at me, he was only trying to find flaws. He certainly made it clear today that he disapproves of me."

"Maybe," Glory said, twisting a red strand of hair that had come loose and pinning it up with the rest. "But there was interest there, too. I have a feeling he's never met anyone like you, and he is more than likely intrigued by you, maybe even fascinated."

Crystal agreed with a nod. "You're at least a mystery to him—a mystery that he wants to solve. And I saw you watching him, Abby, so don't deny it."

"I'm sure he is accustomed to women appraising him. As for me, I have no more interest in him than he has in me. Besides, Quince told me he is engaged to a woman in Philadelphia."

Glory dried a glass and handed it to Abby to put away in the cupboard. She studied her young sister-in-law closely. "Yes, but that puts her back north, and he's here, isn't he? And . . . unless I miss my guess, Major Tremain has just met a beautiful girl he can't get out of his mind."

Abby shook her head. "What the two of you don't seem to understand is that we don't like each other. And furthermore, I am not even pretty, much less a beauty."

Glory gave Crystal a calculating glance. "Let's finish quickly so we can all join the men."

When they had finished the dishes, Abby reluctantly went along with Glory and Crystal. She would much rather have escaped to her bedroom than join the family in their worship of the major.

Her brothers were sitting in cane-bottom chairs, and Jonah was leaning against the wooden porch post. "Where's Papa?" Abby wanted to know.

"At the stable," Brent said, anger lacing his words. "It seems he has a new racehorse that won one of the races yesterday. He said something about hand-feeding the victor."

Both brothers got up and gave their wives their chairs, then seated themselves on the steps. Abby wandered to the other end of the porch, where she stood half in shadow. She was in a good position to study their guest without his knowing it. His posture was as erect as if he were on parade. The brass buttons on his uniform glistened from the lamplight that spilled out the front door. His uniform was definitely not army-issue, but had probably been tailored from quality material. At least he wasn't wearing his sword and holster, as he had been earlier in the day.

Abby noticed that even in repose he kept his coat buttoned; she supposed to remind everyone of his rank. He was lean and tall, his shoulders wide, his body beautiful. His black boots came almost to his knees and held a high polish. She wondered how many aides it took to keep him so splendidly clothed.

Jonah was amused by something Brent had said; his deep laughter sent warmth throughout Abby. She turned to look at the moon, wishing she had gone to bed instead of joining the others. Once again she was reminded how alone she was. Brent looked at Crystal as if she were the only woman in the world, and Quince couldn't keep his gaze from wandering to Glory.

She was so caught up in her own thoughts that she was startled when Quince called out to her. "Abby, you wouldn't mind taking Jonah around the ranch tomorrow morning, would you?" He turned his attention to Jonah. "I would take you myself, but one of our mares has the colic, and she is only weeks away from dropping her foal. Besides, Abby will help you choose the best horse for your needs."

She moved out of the shadows and sat on the wooden rail of the porch. Good manners and her brothers would require that she be gracious. "If you need me to," was all she could manage to say. She didn't enjoy the thought of spending a whole day with the major.

His inquiring gaze locked with hers. "I wouldn't want to take you away from anything pressing."

She would have liked to have told him to find his own way to the north pasture. "I have nothing that can't wait," she said reluctantly.

His brow arched—she didn't fool him for one moment. He knew she didn't want to go with him. "Thank you, Miss Hunter. I'll try not to encroach on your time any longer than necessary."

His tone had been patronizing, but Abby seemed to be the only one who noticed, or was she? Glory looked at her inquiringly and frowned.

"Well, if that is all settled," Quince remarked, standing and reaching for his wife. "You'll be in good hands with my sister tomorrow, Jonah. I'll meet up with you when you get back."

Good-night wishes were exchanged, and Abby watched her brothers leave with their wives. It took her a moment to realize that their guest was standing beside her. She turned, and they looked at each other without saying a word. His breath touched her hair, and she felt a sensation like hot honey running through her veins.

"We should get an early start, Major," she managed to say, stepping away from him. "I'll meet you at the barn at six."

He was still watching her. "Good night, Miss Hunter," he said finally. "I believe I'll just stay out here for a while. It's very tranquil this time of night."

He wouldn't think it was so tranquil, she thought bitterly, if he looked beneath the facade her family had created for others to see.

"I hope you will be comfortable. If you should need anything, just ask Frances."

"You are more than kind, Miss Hunter."

The humor was back in his voice, and she resented him for it; in fact, she resented everything about him.

And yet she felt reluctant to leave him. Something vibrated through her, filling her with such sweetness, she had to swallow twice before she could find her voice.

"I must thank you for not telling my brothers about this morning. They would not have approved of what I did." She was quiet for a moment, waiting for him to speak. When he made no reply, she asked, "Does your shoulder bother you?"

He laughed softly. "Not so much. Rest easy, Miss Hunter; only my pride was hurt." He turned away from her and stared into the night sky.

The screen door creaked when she opened it. "In the morning at six," she reminded him before going inside.

From her bedroom, Abby could hear when her father returned from the stable and bid Jonah goodnight. She found herself pacing between her bed and the door, her stomach knotted. Finally, in exhaustion, she threw herself on the bed and buried her face in the coverlet.

Why did he have to come to the Half-Moon? She was bewildered by him, and she didn't know why. After she undressed and slipped between the sheets, Abby pounded her pillow and closed her eyes. Restlessly she wrestled with her sheet and pillow until long after midnight, and then she fell asleep.

Chapter Six

Abby took a quick sip of milk, staring at Frances over the rim of the glass. She had a sinking feeling in the pit of her stomach. "How long ago did you say he ate?"

"It's been a good hour now. Said he wanted to get one of the men to show him around a bit. He said I was to tell you that he'd be waiting for you."

"He's early," Abby replied sharply. "It's just like him to do something like this."

Frances paused in her biscuit making with dough caked on her fingers. "I like the cut of that man. You balked yesterday when I said he's a real gentleman, but he is. I figured out a long time ago that there are two kinds of people in this world: those who want to talk about themselves all the time, and those who listen to what others have to say. He sat right here in this kitchen and talked to me while he ate this morning—treated me just like he was interested in what I was saying."

Abby cast the housekeeper a disgusted look, grabbed her hat, and picked up the canvas bag Frances had packed with food. "You don't really know him. It would be just like that man to be pacing while he waits for me."

"Then you'd better get going, hadn't you?"

With boundless energy, Abby raced across the yard to the barn. When she entered the dark interior, the sun had just touched the eastern sky, shedding shards of light through the cracks in the wood. It took a moment for her eyes to adjust to the lone lantern that hung from one of the stalls, where Navidad and Curly were deep in conversation with Major Tremain.

Drawing an irritated breath, she took measured steps in their direction, wishing she did not have to be alone with the major today.

Curly must have been telling one of his yarns, because Jonah was laughing heartily. But when Jonah noticed her walking toward him, his amusement faded, and he centered his attention on her. Abby was made more aware of how inadequately she was dressed. There was an expression on his face that she did not understand—probably stark disapproval, which only encouraged her to straighten her spine.

"I've been looking over the ranch," he said by way of greeting.

"I said we'd start at six; it's fifteen till."

Abby stopped so close to Jonah that he could smell her soft honey scent again. He struggled with the smile that threatened to curve his lips. "I'm an early riser—always have been."

He looked far too happy, and it galled her. "Are you ready to go?"

He nodded. "Anytime you are."

She walked past him to the stall where she kept her working horse, Sassy. "How much of the ranch do you want to see?" she asked, slipping the bit between the brown-and-white pinto's teeth.

He felt motivated to help her saddle her horse, but instinct told him she would not appreciate the gesture. "I'd like to see the mustangs Quince mentioned. And he suggested you might show me a couple of horses that could be trained to a sidesaddle."

She paused as she tightened the cinch beneath her horse. "You want a horse for a lady?"

"That's right. Quince said you could train one for me. I don't doubt your ability after seeing you ride yesterday."

"I don't ride sidesaddle."

He gave her an audacious look. "I believe I came to that conclusion on my own."

She led Sassy out of the stall and shoved their lunch into the saddlebags. Why did he have to make her so mad? she wondered, as she watched the way his midnight-colored hair fell softly across his forehead. She wanted to touch it, to touch him. He was so male, so overpowering, that she wanted to walk right into those arms and feel them close around her.

She tossed a rope over her saddle horn in disgust. She could only imagine what his reaction would be if she did such a thing.

Against his will, Jonah's attention was drawn to the sway of Abby's hips, in spite of the baggy trousers she wore. The heat that coursed through him was so powerful it left him shaken. He was stunned that this little vixen, the one woman who was forbidden to him, could stir his passion so fiercely, and she wasn't even trying. He was glad she kept her distance, because he was not sure he could resist her if she had shown him the slightest encouragement. Even now heat swelled his need with such an intensity it left him reeling.

He forced his attention away from her body and watched her take a rifle off the hook, then shove it into her saddle holster. "Are you expecting trouble, Miss Hunter?"

"You always expect trouble out here," she told him, swinging into the saddle. "If there is none, you count yourself lucky."

He smiled. "I see. I hope, if the need arises, you will protect me."

Her lips clamped together tightly as she attempted to suppress the angry words that begged to be spoken. Instead she guided her horse out of the barn and waited for him to join her. With the familiar creak of leather, he rode up beside her.

"Did you fill your canteen, Major?"

Abby's face flushed with indignation when he laughed aloud and replied, "Sometimes you just have to laugh at the absurd." Then his eyes gleamed, reflecting humor. "I *am* in the cavalry, Miss Hunter; I don't go anywhere without water."

She felt like such a fool, and his laughter only made her feel worse. He was an officer who led troops into battle, she reminded herself. Of course he would know the fundamental survival skills that were probably taught to first-year cadets at West Point.

As they rode away, Jonah was still amused, and that further nettled Abby. So far she was not enjoying herself, and the morning had just started. Later she would have some choice words to say to Quince for volunteering her to spend the day with his friend.

The two of them rode abreast and in silence until the house was out of sight. When they came to a fence, Abby bent to open a gate and, after they rode through, fastened it behind them. They rode through the tall grass at a steady pace, scattering a large herd of deer as they went.

Jonah felt the warmth of silent companionship spread through him like a gentle wind. He could imagine himself owning a spread like this one with Abby riding beside— He shook his head. No, not Abby—Patricia.

He had fallen behind and spurred his mount to catch up with her. The sight of that frivolous little braid swaying down her back was too enticing for his peace of mind.

At one point Abby noticed that Jonah kept glancing behind him, and he finally halted. She reined in and raised an inquiring brow at him.

"That's the horse you were riding yesterday; why is he following us?"

A smile lit her face when the stallion galloped up to her and nudged her hand. "Moon Racer is like a pet—he thinks he can go anywhere I go." Her fingers trailed down the stallion's thick mane. "Once he even followed me onto the porch, thinking he could go in the house with me." She ran her hand down the roan's neck. "You should have seen Frances take a broom to him that day."

"Quince told me how you saved Moon Racer's life by bottle-feeding him."

She laid her face against the stallion's neck. "He's still just a big baby who wants affection."

While Jonah watched her with the horse, he felt a tightening in his heart. There were so many aspects to Abby's personality that he couldn't decide who she really was. One moment she could be happy and glowing, like now, then the next moment, saucy and defensive. She was like a spring mist, visible, but untouchable by the human hand. She was intelligent and able to hold her own in a conversation. But there was also a distant, cold part of her that was like a winter wind, intense and relentless.

He could remember, as a child, catching a firefly in his hand—he had felt wonderment at the delicate glow that had spread outward from his fingers. In the end, he had opened his hand and allowed the firefly its freedom.

Would it be like that with Abby if he tried to catch her?

He had a burning need to learn more about her—he wanted to hear her laughter sing on the wind. He wanted to know the real Abby. He wanted to hold her until the deep sadness disappeared from her eyes.

She smiled and leaned closer to him and whispered, "Moon Racer is jealous of any other horse I ride."

Jonah watched her eyes sparkle with devilment, and for the first time he heard her laughter. The sound struck deep, arousing powerful emotions, and ignited an answering happiness in him. She was the most enchanting creature he had ever seen. If he wasn't careful, she would beguile him—if she hadn't already done so.

"You see, Major, I've never told Moon Racer that he's a horse—he thinks he's a person."

The great stallion tossed his head and whinnied, pushing against the pinto and causing the mare to edge sideways.

"Moon Racer, stop it," Abby demanded, trying to guide Sassy away from the aggressive stallion's powerful teeth.

Before Abby could intervene, the roan had already nipped the pinto's neck, and the frightened mare reared and backed away.

When Abby finally calmed the frantic Sassy, she slid out of the saddle and went to Moon Racer. "You should be ashamed of yourself." Even as she scolded him, she drew his head toward her and patted his back. "Why do you have to be jealous? You know how important you are to me."

Moon Racer would have gone after the mare again, but Abby grabbed his mane and yanked his neck toward her. "Don't do that!"

She looked up at Jonah. "I'm sorry about this. If I had known Christmas put Moon Racer in this pasture, I would have taken us in a different direction. I am going to have to change mounts."

Jonah leaned forward in the saddle. "So you let the stallion have his way?"

"Not always, but I will today." She went back to the mare and unsaddled and unbridled her. Looking Sassy over to make certain that the stallion had not drawn blood, Abby nodded in satisfaction when she saw no injury. With a gentle pat on the mare's rump, she sent her galloping across the pasture. "I'll have Christmas bring her home tomorrow."

Before Jonah could offer his help, Abby had already thrown her saddle over Moon Racer and cinched it. He watched her smile at the horse, dimples dancing in her cheeks.

"You can't always have me to yourself," she said to the stallion before climbing into the saddle. Then she turned to Jonah. "I know he's spoiled, but he almost died as a colt. He grew up without a mother, like I—"

Even though Abby had clamped her lips together, Jonah knew she had stopped short of telling him about her motherless childhood. She was tugging at his heart, and other lower extremities, and he didn't seem to have any defense against her.

He found himself thinking how difficult her life must be, knowing her father had murdered her mother. The woman in the portrait had definitely been a lady, and if she had lived, her gentle guidance would have helped her daughter. He wondered if Abby dressed in trousers because she had never learned how to be a woman, or if it was her way of defying convention.

He tried to think of Patricia, but her image was blocked by Abby's mischievous green eyes.

He had to concentrate on something else, say something, anything, to distract himself. "Now that I see how much the stallion means to you, I know why you were offended when I offered to buy him."

Her mood changed from somber to hostile. "Moon Racer is as much a part of this ranch as the soil itself. Many of the horses you see here were sired by him, and many of our neighbors' horses as well."

She nudged the stallion forward, and they rode away from the pasture, through another gate, until they finally reached a hilly meadow.

"The two horses you asked to see are just over the next hill," Abby told Jonah. "If you choose one of them, I'll train it for you."

He glanced out at a land that looked like Eden, but there were thorns and secrets in this paradise. The woman who rode beside him was like an unbroken horse herself, wild and untamed.

Abby Hunter had disturbed him almost to the brink of madness. He'd had trouble going to sleep the night before, knowing that she was in the room next to his. He had been awake to hear her restless pacing and wondered at the reason for it.

She reined in the powerful stallion. "After lunch I'll take you to see the mustangs," she told him.

Jonah nodded, his attention centered just above her head because he dared not look into those mesmerizing eyes. "I'll look forward to it," he answered, wishing she had never come bounding out of that tree at him, disrupting his orderly life.

Chapter Seven

Frances had prepared a feast.

She had certainly outdone herself for the major's benefit. Abby thought of the sandwiches and fruit the housekeeper usually packed for her on the days she couldn't get home for lunch.

"You have a choice of spiced beef, chicken, block cheese, and apple or cherry tarts. What would you like to start with?"

He had sat down with his back against a tree trunk, watching her. He bent forward and looked into the bag. "Is there a chicken leg in there?"

"As it happens, there is." She handed him a red-and-white-checked napkin along with the chicken leg he had asked for.

Abby took a chunk of cheese and nibbled on it while she watched the way the breeze danced through the high grass, all the while feeling the major's eyes on her.

At last he asked, "What do you do for fun?"

"Fun?"

"Yes, fun—interest, hobbies, pastimes."

She had to think a moment. "I like riding, of course. I try to draw when I have time. I used to spend a lot of time visiting Iona Montgomery—you met her husband yesterday."

"Used to?"

She frowned and glanced up at the sky. "Iona was a good friend." Abby looked at him. "She died a short while back."

"I'm sorry. I wouldn't have brought up a painful—"

She stood, feeling pain in her heart for the woman she had loved like a mother. "No. It's all right. Iona had been ill for some time before she . . . died."

"What is your impression of Mr. Montgomery?"

"He's my father's friend. The whole town of Diablo seems to think highly of him."

It did not escape Jonah's notice that her voice was cold when she spoke of the banker.

"Let me ask you a question," Abby said, wiping her fingers on a checked napkin. "You knew Quince before he met Glory—do you find him much changed?"

He paused for a moment. "I suppose he is more contented than he was when he scouted for me. Yes, I would say Quince is very contented."

"Yes, he is that, but it's more than just being content. He's happy, I mean, really happy. And so is my brother Brent." She met Jonah's gaze. "Is it the same for all men when they marry? Is that the way you feel about the woman you are going to marry?"

Jonah was taken aback by her bold questions. His lips twisted, and he arched an eyebrow. "My, aren't we being inquisitive?"

"I don't mean it that way—I'm not prying. I'm trying to understand why Quince, who never wanted to be tied down to anyone, has become so domesticated. I see a softness in him that was never there before. Glory can just come into a room, and Quince is all smiles."

"Yes, I have noticed their closeness. Perhaps he feels more responsible now that he's married."

"It's not that—we all feel responsible and dedicated when it comes to the Half-Moon. It's simply that Quince cares more about Glory's happiness than his own."

Jonah's voice deepened as he stared at her. "Some would call it love, but I'm not sure I know what that word means."

Abby drew in a deep breath. "I'm glad someone else sees it the way I do. I would never allow any man to order my life, like Glory and Crystal do. I can't see me grinning and getting all soft over any man."

Jonah took a bite of chicken and chewed it for a moment, not trusting himself to speak. He looked at her guardedly. "There must be some man of your acquaintance you would be willing to settle down with."

"There isn't. I don't even like men, except for my brothers."

He frowned. "Someone has hurt you, haven't they?"

"Why would you say that?"

"You are always on guard, as if you are expecting people to be critical of you. I believe you dress and act the way you do out of defiance."

Abby glared at him. "You don't know me well enough to say that. And I don't need your opinion on the way I dress."

"I am sorry. I didn't mean it that way. But you see, I knew you a long time before we met. Quince talked a lot about you. He's proud of you, you know."

"Yes, I know he is."

"I haven't met your brother Matt, but between Quince and Brent, I would say you are more like Quince—at least in looks and actions."

"We both favor our mother in coloring."

Abby chewed on her bottom lip for a moment and then met Jonah's clear gaze. "So you don't love this woman you are supposed to marry?"

He was startled, because he had been trapped by his own words. Abby didn't miss a thing. "I respect and admire her."

She was profoundly puzzled. "Is that any reason to marry someone? I respect Charley Herbert, and I admire Mr. Spindle, who owns the general store, but I wouldn't want to marry either one of them."

"Is there more chicken?" Jonah asked, trying to change the subject, because her questions had caught him off guard. He was accustomed to women who were coy or flirtatious. If she would faint or have the vapors, he would know exactly what to do. But he had no defense against her candid outspokenness, and her total disregard for him as a man.

"Frances likes you," Abby said matter-of-factly. "Because of you she gave us enough food to feed ten hungry men."

He smiled. "It's always wise to please the cook."

Later, when they had both satisfied their hunger, and Abby had packed away what remained of their lunch, Jonah leaned back against a tree and closed his eyes, contented for the first time in so long he could not remember.

After a while, Abby wandered to the top of a hill and shaded her eyes against the sun as she glanced at the valley below. There was a restlessness in her that she couldn't understand. She looked back at Jonah, who appeared to be sleeping, then walked back down the hill, knowing she should wake him soon if they were going to see the mustangs while it was still light.

She dropped down on the grass; her gaze eventually turning to him. He had an aristocratic profile and a strong jawline, and he was so handsome she wondered if he were spoiled by the attentions of the ladies. She had an almost overwhelming urge to touch him, to lay her face against his, to feel his arms encircle her. He had removed his coat and unbuttoned his shirt, and she could see the sweat gathered in the hollow of his throat.

What was there about him that made her feel such anguish and uncertainty?

She lay back in the grass, watching the sun peeping through the branches of the tree. All around her were familiar sounds and smells: the scent of wildflowers, a mockingbird trilling in a nearby live oak, the scrabbling of squirrels playing tag up the thick oak trunk.

Once again she looked at the major, watching the rise and fall of his breathing. A woman could feel safe with her head resting against that broad chest. She looked at his beautiful lips and wondered what it would feel like to have them pressed to hers.

She was startled when he opened his eyes and gave her a lazy, provocative smile, as if he had known she had been studying him.

There was not enough breath in her to do more than whisper, "You were sleeping, and I didn't want to disturb you."

"I wasn't asleep; I was thinking."

"What about?" she couldn't help asking.

"What would it take for a man to start a spread like the Half-Moon?"

She spoke without thinking. "Good land and prime stock."

He sat up. "That's not what I mean. What would it take for a man like me, who has a limited knowledge of ranching, to become a rancher?"

"Hiring a good foreman and wranglers who knew what they were doing—land, water. . . ."

"I don't see myself raising horses." His voice took on an excited tone. "I would be more interested in cattle breeding."

She sat up straight in shocked surprise. "You can't be serious."

"Probably not." He looked at her for a long moment before he spoke. "When I arrived at this ranch yesterday, it just felt right to me." He didn't know why he was telling her how he had felt, but he wanted her to know. "Does that make any sense to you?"

"Not really. You are a high-ranking officer, and your slightest wish becomes a command, while we work hard just to hang on to what we have. This is the West; you are from the North—"

"East."

She looked as if she would like to argue the point, but relented. "I don't understand why you would even consider giving up what you have"—she waved her hand around—"for this."

"Wouldn't you?"

"I belong here—you don't."

"Yes." He glanced into the distance. "It was just a fleeting thought."

Abby tried to imagine him as a rancher, but she just didn't see it. From their first meeting she had felt that he was the most authoritative man she had ever met, and nothing that had happened since had changed her mind. He was a commander of men, not a cattleman.

"What would the lady you are to marry think about moving to Texas?"

He looked as if he were pondering that thought. "She probably wouldn't like to live anywhere but Philadelphia."

For reasons she couldn't understand, Abby instantly disliked his fiancée. She frowned, knowing she had no right to feel that way about a woman she had never met. And, after all, she didn't even like Jonah Tremain.

"Miss Hunter," Jonah said as he pulled on his blue jacket and buttoned it, "which of the two horses you showed me this morning do you recommend for Patricia?"

"The white mare is spirited, but I can gentle her down. The Arabian gelding, however, has an inclination to be willful, so he will need a firm hand. He also has a tendency to be nervous, and shies when he's startled. I would recommend the mare for your bride-to-be."

He looked at her for a moment. "Which horse would you choose for yourself?"

She knew that he expected her to say she would choose the Arabian. "Neither of them would suit me. The mare is too tame, and the Arabian is not spirited enough either."

He remembered the sight of her astride Moon Racer, a memory that would always be with him. "That's pretty much what I thought."

"Have you decided which horse you want?"

"I'll take the mare, if you will train her for me."

"Yes. I said I would." A pain shot through her heart at the thought of training a horse for his lady, and she did not understand why.

Why should she care that he was going to marry some Yankee and raise other little Yankees? she thought bitterly.

* * *

Jonah caught a glimpse of blue sky through the gently swaying branches overhead. He couldn't explain to her how he felt because he couldn't even explain it to himself. He had the feeling he had finally found what he had been missing in his life. If he had not come to the Half-Moon, he might never have known there was an emptiness inside him.

He had sensed something extraordinary about the Hunter family the night before. He hadn't missed Quince's pride in his sister, or Brent's inflexible misgivings about her recklessness, and his fear that she might have been hurt. The Hunters had survived a terrible tragedy that would have torn most families apart, but it seemed to have bonded those three together. Even though they might disagree among themselves, they held on to each other and they fought to hold on to their land. The father was another matter—he was a pathetic figure, on the outside looking in, but that was to be expected.

A strand of hair had come loose from her braid, and she pushed it impatiently out of her face in an innocent movement that fired Jonah's blood. He ached inside for something that was just out of his reach, something he could never have.

"It's getting late. If you want to see the mustangs, we had better leave now," she told him.

When Abby stood up, she innocently stretched her arms over her head, a move that pushed her breasts tightly against the front of her shirt. It was such a tantalizing sight that it was almost Jonah's undoing.

He turned his back to her, and his eyes closed. "Yes, we should leave now."

Every move she made was provocative—she was half wanton and half woman. Abby seemed to have no knowledge of how easily she could torment a man; she was totally at peace with who she was, while he felt as though someone had just slammed a fist into his gut and twisted his heart into a knot.

Chapter Eight

It was an hour later when they arrived at the pasture where the mustangs should have been grazing. At first Abby was not concerned when she didn't see them; she just assumed that they were probably grouped at the water hole. She nudged her horse forward, and Jonah followed her down the hill.

When they reached the water hole, Abby drew back on her reins and shook her head. "They are not here!" she said in stunned amazement.

"Could one of your brothers have moved them elsewhere?"

She stood in the stirrups, shaded her eyes, and looked all around. "No, they haven't been broken yet. And we always keep them here and don't let them mix with the other stock until Brent has them examined for disease."

Abby had a sick feeling inside; she didn't want to believe what her eyes were telling her. "Lately there has been some trouble with rustlers, and some of our neighbors have been hit hard." She frowned. "My brothers aren't going to like this."

She whirled her mount around. "I have to get back to the ranch and let them know at once!"

"Wait!" he called out, stalling her, the commander in him taking over. "I need to look for evidence while it's still light. If we take the time to ride to the house, we'll lose the light, and the trail might be cold by tomorrow."

"Quince will be able to track them."

He gave her a brief glance before he rode slowly forward, his head bent while he studied the ground intently. "Were they shod?"

She maneuvered her horse beside him, looking down for signs. "No. This was a new string that the hands drove in last week. They wouldn't be shod until they were ready to break."

"I see signs here of some twenty-odd unshod horses."

"That's right. Twenty-three."

"I see something else," he said, dismounting, bending down to touch a broken blade of grass and rub it between his fingers. Then he traced a hoofprint with his finger. "There were at least three shod horses among the stock. Whoever was driving the mustangs took them toward the west, and it wasn't more than an hour ago." He stood and gazed about him. "We just missed them."

Abby trusted Jonah to know what he was talking about. "We must let my brothers know as soon as possible!"

Before he could mount his horse, two shots rang out in quick succession, kicking up dust in front of Abby and causing Moon Racer to back away. Two more shots followed, and the stallion reared, his eyes wide with fright.

Without thinking, Jonah rushed to her and lifted her off the horse. He shoved her toward a nearby oak, then pressed her against the trunk, shielding her with his body.

He lightly touched her shoulder. "Don't move."

She tried to squirm away from him, but his grip tightened. "I have to get my rifle."

He unsnapped his holster flap and drew his gun. "You aren't going anywhere. Whoever fired those shots is either a bad shot, or he was aiming at you. He shot too wide to be aiming at me."

Another shot rang out near Moon Racer, and Abby watched helplessly as the giant horse backed away. "Jonah," she cried, "they want to shoot my horse. I have to do something to help him!"

Another shot rang out, and the roan shied, tossing his head in defiance.

She frantically cried out, pushing against Jonah's chest. "Don't you understand—he won't leave me! He'll stay until they kill him!"

His grip on her tightened. "Abby, listen to me. I don't think the rifleman is trying to hit the horse. It appears he only wants to frighten it, or maybe draw you out. I am not going to let you be a target." He tensed, his attention on the next hill over, where he saw the sun reflecting off the barrel of a rifle. His keen sight picked up the dust from at least one rider.

"Let me go," she said, wiggling against him, trying to slide past his body.

"Don't move." He pressed his body tighter against hers. "He's still out there."

"I can't just do nothing while he shoots Moon Racer. What kind of twisted person would want to hurt a helpless animal?"

"If we knew the who, we might know the why." He glanced down at her. "Do you have any enemies you know of?"

"Not anyone who would want to kill me."

The man must have reloaded, because shots rang out again; this time Moon Racer edged closer to Abby.

Jonah glanced down at her. "I'm going to have to shoot close to Moon Racer to make him leave. He's too easy a target."

She nodded, trusting his aim. "Do it quickly."

Jonah turned slightly so he could take better aim and shot three quick rounds near the stallion's front legs, but still the animal would not leave. Jonah aimed closer, and the stallion reared on his hind legs, his front legs pawing at the air. Another shot from Jonah's gun sent him galloping away.

Abby held her breath until she saw him at the top of a hill, and then he disappeared safely behind it.

Her legs felt so limp they could scarcely bear her weight, and she collapsed against Jonah.

He grimly studied her face. "We can't leave until we know the gunman is gone."

Jonah arched to removed bullets from his belt, and his body ground against her. She caught her breath as he loaded the pistol, suddenly feeling the heat of his body. She felt the wall she had erected around her feelings begin to crack and crumble. She moved her head the merest bit to rest her cheek against the roughness of his jacket. "I've never had anyone shoot at me before," she managed to say.

"I have." Jonah released the hammer of his gun and rested his chin on the top of her head, his arms going around her. "Don't be frightened. I won't let anyone hurt you."

When she tilted her head and looked into his eyes, the rifleman was forgotten, and all she could think of was the male body pressed against hers. Sweetness, raw and deep, wound its way through her, and she wanted to hold on to the moment forever.

They heard the sound of hooves as the gunman rode away, the noise growing fainter in the distance. Then she sensed a sudden change in Jonah. His hand clamped around her waist, bringing her closer to him. She moved her head at the same moment he lowered his, bringing his mouth near hers. If she moved the merest bit, their lips would be touching. In a movement that took her by surprise, he laid his face against hers, and she closed her eyes while her breathing became shallow.

She felt an urge to slide her fingers into his thick black hair, but resisted it.

His breath became trapped in his throat, and his arousal was so quick and violent it took him by surprise. He wanted her so badly his hand moved to the clip that held her braid in place. Strong emotions stirred within him as he fought to resist the temptation. Even battling with himself as he was, he brought her tighter against him, and she did not object. He touched her face, trailing a finger across her lips, and his breathing caught even tighter. He had the strongest urge to touch every part of her satiny body.

"Abby," he whispered. "You have driven me crazy since the moment you came swinging out of that tree at me."

She was too honest to deny what was happening between them. "Yes," she admitted in a velvet-soft voice. "I know."

Her blood was singing through her veins, and she could feel her heart pounding fiercely. He held her so tightly she could feel his body tremble and swell with his need.

Her lips quivered, and she could not utter a word as his mouth crossed her jawline and lightly caressed her lips, not lingering long enough for a kiss, but long enough to make her want more.

Jonah shifted his weight and nudged her legs apart, fitting his hardness between her thighs. His hand slid up her arm, and he heard her uneven breath against his ear.

His heart was slamming as if it would break out of his chest. He cradled her head against his shoulder. She had tapped into something primitive and possessive within him, and yet he felt overwhelming tenderness that made him want to protect her. He held her to him for a moment, filling his soul with her sweetness—yet knowing he must let her go.

"I didn't mean for this to happen," he said in a hoarse voice. "I can't explain it."

She choked on her reply. "I know."

He raised her chin and studied her face, tracing her mouth with a lover's touch. He wanted to kiss the dimple in her cheek and to loosen her hair from its confines. His hand slid up her ribs, but he forced himself to stop before he touched the tempting swell of her breasts.

"We had better go," he said regretfully, still unwilling to loosen his hold on her.

"Yes," she said thickly, pushing lightly against his chest and feeling him step away from her. "As it is, it will be nearly dark when we get home."

He took her hand and held it for a moment. "Abby, I'm sorry for what just happened between us. I went too far." He was struggling for the right words. "I hope you will forgive me."

"It was nothing." Abby didn't want him to be sorry, and she didn't want to forget what had just passed between them. For a brief moment they had shared something fragile and wonderful. She had felt warmth in him, and he had touched her heart in a way that no one else ever had.

Now the ice-blue eyes she looked into held no warmth. "I . . . we should leave now, Major."

He nodded. "We'll have to ride double."

She quivered, and her pulse quickened at the thought of being that close to him again. But she had no choice unless she wanted to walk back to the ranch. Her breathing became shallow as she approached his horse. She tried to distract herself by contemplating his McClellan cavalry saddle—it had no saddle horn, and it wasn't as deep as the western saddles she preferred.

Jonah felt her hesitation, so he gripped her waist and lifted her onto the saddle. He brushed against her as he climbed on behind; then his arms came around her when he gathered the reins.

She was in his arms again, and she thought her heart would burst free of her body. She felt the hard wall of his chest against her back, and she could feel the intake of every breath he took. Her head drifted backward to rest against his shoulder, and the world seemed to shift around her.

Abby's eyes closed, and she was enveloped by his masculinity. She was puzzled by new and unwelcome sensations. How could the one man she had disliked on sight be the first man to bring out such feelings in her?

There could be no future for her and Jonah. He would marry the woman in Philadelphia who was probably of his class and breeding. She bit her trembling lip. Probably every female who came in contact with him felt the same overpowering attraction that she had, and the same devastating hopelessness.

Abby straightened her spine and pulled away, trying not to think about him in that way. Today she had experienced a new awareness of her own body.

She had a consciousness of what it felt like to be touched by a man—the memory of his lips brushing hers was so keen that it ripped her apart inside. She wanted him to press her to his body and do all the things a man did to a woman.

Her transformation from child to woman had been a painful one.

"Are you comfortable?" he asked against her ear.

"Yes, thank you," she answered, barely able to find her voice.

He slowed his horse to let it rest, since it was carrying double.

"It's all right if you relax against me. There is no need to keep yourself so stiff."

Her head was against his chest but she did not relax—if anything she was more rigid than ever.

His mouth touched her ear, and he whispered, "You haven't been this near a man before, have you?"

She could not speak, so she shook her head.

"It's all right, Abby," he assured her. "You are safe with me."

Her eyes drifted shut as his thighs pressed against her.

"Abby."

"Yes."

"I really won't hurt you."

Hurt her—her heart was having to pump twice as hard just to keep up with the blood that flowed through her body. "I know."

They both fell silent.

Jonah did not understand how he had almost lost control, something that had never happened to him before. He had never felt such a deep yearning for any woman, not even Patricia. In spite of Abby's unconventional behavior, he now considered her the most feminine woman he had ever met. She fit perfectly in his arms, as if she belonged there. A powerful craving tore at him, and he wanted to touch his mouth to those sweet lips. He wanted to teach her what it felt like to be a woman—his woman.

He mentally shook himself. He must be out of his mind—he was supposed to be her brother's friend.

Quince trusted him with Abby.

Hoping to guide his mind back to sanity, he attempted to conjure up a mental picture of Patricia. But his mind was locked on the green-eyed minx who probably wanted nothing more than to get off his horse and as far away from him as possible.

"Could we hurry?" she asked, proving his conjecture and straightening away from him.

He nudged the horse faster with the heels of his boots. She had stormed into his world and turned it upside down.

When they reached the house, Brent was just leading his horse out of the barn. When he saw them, his frown eased into an expression of relief.

"I was just going to look for you. When Moon Racer came back riderless, I knew something had happened. Are you all right, Abby?"

Jonah lifted her down, and she went into Brent's arms. "Someone shot at us, and the mustangs are gone!"

Brent turned to Curly. "Round up everyone who can ride and send someone for Quince. I'll want to leave within the hour." He looked at his sister. "Abby, I want you to get in the house. If someone is shooting at us, I don't want you in the way."

Usually Abby would have argued the point, but she merely nodded. She looked at Jonah. "Thank you for what you did today."

Before he could answer, she had turned and walked swiftly toward the house.

"Brent," Jonah said, "whoever it was deliberately shot at your sister."

Brent's jaw tightened. "Then he's a dead man if I find him."

Chapter Nine

Edmund closed the front door and hung his hat on the hatrack in the entryway. He sorted through the mail on the hall table and saw nothing interesting there.

The house was eerily silent because it was Hilda's day off. She had likely left a cold dinner for him, but he wasn't hungry. He wanted to go over his ledger again and see just how much money Jack Hunter and his brood owed him.

Jack was so gullible, it was easy to maneuver him into spending money he couldn't afford, thus helping Edmund along with his plans to bankrupt the Half-Moon. Jack's ignorance and naivete only proved what Edmund had known all along—he was superior to Jack in every aspect. His real problem had been Brent, who was shrewd and not so easily fooled. And now there was Quince to contend with as well. He'd outsmart them all—the deed to the Half-Moon was almost within his—

"I always wanted to live in a house like this."

Edmund was startled by the voice and turned to see a man sitting in his desk chair, his muddy boots propped on the oak surface of his desk.

Kane had a malevolent air about him, and seemed to contaminate the atmosphere around him. His black eyes caught the lamplight and were glowing like red coals. There wasn't anything Kane wouldn't do for money, and that made him invaluable to Edmund. However, Edmund didn't want anyone to think they were on friendly terms—he had stressed many times that Kane would not be welcome in his home.

"What in the hell are you doing here?" His face was reddened by the anger that fired his blood. "I don't want you here!"

Kane swung his legs to the floor and shrugged. "I thought you might like to know the job's done. I drove the Hunters' mustangs to Echo Canyon like you wanted. I also took some scattered shots at the Hunter gal."

Edmund stalked across the space that divided him from the swarthy bastard and yanked him to his feet. "If you ever so much as look in Abby Hunter's direction, or go anywhere near her, or do anything like that again, it'll be the last thing you ever do!"

Kane laughed unpleasantly. "I think the day will come when we are going to have a serious disagreement. But," he said, shrugging, "this is not that day.

And by the way, you needn't worry about Abby Hunter. That handsome young officer is looking out for her. In fact, I probably did that officer a favor. When I watched them eat their lunch, neither of them seemed to be having a good time. But when I shot at that little gal's horse, he charged to her rescue and became very protective of her. He had to get real close to her to do that. I bet you couldn't have pushed a straw between the two of them."

"I could kill you!" Edmund's face grew even redder, and his rage was almost out of control. Having difficulty catching his breath, he dropped down on a chair. "If you do anything like that again, I *will* kill you."

"I don't think so." Kane laughed, and the sound of it was pure evil. "How does it feel to be old, and to realize that pretty little thing won't have you? She is surely sweet, but you'll never have that sweetness." His smile deepened the lines in his jaw. "But . . . that handsome young officer probably will."

"You bastard!"

Kane looked pensive for a moment, and then said icily, "You are probably right—I don't think my mother knew who my father was. If I am a bastard, that makes me dangerous—so don't ever push me too far."

"Get out! You have let the Hunter bunch check you at every move. If this one doesn't work out, you're through, Kane."

Kane's black eyes narrowed, and he cast Edmund a look so dark it made him shiver. "Not until I have all the money you owe me."

107

Edmund stood up, grasping the back of the chair. "We agreed you would sell the mustangs and keep the money you got for them, and I would deposit the rest in the account I set up for you."

Kane's smile did not touch his lips. "I wonder what the good people of this town would do if they knew about some of your dealings?"

Edmund stared at him, and then laughed aloud. "And you are going to tell them? I don't think anyone would take your word against mine. You don't frighten me, Kane. You'll do what I say, when I say it."

Kane shrugged. "For the moment, my interests are tied to yours." He paused with his hand on the door. "You are lucky that I don't like the Hunters."

"Yeah," Edmund said, feeling satisfaction stir in him. "It still sticks in your craw that Quince Hunter stopped you from taking his herd of mustangs, and you got all your men killed in that little struggle. They also rounded up the herd when you scattered them, didn't they?"

"Don't push, banker." Though spoken barely above a whisper, the warning was clear.

Edmund looked into cold black eyes and knew he'd struck a nerve, so he pushed further. "Isn't it strange how many of your men end up dead? I wonder if the ones you hired this time know to watch their backs?"

Kane took a step toward Edmund, reconsidered, and paused. "I know to watch my back with you, banker."

"That very well may be—but you are safe as long as I need you," Edmund said quietly, almost too quietly. "What you need to remember most is to stay away from Abby Hunter."

Kane touched the brim of his hat and smiled. "She's not the kind of woman I crave—she's too tame for me. But the major, he seems to like her just fine." He walked out of the room with Edmund following behind. "I'll be seeing you."

"Not that way," Edmund said. "Leave the back way, and don't let anyone see you go. And don't ever come here again. If I need you, I'll find you."

Kane's laughter followed him out the back door. When he had gone, Edmund sank down on a chair, his hands trembling. He thought of what Kane had said about Abby and that uppity major. Could Abby be interested in the man?

He had to find out, and there would be hell to pay if Major Tremain got in the way of what he wanted.

Abby hadn't been able to sleep for worrying about the stolen mustangs. Just before sunrise she tossed the covers aside and slid out of bed. Most of the men would be with her brothers, so she would help them out by tending the stock.

It took her only a few minutes to dress and braid her hair. She heard Frances stirring in the kitchen as she walked through the house, not wanting any breakfast. When she stepped off the porch, she stared worriedly at the clouds that hung low in the slate-gray sky. It would probably rain before the morning was over, and that wouldn't help her brothers track the mustangs.

When she reached the barn it was dark inside, so she lit a lantern and went to pump water. After the horses had been watered, she took the pitchfork off the hook and, with practiced aim, tossed the right amount of hay to each horse.

She had reached the last stall when she heard someone at the front of the barn. When she caught a glimpse of a blue uniform, she thought it might be Jonah. But when the cavalry trooper stepped into the lamplight, he was a stranger to her.

"Ma'am," he said, touching his flat-brimmed hat. "I'm Private Davies, and I was sent to get Major Tremain."

She paused and leaned her cheek on the handle of the pitchfork. "He was here, but he rode out with my brothers. I can't tell you when to expect him back." She went on with her work and tossed hay over the last stall. "If you will wait until I am finished, Frances will give you breakfast."

Davies grinned, his eyes following her graceful movements as she worked. "I don't mind waiting."

Jonah and the men of the Half-Moon Ranch had been out all night attempting to follow a cold trail. There was not a tracker anywhere better than Quince, and even he had lost the trail when they came to the limestone hills. Whoever had taken the mustangs certainly knew what they were doing.

Quince and Brent exchanged weary glances. They both knew that it was going to be nearly impossible to meet the army contract unless they rounded up more mustangs, and there wasn't time for that.

It was a bedraggled-looking group who gave up the chase and returned home just after dawn. Everyone went in different directions, each hoping to get a few hours of sleep.

Jonah was walking in the direction of the house when he saw the horse with the U.S. Army brand. He turned to look at the barn and, seeing the lantern glow, hurried in that direction.

Abby was aware that the private was watching her, but she chose to ignore him. He had a look in his eyes that spelled trouble for someone—for her.

"You look like you know what you're doing. I never saw a girl wearing britches and doing that kind of work afore."

"Is that so?"

He grinned and moved closer to her, lifting her braid and working it through his fingers. "You ever do anything fun in the hay—anything with a man who knows what he's doing?"

She turned to him, and at the same time brought the prongs of the pitchfork within inches of his chest. "If you think I won't use this, you are sadly mistaken. Let go of my hair—now!"

He dropped her braid and stepped back, coming up against the stall gate, unable to move any farther away. "I was only funning. I wouldn't of done anything unless you'd of agreed to it."

The pitchfork moved up to his neck, and she rested the sharp points against his throat. "Let's just say I don't like your idea of fun—I don't find you humorous at all."

Abby heard the crunch of boots and glanced into Jonah's glacier-blue eyes. He seemed to be assessing the situation before he stepped forward to take the pitchfork from her, throwing it harmlessly to the ground.

"Have you nothing better to do than to terrorize my men?" Jonah said bitingly.

"Just keep him away from me." Abby was furious at the trooper for taking such liberties with her, but angrier with Jonah because he was defending the man.

She shoved past him and stopped to glare at Private Davies. "Never set foot on the Half-Moon again. If I see you here, I will finish what I started."

Jonah watched her stalk out of the barn before he turned his attention to the private. "What did you say to her?" Jonah demanded, ready to disembowel the private. Now that he'd had a moment to think, he knew Abby would not attack anyone without a reason.

He snapped to attention. "I . . . just . . . implied that I'd like to . . . that . . . do something in the hay. Maybe I touched her hair a bit, sir."

Jonah grabbed Davies by the shirtfront and jerked him forward, his jaw muscles taut with anger. "You just bought yourself more trouble than you can handle, trooper. You are never to go near Miss Hunter again, or even speak to her. Is that clear, soldier?"

"Yes, sir. But she's so pretty she got my blood to boiling."

"Cool down, mister. I will deal with you later. But for now, do you have a message for me?"

Davies knew he was in real trouble when he saw the anger brewing in the major's eyes. Yep, trouble was coming his way, all right, but Major Tremain would tend to business first. "Yes, sir. Sergeant MacDougall said I was to tell you there's a ranger in town, sent to help . . . you, sir."

Jonah released him, and he fell backward, catching himself on a railing to break his fall.

"Go back to town and tell the sergeant I will be there directly. Then you can wait for me in the hotel room."

The young trooper saluted and hurried away. Yeah, he was in bad trouble.

Abby scrubbed with wide strokes, taking her anger out on the oak table. She dipped her cloth in the suds, wrung it out, and continued her task.

She heard bootsteps outside the kitchen and didn't bother to look up when Jonah entered the room.

He leaned a shoulder against the wall and watched her for a moment before he said, "If you continue scrubbing that hard you'll likely take the finish off the wood."

She blew a stray strand of hair out of her face. "It's nothing to you."

He pushed himself away from the wall and came up beside her. "Do you want to tell me what Private Davies did or said that forced you to defend yourself?"

"No."

She dipped her rag in the water, not bothering to wring it out and not caring that she splashed sudsy water on Jonah's nice shiny boots. "All I ask of you is to keep that vile man away from me."

He reached for her hand and took the rag, tossing it into the water. Turning her resisting body toward him, he looked into her eyes. "I need to know what he did so I can make the punishment fit the crime."

"Then ask him."

He released her and stepped away, and his restless pacing seemed to fill the room. "The private has already indicated he behaved improperly toward you."

She watched him take a limping step, and he looked so weary her heart went out to him. It was with effort on her part that she was able to keep her head up and her spine straight. "This has happened to me before with men who think they can say anything to me. I can take care of myself, as you saw when you entered the barn."

He inhaled softly. "What would you have done, Abby—run him through with the pitchfork?"

She shook her head. "I wouldn't have hurt him, but I wouldn't have let him hurt me either. I'm so tired of men thinking they can touch me and say improper things to me just because my father . . ." Her lips trembled from the effort she was expending to keep from crying. "If my brothers knew what your trooper said to me, they would . . . they would . . ." Her eyes widened with concern. "Please don't say anything to them about what happened."

He stopped in front of her and took her into his arms. He felt her melt against him. "I myself would kill anyone who harmed a hair on your head, Abby."

She closed her eyes, feeling the comfort of his shoulder beneath her cheek. A sob was building up inside, so she clamped her lips shut.

His hand drifted across her shoulder, and he planted a soft kiss on her hair. "I have to leave now. I'll be in Diablo for a few days if you should need me for anything."

She frowned. "Why are you going away?"

"Something needs my attention at the moment. But tell Quince I'll be back by Thursday so I can help him look for the mustangs. He said there were several hidden canyons and valleys where we could look."

"It could take a long time, or we may never find them."

He stepped away from her. "Be assured I will deal with the private in my own way, and please accept my apology. I am sorry that someone connected with me has caused you distress. And I'm sorry for what I said at first."

She moved stiffly back to the bucket and dipped her hand into the soapy water to retrieve her scrub rag. She centered her concentration on the table as she listened to him walk out of the room. In her mind she could picture him packing his gear and riding away.

Throwing the rag down, she ran out the back door and toward the barn. She didn't want to watch him leave, because she might never see him again.

He said he would come back, but what if he didn't?

She covered her eyes with her hands. And what if he did come back—what then?

Chapter Ten

When Jonah reached the hotel, he took the steps two at a time in spite of his limp. His anger had been smoldering during his ride to Diablo, and it was now in full flame. Without knocking, he thrust open the door to Davies's room and stood on the threshold, glaring at the private.

"You have some explaining to do, trooper!"

Davies had been nervously polishing his sword and rose to his feet, the sword clattering to the floor. "Yes, sir."

MacDougall, whose room was across the hall, heard the commotion and came to see what was happening. "Is there trouble, Major?"

"He didn't tell you?"

MacDougall shook his head. "No, sir, he didn't."

Jonah glared at his sergeant. "I told you to choose someone to come with us who would be of use to me." He pointed at Davies. "That man is a disgrace to the uniform he wears."

MacDougall's head snapped around, and he stared hard at the private whose body now visibly shook with tremors. "Can I ask what he's done, sir?"

"You tell him, Private," Jonah ordered, feeling sick inside for the pain the young man's actions had caused Abby.

Davies couldn't seem to find a comfortable place to put his hands—he straightened his collar, fidgeted with the buttons on his shirt, and, at last, clasped them behind him.

"I'm waiting," MacDougall's voice boomed out.

"I . . . there was this pretty gal—she wasn't a lady or anything, 'cause she was wearing britches. I saw her there in the barn, and I wanted to . . . I thought she might oblige me by taking off her—"

"Enough," Jonah said, his voice filled with fury. "That woman you are referring to is very definitely a lady. You insulted Quince Hunter's sister, and you insulted the Sixth Cavalry. Do you have anything to say for yourself?"

MacDougall's expression was murderous. "Stand at attention when the major speaks to you, soldier, and answer his question."

"Yes, sir." Davies snapped to attention, his body stiff, his eyes darting from one man to the other. "I didn't mean no harm. I just haven't been with a woman in a long time, and—"

118

Jonah turned to MacDougall. "Get him out of my sight. I want him gone by the time I get back to the fort. I won't have a man under my command who insults a lady. Go with him and arrange his transfer to Fort Leavenworth. If I could, I would have him brought before a tribunal for what he's done. But I don't want Abby Hunter's name brought into it. Make sure his punishment will remind him of what he did today."

MacDougall had never seen the major so angry, and he knew there had to be a good reason for it. His eyes were hard as his attention fell again on Davies. "You heard Major Tremain. Pack your kit and meet me out front in half an hour. From here on out, soldier, you won't know a peaceful day till you learn never to insult a lady."

Jonah stared hard at his sergeant. "Where is the ranger I'm supposed to meet, and what is his name?"

"His name's Grant Zachary. He's staying in the room next to mine, sir. But I believe you'll find him at the Lone Star at the moment. I've heard of him. He's got a good reputation."

"See to your prisoner, and come straight back here when he has been transferred." Jonah moved slowly out of the room, his anger still smoldering. He didn't want anyone to touch Abby but him. He paused on the stairs, thinking he was little better than Private Davies because he wanted to kiss those soft lips and touch her soft skin—

"Damn," he ground out. He had to get her out of his mind.

That seemed to be the hard part.

*   *   *

The bartender at the Lone Star eyed the stranger. He could usually tell a lawman at first glance—there was something in their stance, the way they wore their guns, and the way they watched the people around them without seeming to watch them. What Ken O'Malley didn't know was what branch of the law the stranger served.

He slapped a coin on the bar and smiled in welcome. "This here silver dollar is me betting I can guess who you work for."

Grant Zachary was tall and rugged-looking, rather than handsome. He had sandy hair and clear gray eyes that shone with an honest, almost boyish light. "I don't make enough money to throw it away on another man's bet. But I don't have any objections if you guess, and if you're right, I'll buy you a drink— if you aren't, you can buy me one."

"Fair enough." O'Malley stroked his mustache as he intently studied the man. His gun was slung low, meaning he was a quick draw. The handles of his guns were pearl, which meant he valued them and could afford them. He was lean, so he must spend a lot of time in the saddle.

"My name's Ken O'Malley—most people just call me O'Malley—and my guess is that you're either a U.S. Marshal or a Texas Ranger. My money's on your being a ranger."

The stranger opened his coat to show his badge. "Well, O'Malley, it looks like I owe you a drink. Name's Grant Zachary."

O'Malley's face slid into a grin. "I heard of you by reputation. It's said that you sometimes work hand in glove with the army. It's also said that when you get on the trail of an outlaw, you don't come back without 'im."

"Now, that there's more fiction than fact. I have gained a reputation I don't quite deserve."

"Keep your money, ranger. It'll be a pleasure to buy you a drink, and maybe you can tell me what brings you to Diablo."

"I'll take the drink, but I don't have any information to give you."

"So that's the way it is?"

"Yeah. That's the way it is."

The bartender placed a drink in front of the ranger before his attention was drawn to the high-ranking officer who came through the bat-wing doors, leaving them swinging behind him. Here was another part of the puzzle, he thought.

Jonah waited until his eyes adjusted to the smoke-filled dimness. His gaze swept over the crowd and stopped on the man at the bar who looked back at him with a smile.

"Are you Grant Zachary?"

"I am—and you'd be Major Tremain."

"Let's take one of the back tables so we can talk privately," Jonah said, shaking hands with the ranger.

O'Malley watched the two men move away from the bar. Something was in the wind if a ranger was in town, and still more, a high-ranking cavalry officer. If he was taking odds on the reason for their presence, he'd bet they were joining forces, looking for the men who'd been robbing the army payrolls.

When they were seated at a table in a secluded corner, Jonah asked, "Have you anything to tell me?"

"I did some checking up Uvalde way. Someone thought they recognized one of the men in the holdup, but the man had left town by the time I got there, and I haven't picked up his trail. Yet."

"Have you ever heard of Norman Williamson?"

"Yeah, I have, but nothing good. He used to be a gunslinger, but I hear he's an Indian agent now. Seems to me the government isn't so particular about who they hire these days."

Jonah nodded in agreement. "Some would say he does the Indians more harm than good. Some say he has lately come into money that he can't account for."

"You want me to poke around and see what I can turn up on him?"

"No. I already have someone watching him." Jonah looked clearly into the ranger's eyes. "What I want you to do is find out anything you can about the local banker: What is his background, where does he come from, how does he spend his time?"

Grant reared back in his chair. "Edmund Montgomery."

"You know him?"

"I know he's respected around here, but I heard that New Orleans doesn't hold him in such high regard."

Jonah absorbed that bit of information. "I need to know what places he frequents so I can ask questions of the right people. So far it seems Mr. Montgomery just goes from the bank to his house, never deviating from his daily routine."

"I should think he would go to most of the local functions."

"Like what?" Jonah asked.

"I hear they are having a shindig next Saturday. It's the town's birthday or something like that." Grant lit a cigar and blew the smoke into rings above his head. "How's your dancing, Major?"

Jonah was awakened the following morning by a loud commotion outside his window. He groaned, rolled to his feet, and looked down on a group of young boys gathered in front of the hotel. Two of them seemed to be on the verge of fighting, and they were being urged on by several other youngsters.

The larger boy's victim was a young lad who was at least forty pounds lighter than he was. The bully shoved his young opponent and sent him sprawling on the ground, giving the onlookers a reason to cheer.

"Come on, coward, fight me," the larger boy taunted.

Jonah had seen this same kind of baiting among some of his soldiers—he hadn't liked it then, and he didn't like it now. He left the room and went down the stairs.

* * *

Abby helped Rob Herbert to his feet and dusted him off. She then took her handkerchief and wiped the dirt from his face. "Rob," she said pointedly, "Johnny Brisco is two years older than you, and he's bigger, and until you prove to him that you aren't afraid of him, he will continue to make your life miserable."

The young boy's eyes were shimmering with tears, and she could feel him tremble. "I . . . am," he said, hiccupping, "a-afraid of him."

Abby knew she was not helping Rob's cause by coming to his aid. Already the aggressor was sneering at Rob from several yards away and making rude comments about his needing to be rescued by a woman.

"Listen to me, Rob." Abby raised his chin and looked into tear-dampened eyes. "It's not size that matters—it's how much you want to win. Remember your Sunday school lesson about David and Goliath?"

"Uh-huh," he muttered, but again lowered his head.

"You aren't listening," she said firmly but quietly. "You can beat him, Rob. But only if you believe in yourself like I believe in you."

There was hope in the gaze he raised to her, and he was listening intently. "How?"

"I happen to know you are left-handed, so keep your right fist up and aim low with the other one. You can't reach his jaw with any power, so aim for his stomach. Hit him hard!" She smacked her fist against her hand. "Put everything you have into the blow. I promise you if you take him to his knees, he'll never bother you again. It's always the same with bullies—they only pick on those who fear them. Don't be afraid, Rob."

He acknowledged what she was telling him with a slight nod of his head, but there was still doubt clouding his eyes.

Johnny sauntered up to Rob and tapped him on the shoulder. "Are you going to fight, freckle-face, or run home to your ma?"

Rob drew in a determined breath and lunged forward with his fists flying. He hit Johnny so hard that it surprised the older boy and made him double over in pain. He struggled to catch his breath and dropped to his knees, his eyes on Rob, fearing he would hit him again.

The younger boy stood with doubled fists, his feet planted wide apart and a fearsome expression on his face. "If you get up, I'll hit you again!"

Abby watched young Rob's head come up in pride when he looked at her, and she nodded her approval.

Johnny was groaning and holding his stomach, so Abby offered him some advice: "I wouldn't do anything to provoke Rob again, if I were you. He's probably only been holding back so he wouldn't hurt you. Guess you pushed him too far this time."

The other boys had already taken to their heels, leaving Johnny to fend for himself.

"You ain't gonna let him hurt me, are you?" Johnny asked, dragging gulps of air into his lungs.

Abby bent down beside him to make sure he wasn't badly hurt. She concluded he was merely winded. "I don't know if I could stop him. He's pretty mad at you."

Johnny nodded as he glanced at his red-faced adversary, who looked as if he wanted to tear his head off. "Would you ask him not to hit me again?"

"Yes. I could do that." Abby stood up. "What do you say, Rob—if Johnny leaves you alone, will you leave him alone?"

Abby saw Rob's fists tighten, and he took a step toward Johnny, who cringed and closed his eyes as bullies always did when they were challenged.

"I guess so. If you don't talk to me and don't even look at me, I might leave you alone."

Johnny stood up slowly and ducked behind Abby. "I'm going to be leaving now," he said, his eyes darting to Rob's still-clenched fists. He inched past the hotel, hurried past the general store, and then quickly disappeared behind the doctor's office.

Rob came up to her grinning, his shoulders straight and confidence in his stance. "You was right, Miss Abby. I hurt him, didn't I?"

"You did, Rob. But don't take too much pleasure in the deed, or you could become just as bad as Johnny."

He looked puzzled for a moment, the freckles on his face more prominent. "Can't I be just a little happy?"

Abby laughed and tousled his dark hair. "Perhaps just a little."

"Miss Abby, will you wait right here? I just want to run home and get something for you."

"You don't need to give me anything, Rob. We're friends, aren't we?"

"Yes, ma'am—I'm surely your friend." He backed up. "Don't leave till I get back." With that, he turned and ran in the direction of his house past First Street.

"Nicely done," came an amused voice behind Abby.

She turned to find Jonah leaning against a supporting post, his arms folded across his broad chest. "Have you been there all this time?"

"Mostly." He levered himself away from the post. "I have come to the conclusion that if the army took you along to act as diplomat, we might not have to fight Victorio."

"You might find this humorous, Major, but I can assure you I don't. Poor Rob has been hounded and terrorized for years by Johnny Brisco."

Jonah liked the way her green eyes flamed with indignation when she was passionate about something. "So you took matters into your own hands."

Abby's attention was caught by Rob, who was running toward her with the mangiest, scraggliest-looking dog she'd ever seen bouncing in his arms. "Oh, no," she said with a sinking feeling.

Rob's eyes were shining as he held the dog out to her. "Clover had three pups a while back. I was able to give them all away but this one—no one seemed to want him. I want you to have him, Miss Abby."

She was aware that Jonah was silently laughing, and it infuriated her. "I'm proud to have this pup," she told the young boy. "And I thank you for your generosity."

"It's my only way to thank you, Miss Abby."

Abby got a whiff of the animal and held it a little away from her. "You had better run along home, Rob. Your mother will be expecting you."

"I think you're mighty pretty, Miss Abby." His eyes were shining with earnestness. "Real pretty."

Abby smiled at him. "Thank you. Now go."

She watched him race up the street before she turned back to Jonah.

"I think you have a friend for life," Jonah said, smiling.

She held the animal up and examined him. He was lop-eared, with one rheumy eye and scraggly whiskers. It was hard to tell what color he was, but she would say he was yellow, mottled with brown. His feet were so big he was sure to trip over them every time he tried to take a step.

"What am I going to do with this dog?"

Jonah laughed in amusement. "That is the ugliest dog I have ever seen. I don't think you will find anyone to give him a home. It looks like you are stuck with him."

Abby glared at him. "This dog might look ugly to you, but Rob gave me something he treasured. I am going to take him home with me. It was a beautiful gesture."

Jonah looked at the mongrel clutched to her chest. "What you did for the boy was a compassionate and beautiful gesture," he said quietly. "And the boy was right—you are mighty pretty, Miss Abby."

Chapter Eleven

Abby drew in a deep breath, stumbling for the right words, but they were stuck in her throat. Why did Jonah always catch her at her worst, and why did she care so much? "I have to go now. I've got supplies to order."

Jonah would have said more, but Grant Zachary came out of the hotel at that moment and stopped beside him.

"Abby? Abby Hunter? Can that be little Abby all grown-up? It can't be anyone else with those dazzling eyes."

The ranger's infectious smile was well known to her. "Grant," she said with affection warming her voice, "what a pleasure it is to see you again." She reached out, and he took her hand, dwarfing it in his giant one. "Does Brent know you are in town?"

The laugh lines at the corners of his eyes deepened. "Not yet. I thought I'd ride by and see him later on. I heard about him getting hitched."

Abby was wrestling with the dog, and she finally solved her dilemma by shifting the animal over her shoulder. "It's been much too long since we have seen you. I imagine Frances would make you her famous chocolate cake if you came by the ranch."

"Tell her I'll be coming by Saturday next. I hear Diablo will be celebrating an anniversary with fireworks and a dance. I'm hoping you'll go with me." He nodded at Jonah. "You might even save the major here one of your dances."

She shook her head. "I don't usually attend the town dances."

Grant remembered all too well how the townspeople had treated Abby after the family tragedy. In the past he had defended her name on more than one occasion. "I can't believe you are all grown-up now." He shook his head and held her at arm's length so he could see her better. "I want you to go to the dance with me, and I won't take no for an answer."

Jonah was irritated by the happy reminiscing between the ranger and Abby. "How does it happen that the two of you know each other?"

"I've known this pretty little gal since she was no more than knee-high to a stump, and I've just been waiting for her to grow up so I could dance with her."

Jonah glared at the man. "You are full of surprises, ranger."

Abby didn't want to admit to either of them that she didn't know how to dance and that she didn't have a dress suitable for the occasion. "Grant, I don't think I—"

He stopped her before she could refuse him. "I'll be coming for you, Abby. I think I can get there in time for supper if you ask me nice-like."

He left her no way to refuse, because she wanted him to come to the ranch so everyone could see him. "I'll tell Brent you're coming so he can be there, too." She was still wrestling with the dog. "I have to go now." She nodded at Jonah and then at Grant.

Grant reached out and took the pup from her until she could mount her horse, then handed the animal up to her. He touched the brim of his hat. "Good day to you, Abby. I'll be seeing you Saturday."

Jonah wondered why he hadn't thought to help Abby with the dog. He had been deeply troubled when Abby smiled at Grant the way she never had at him. Although he had no reason to object, he didn't like the idea of her dancing in the arms of this man—or any other man, for that matter.

Grant waved as she galloped away. "She's 'bout as pretty as a speckled pup. A man would consider himself lucky if he could win her affection."

Jonah glowered at the ranger. "How long have you known her?"

"Her brother Brent and me are friends. We met when we were just boys at the fishing hole south of town. I spent a lot of time at their ranch."

"You lived here in Diablo?"

"For the better part of my youth." He watched Abby ride out of sight. "She has grown into one very fine-looking woman. I reckon she's about the prettiest gal I've seen in a long time. Do you know if she's spoken for?"

Jonah stared up at the clear blue sky, feeling a sudden possessiveness toward Abby and knowing he had no right to feel that way. "You would have to ask the lady."

Grant, hearing the biting tone in Jonah's voice, turned to him. "I intend to, Major—I certainly intend to. When I saw her just now, after not seeing her in over three years, something hit me like a train. I certainly have it in mind to go courting at her door. Lately I've been thinking about taking me a wife and settling down somewhere, buying a little spread and raising kids and cattle."

There was a hard lump in Jonah's throat. At the moment he wanted nothing more than to smash his fist into the ranger's face. "You think you can come riding into town and expect Abby to marry you?"

Grant thumbed his hat back and shook his head. "Well, no, it won't happen quite that easily. I'll have to do some dedicated sparking."

Doubts tore at Jonah's mind. Abby did seem to be fond of the ranger, and Grant appeared to be a good sort of man. Needing to distance himself from the situation, Jonah stepped into the street. "There is something that needs my attention."

Grant nodded, blissfully ignorant of the turmoil that churned inside Major Tremain.

* * *

Abby met Glory at the front door and took her hand, pulling her inside. "You have to help me!"

Glory looked puzzled—she had never seen her sister-in-law like this before. "You know I will. But what do you need me to do?"

Abby ran her hand through her hair, untwisting the braid and allowing the wavy mass to sift through her fingers. "Everything is wrong about me! I want to cut my hair. I don't have a proper gown to wear to the dance, even if I knew how to dance, which I don't."

Glory removed her hat and tossed it on a chair. "Halt, stop, slow down. I haven't understood one word you've said."

"Grant Zachary has asked me to the dance next Saturday night, and I don't know how to dance!"

Glory was dumbfounded. "I want to meet the man who has made you want to wear a gown and cut your hair. Tell me all about him."

"Who?"

"Abby, you can be so maddening at times. Tell me about this Mr. Zachary. What's he like?"

Abby was puzzled. "Grant is Brent's friend, and he's a Texas Ranger. I've known him most of my life—he's like a big brother to me."

Glory stared at Abby in bemusement. "He's like a brother to you, and yet you are willing to cut your hair for him?"

Abby led her confused sister-in-law down the hall-way to her bedroom. She searched in her mending basket until she found her scissors, then placed them in the palm of Glory's hand. "Please, just cut it."

Glory was still puzzled when Abby sat down before the mirror.

"I like the way you do your hair. Cut mine like yours."

The redhead felt as though a tornado had just swept through her life—sometimes Abby had that effect on people. She lifted a long black strand of hair and shook her head. "I can't. It's too beautiful to cut."

"Close your eyes and do it," Abby urged.

Glory met Abby's gaze in the mirror. "I'm not sure closing my eyes to cut your hair is a good idea." She took a tentative snip. "Quince is going to kill me for this."

Abby closed one eye and stared at the reflection of the scissors with the other. "Just do it before I change my mind."

Glory drew in her breath and snipped, still wondering what in the world had come over Abby.

Soon long black tresses lay at Glory's feet, and she stepped back to observe her handiwork. Now that the weight was off Abby's head, the rest of her hair curled about her shoulders and face in ringlets.

"I never knew you had curly hair."

Abby ran her fingers through her hair in amazement. "The curls have been a source of irritation to me for as long as I can remember. Since I didn't know what to do with them, I found it easier to wear my hair braided."

Glory pulled the curls away from Abby's face and studied her attentively. "You look very different."

Abby turned to look at her sister-in-law. "Will you help me find a gown and teach me to dance?"

Glory stood back and studied Abby closely. "We are about the same size, except you are a few inches taller than I am. I have a yellow gown that would look good on you. I would have to lower the hem a bit, and maybe put lace around the bottom."

Abby stood up. "Now teach me to dance."

"I'll try," Glory said doubtfully. "But I don't know how to lead—you would need a man for that." Glory suddenly frowned. "We don't have music. I can't sing, can you?"

"Not so well that anyone would want to listen," Abby admitted. "If only Crystal were here, she could sing or hum for us."

"Let's find a room with more space," Glory said, getting into the spirit of adventure. "It's too crowded in here."

Glory walked out of the room, and Abby followed her to the parlor. Under Glory's direction, they moved furniture until they had cleared a wide area.

"Let me see," the redhead said, taking Abby's hand. "You put your hand on my shoulder, and I'll— No, that's not right. I put my hand on . . . I'm confused, Abby. We need one of your brothers."

"Will I do?" Jack said, poking his head around the corner.

Glory beamed at her father-in-law as she went forward and dragged him into the room. "You are just the person we need. I want you to teach your daughter to dance."

Jack looked at Abby in wonderment. Something about her was different. She still wore her trousers, but . . . "You cut your hair!"

Abby fluffed it and smiled. "Do you like it, Papa?"

He studied her for a long moment, and then had to clear his throat before he could speak. "It's almost like I was looking at your mama." He shook his head and went toward her. "I think we should start with a waltz, since it's the most fun."

At first Abby felt nervous because she had been consciously avoiding her father for so long. But she had not seen him drunk in several weeks; he seemed to be trying to stay sober. He had stopped muttering about Matt under his breath, something he did only when he was drinking.

He smiled down at her and gently instructed her with patience as he led her through the dance steps. Abby began to relax a bit. He hummed softly while he whirled her around the room, and she became caught up in the dance.

"You learn fast," he commended her. "You follow my lead like a born dancer." He could have told her that her mother had been a fine dancer, but she didn't want to hear any more about her mother from him.

After a while, Jack was taking Abby through the steps of a polka. Then he showed her the motions of a slow dance. "You won't have trouble following any man's lead. Your moves are natural."

"Thank you, Papa," she said, laying her head against his shoulder, warily at first, and then experiencing a glimmer of the same love she had felt for him as a child.

Glory was beaming at her sister-in-law's progress. "Now we just have to get you into a gown and shoes. I'll come over early the day of the dance and dress your hair."

Jack held Abby away from him. "You will be the prettiest one at the dance."

"Will you be going to the dance, Papa?"

"No, I won't, Abby. But I'll picture you there dancing with all the young men and stealing their hearts away."

Abby smiled and snapped her fingers. "I almost forgot. I have something for you. Wait right here with Glory until I get it out of the barn."

Jack looked inquiringly at Glory, but she shrugged her shoulders.

Moments later Abby returned carrying a dog, which she shoved into Jack's arms. "He's yours, Papa, a thank-you gift, or maybe a birthday gift."

Jack held the dog away from him. "My birthday isn't until January."

"I know that, but it could be an early birthday present."

Lifting the dog, he could only stare at the homely creature. He preferred pedigree in any animal, whether it was horses or dogs. This pup was certainly at the bottom of the ladder in breeding.

"He's a mongrel," he said, shoving the dog back at Abby.

"Yes, I know," she said, shoving the pup back to him. "But he has personality and character. Look how he's wagging his tail—he wants to belong to you."

"Abby!"

She grinned at him. "What will you name him, Papa?"

Jack was at a loss for words to describe the dog. "With his scraggly whiskers he looks something like a catfish with fur."

The dog chose that moment to lick Jack's face, and Jack pulled away in disgust.

"I think you just named him, Papa. He seems to like to be called Catfish."

"Charming." He placed the dog on the floor, but it stayed right at his feet, bouncing and wagging its tail.

"I think he likes you, Jack," Glory said, catching Abby's eye, and they both laughed.

"Frances will never allow him in the house," Jack warned, bending down and reluctantly patting the dog on the head.

"Oh, he's housebroken, Papa. But he is a bit clumsy. When he wags his tail he knocks things off tables. He would benefit from training."

Jack grumbled as he walked out of the room with Catfish sliding and scrambling after him.

Chapter Twelve

Jonah sat in the straight-backed chair in Sheriff Dawson's office, posing questions to the middle-aged man with graying hair.

"Have you happened upon a man here in Diablo by the name of Norman Williamson?"

The sheriff shifted in his chair and nodded. "Yeah, I have. I believe he's friends with Edmund Montgomery. At least, I saw them together a few times here in town."

"Did you notice anything suspicious about Williamson—has anyone commented on any unusual actions?"

The sheriff was thoughtful. "Not suspicious exactly—more like unusual. From what I've heard, him and Edmund have a joint venture of buying up land. I thought it was kinda odd that an Indian agent would have that kind of money. I overheard them talking about the Taylor ranch, which is the biggest cattle spread hereabouts. I didn't even know Lester Taylor had his place up for sale."

"Could you give me directions to the Taylor ranch?"

"I'll do better than that, Major." Dawson stood up, hung the jail keys on a peg, and then straightened his gun belt to a more comfortable position. "It's a slow day, and my deputy can watch things here in town for a few hours. I'll ride out with you."

It had rained on the ride to the Taylor ranch, but the sun had burst through the clouds before they arrived, and the rain had soaked into the thirsty ground without leaving a trace.

Jonah, Sheriff Dawson, and Lester Taylor were seated in rustic chairs on the front porch of the sprawling brick ranch house. Lester was a tall, thin man of advanced age, and he had the haunted look of someone carrying a heavy load on his shoulders. Jonah recognized the unmistakable signs of a beaten man.

"In three weeks I'm going to lose everything I've worked all my life for, Sheriff." He lowered his head to his hands and shook it. "Since my wife's dead, and we had no kids, I have nowhere to go when I leave here."

"You don't know me, Mr. Taylor," Jonah said, "but would you mind answering a few questions for me?"

The old man raised dark eyes that held a defeated look. "I don't mind if I do."

"I don't know much about ranching, but I saw a large herd of cattle grazing when we rode up. I can see that the house is a fine one, and the bunkhouse and barns seem in good repair. I guess what I'm asking is, how did you come to this pass?"

"You mean the foreclosure?"

"That's right."

"I trusted Edmund Montgomery, that's how." For a moment his eyes flamed with indignation, and then he shook his head. "He was always acting like my friend and getting me to buy more cattle and more land. I always prided myself on having a good business head, but Edmund came in through the front door like a friend and went sneaking out the back door taking everything I own with him. You can call me a fool if you want to, but I never saw what he was doing until it was too late."

"Have you heard of, or had any dealings with, a man by the name of Norman Williamson?"

The old man nodded. "He came here with Edmund once. Said he wanted to buy the place. That was before the trouble, and I told him I wouldn't sell." He lowered his head again, his shoulders slumping. "Now I wish I had taken his puny offer. At least I'd have had something to show for my years of sweat."

Jonah absorbed all he was being told. He stood up and walked to the edge of the porch that wrapped around the house, and gazed out over the land. It was beautiful, with a lot of tall oaks and meadows.

He could imagine children, his children, running across the grassy lawn—a strong son and a green-eyed daughter. His breath shuddered. No, his daughter would not have green eyes. Patricia's eyes were blue.

He swiveled around and faced the older man. "Mr. Taylor, if you were to sell your ranch today, what would be a fair price?"

"No one 'round here has that kind of money."

Jonah gave him a shrewd glance, thinking about the large inheritance that had come to him through his mother's estate. "I have."

Sheriff Dawson stared at Jonah. "Are you making a bona fide offer, Major Tremain?"

Jonah had known almost from his first glimpse of the ranch that he wanted to own it. He wasn't usually one to make a quick judgment, but this situation called for haste. "Name a price, Mr. Taylor, and I will expect it to be fair for both of us."

"You aren't funning me, are you?"

"I have too much respect for you to be anything but honest with you. I want to buy your ranch."

The old man's eyes filled with hope. "There is that large lien on it from the bank."

"Sheriff Dawson tells me you are an honest man, so take that into consideration when you set your price. But before you agree to anything, I will need you to stay on here and run the place and teach me all you can. I know very little about ranching."

There was cautious expectation in the old man's dark eyes. "You mean if you bought the place, you'd let me stay on here?"

"It would be part of the transaction. I would give you the control to buy cattle and hire what men you need to work the place."

Taylor sat forward and grinned. "Major Tremain, I could move into the foreman's house, and he could bunk in with the hands, since his wife left him for some northerner."

"I have more considerations before you decide." Jonah leaned against the porch railing and watched the old rancher's face. "Two more, actually; I will want all transactions to go through a bank in Fort Worth, because I don't want any dealings with Edmund Montgomery's bank. And I don't want anyone to hear that I bought the ranch until I have decided to let it be known."

"No one will hear a word from me, and I know the sheriff here won't say anything either."

Dawson nodded in agreement. He'd never liked Montgomery, and it did him good to see someone get the better of the banker.

Lester suddenly shot out of his chair and laughed with pure joy. "Damn if I ain't gonna get back at Edmund, and there's nothing he can do to stop me." He stuck out his hand to Jonah. "Son, you just bought yourself a ranch!"

"Call me Jonah."

"I'll call you Jonah, boss, king of the hill, anything you want me to call you. When I woke up this morning I didn't have a hope in the world—when I go to sleep tonight, I'll put my worries behind me."

* * *

Jonah stepped out of the telegraph office and right into the path of Edmund Montgomery.

"Major, what a coincidence, running into you. I have been wanting to speak to you about something."

"Mr. Montgomery."

Edmund heard the coldness in Jonah's voice, but he couldn't retaliate as he would have liked. He needed information that only the arrogant bastard could furnish. "I see you got a telegram."

"That's right."

Edmund watched him fold it and place it in his breast pocket. "I guess you won't be staying here much longer. I'd wager they'll be needing you at Fort Fannin, with the Indian trouble and all."

"We in the cavalry are practically vagabonds, Mr. Montgomery—we never know where we are going to be from one day to the next."

Edmund bit back the angry words that came to mind. He wasn't getting anywhere with this Major Tremain. He wanted to ask the major if he had touched Abby. He wanted to shove a gun in the man's face and pull the trigger. "I know you're looking for the men who robbed the army payroll—that's right, isn't it?"

Jonah detested the banker even more now that he had learned about his crooked dealings with Lester Taylor. And he was offended by the way the man was always prying into his affairs. "Mr. Montgomery, the government pays me to do my duty and to keep my mouth shut while I'm about it. I'm sure you can understand that."

It was becoming a real struggle for Edmund to hold on to his composure. "Will you be staying much longer at the Half-Moon Ranch?"

Jonah stared coldly into the man's eyes. "If you will excuse me, I have matters that need my attention." He stepped around Edmund and walked in the direction of the livery stable to get his horse.

The banker's fists were balled at his sides. That bastard was after Abby—he knew it.

Something had to be done about him.

He ground his teeth and entered the telegraph office. His smile was in place when he faced the young operator, Ira Billings. "How's everything going today, Ira?"

The young man was tapping out a message on the keys, so he held up his hand to silence the banker. When he was finished, he turned his attention to Edmund.

"I'm just fine, Mr. Montgomery."

"I noticed Major Tremain was just in here."

"Yes, he was."

"I know the major is in town on a mission, and I think I can help him, if you'll help me. But to do that, you'll need to tell me what was in his telegram."

"No, I can't do that. All messages that come through this office are confidential."

Edmund was growing more frustrated by the moment. "You can tell me if he sent a wire to anyone, can't you?"

"Yes, he did."

"But you can't tell me what was in it, or whom he sent it to?"

"No, I can't."

Edmund leaned even closer. "How would you like to come and work for me at the bank, boy?"

"I wouldn't like that at all, Mr. Montgomery." There was indignation in the young man's tone. "It was you and your bank that took my folks' farm. I wouldn't want to work for such a place."

Edmund whirled around and stomped out the door just in time to see Major Tremain riding in the direction of the Half-Moon.

That imperious officer would one day feel the heel of his boot on his neck—that or a bullet in the back; it didn't much matter which to Edmund. For the right price, Kane would be happy to accommodate him.

And as for young Ira, he'd put pressure on his boss to fire him.

Chapter Thirteen

Frances heard Jonah ride up, and stepped out onto the porch to greet him as he dismounted.

"I'm the only one home, Major. The men are all out helping Quince look for the mustangs."

"And Abby?"

Frances eyed him craftily. There was a situation developing here, but it might not bode well for any of those concerned. The major was developing an attachment for Abby, and Abby was already moping about because of him. "You can't never tell with her. The last time I saw her she was riding past the barn."

Abby braced her back against a wide tree stump and held her sketch pad on one drawn-up knee. Moon Racer was wandering about, grazing on sweet clover, so she was able to sketch him from every angle.

She always found solace in drawing because she had to concentrate on what she was doing and couldn't think of anything else—like worrying whether Jonah were going to come back, and wondering why she should care.

Abby heard a rider approach, and her heart contracted when she watched Jonah dismount and walk toward her with long strides. She noticed that his limp was barely visible.

She lowered her head and her hair fell forward, masking her face. One black boot came into view. "You are blocking my light," she mumbled as her hand flew across the tablet, making bold strokes.

He moved to her other side and crouched down beside her. "What have you done to your hair?" he asked with quiet intensity.

She allowed herself to look at him only at chin level. "I asked Glory to cut it for me."

He reached out and took a black strand and tucked it behind her ear, suddenly tormented by the thought that she had cut her hair to please Grant. He tilted her chin up and looked at her closely. "I like it. But I'll miss that saucy little braid."

She ducked her head and reminded herself to concentrate on her drawing and not on the thundering of her heart.

"Let me see what you are doing." He took the pad from her and studied it, then flipped back to other pages and marveled at her talent. "You are good, Abby. You captured Moon Racer's muscles, and you managed to make horsehair look real enough to touch."

She felt uncomfortable under his praise and wished he would just go away so she could breathe again. "I always draw when I'm irritated." She raised her gaze to his. "Or when I'm mad."

He watched her eyes flame with indignation. "Who has made you angry, Abby?"

"Quince. He wouldn't let me go with them to search for the mustangs. He thinks I would be in danger just because someone shot at Moon Racer."

His fingers slid through her silken hair, but when he realized what he was doing, he pulled them away and reached into his inside pocket. "That's irrelevant now, Abby." He handed her the telegram. "This came this afternoon. The mustangs have been found."

She read it quickly, but the sentences were short and choppy and made little sense to her. "What does it all mean?"

"A man called Buddy Pratt, who apparently helped rustle the horses, was caught trying to sell them in Scurry County," he told her, filling in the blanks. "Pratt admitted that the horses had come from the Half-Moon, so he was arrested. I think Quince should send someone to Scurry County to drive the horses back and question this Pratt."

She stood up slowly, and he stood with her. "Jonah, you did this for us, didn't you?"

"It wasn't difficult. I have the resources to reach out to the authorities all over the state. It was Quince who mentioned that whoever took the horses would probably try to sell them. It was just a question of waiting and having others keep watch."

He was near enough that she could reach out and touch him if she wanted to, and she did want to. "You have helped my family once again, and I don't know how to thank you."

He smiled slowly, that devastating smile that turned her insides to a quivering mass.

"You could reward me by giving me that picture of Moon Racer, and we'll call it even."

Her eyelashes swept upward, and she perused his face discreetly, trying to gauge this new and lighter mood. This was a side of him she had never seen before, and she had no defense against it. She nodded and handed him her sketchbook. "Take the whole thing. I have others."

He laughed and tucked it under his arm. "One day, when your talent is hailed by one and all, and you are famous the world over, people will beg me for these drawings."

She carelessly brushed her hair out of her face, and her laughter joined his. "Thank you for what you did about the mustangs. Only a friend would go to so much trouble."

"Am I your friend, Abby?" His tone deepened. "Am I?"

"Yes," she admitted. "A good friend."

He stared at her for a moment. More had changed about her than her hair. There were other subtle differences. She was still wearing those damned trousers, but she looked more feminine somehow. She was so small, he wanted to protect her. He wanted to make her days happy and her nights—

"I was on my way to tell Quince about the mustangs, and I thought I would detour to tell you first. I know how distressed you have been about the horses."

"Will you be coming back to stay with us?" she asked, hope creeping into her voice.

He nodded. "I would like to very much, if it's not too much trouble."

"You'll always be welcome with us."

"Then I'll take you up on your offer tomorrow night. I don't want to be seen too often in town. Certain people are starting to notice and ask questions."

"Consider Matt's room yours anytime you want it."

"Matt is the only one of your brothers I don't know. What is he like?"

She thought about Matt, who had been wild in his youth, and had always been in trouble. Of course she would not say this to Jonah. "I think Matt took our mother's death even harder than the rest of us." She smiled up at him. "I miss him so much. I just want our family together again."

"Family is important." He took a long breath. "I have to leave now if I'm going to ride by the Diamond C and tell Quince about the horses. Afterward I have something to do in Diablo."

"Jonah, what can you be doing in town that you don't want people to know about? Everyone is talking about you."

"There isn't anything I can say at this time." He was anxious to tell her about the cattle ranch he had bought, but instead he said, "I'll see you when I get back."

Kane was skulking about in the shadows, watching the major and Miss Hunter. He liked nothing better than to torment Edmund with tales about the young Hunter gal and the army officer. He might even embellish some when he explained today's situation to the banker. In truth, nothing had happened between those two that could be considered intimate, not as he understood intimacy. But Edmund didn't have to know that.

He watched Major Tremain ride away, and shortly thereafter the woman left, too. He waited a bit until she was out of sight before he mounted his horse and rode to the tree stump where she had been drawing.

He dismounted, smiling. The two of them must have had something else on their minds, because they'd left the telegram behind. He read it quickly and then frowned, wadding it in his fist. He hadn't expected the telegram to concern him—he was getting careless.

He had little doubt that the Hunter brothers would make tracks for Scurry County; he would have to get there ahead of them and permanently shut Pratt's mouth.

Chapter Fourteen

Frances was kneading bread dough when Abby walked into the kitchen, still wearing her trousers. "Don't tell me you're wearing that garb to the dance tonight."

Abby opened a jar, removed a pickle, and bit into it. "Since you asked so politely, you might like to know I'm wearing one of Glory's gowns."

The housekeeper wiped her floured hands on a dish towel. "I'm glad you decided to cut your hair."

It had been three days since Glory had cut her hair, and it had taken Frances this long to mention it. "Do you really like it?"

"I surely do, and you know it. And I'm glad you've decided to go to the dance with Grant. He's such a nice young man." Frances watched Abby's face closely as she said, "The major came in with Quince today. He's going to stay a couple more days. But he rode off, saying he had a meeting with someone in Diablo."

"Did he say if he would be going to the dance to-night?"

"He didn't mention it to me," Frances answered. "But then why should he? I ain't going."

"I didn't really want to go to the dance myself. But Grant left me no choice. I'm not sure how everyone will react to my being there," Abby admitted, remembering painful times when she had been all but ignored. "If you had a son, would you want him to dance with me?"

"If I had a son, I'd be proud to have you for my daughter-in-law."

"I'm not going to marry anyone—it's merely a dance."

"And it's about time you had some fun." Frances looked Abby over, and her voice softened. "When those hateful women whisper behind your back, they'll only be jealous, because you'll be the prettiest one there."

"I don't think they will be commenting on how I look."

"Seeing you standing there with the light shining on you, it strikes me how much you favor your ma's picture."

"Why do people always say that to me? Mama was beautiful, and I'm certainly not."

"Because you not only have her inner beauty, you also have her features," her father said, entering the kitchen and lingering in the doorway.

Abby gave him a half smile. Sometimes, like now, she caught an expression on his face as if he were asking for some small show of affection and kindness, so she moved forward and put her arm around his shoulder. "How was your day, Papa?"

"Busy, as always," he said, hugging her to him, then releasing her almost too quickly.

"Jack," Frances said gruffly, pointing one dough-covered finger at him, "if you don't keep that dog out of my kitchen, I'll be serving you dog meat stew one of these nights."

He laughed, something he had rarely done since he came home from prison. "I can't make that hound do anything. He's useless and a pest." He winked at Abby. "But I guess I'm stuck with him, and he's stuck with me."

Abby took another bite of pickle and moved to the back door. "When Glory gets here, tell her I'm in the stable with Quince."

Quince was hunched near one of the mares, with her foreleg resting on his knee. He glanced at his sister when she approached. "She's been limping, and it looks like she picked up a stone." He ran his pocketknife around the horseshoe and nodded in satisfaction when the offending object popped out. "That should do it. Make sure you tell Navidad not to let anyone ride her for a few days; it looks like she's got a slight bruise."

Abby bent down to hold the mare's leg while he applied ointment. "Did you get the horses back?"

"Curly and Red just sent word that they found them. They said the mustangs were skin and bones, and we would probably lose some on the drive back." He screwed the cap back on the ointment and stood. "It's a funny thing—Jonah got word that the man who helped rustle the mustangs was found dead in his cell in Scurry County. Someone shot him right though the bars of the jail."

"Who would do such a thing?" Abby asked in horror, standing and giving the mare a comforting pat.

"Someone who didn't want him to talk to the sheriff, I should think," Quince told her.

"It's a fine thing that Jonah has done for this family. I don't know why I didn't like him when we first met."

"I don't understand it either." He watched her closely. "Have you started training that mare to the sidesaddle?"

"I . . . have been gentling her down first and gaining her confidence." She couldn't tell Quince that the thought of training a horse for the woman Jonah was to marry was extremely painful for her.

"Don't let yourself care about Jonah too much, Abby," he said with a brother's insight into his sister's feelings. "Jonah will marry that woman in Pennsylvania, and I don't want you to get hurt."

She knew it was already too late for his warning. "I'll start saddle training the mare Monday."

Quince nodded. "Patricia Van Dere and Jonah's pa will be arriving in Diablo in two weeks' time. He'll want the mare trained by then."

"Don't worry about me. I'm a Hunter, and everyone knows Hunters are uncrushable."

The lunch hour found Grant and the Hunter family members gathered around the kitchen table.

"Abby," Grant remarked with his fork halfway to his mouth, "why did you cut your pretty hair?"

"She didn't," Quince spoke up. "My wife here is the culprit."

"I like it," Crystal said. "Don't you, Brent?"

Both her brothers looked their sister over. "Yeah," Brent said at last. "But I liked it the other way better."

Quince agreed with a nod until Glory jabbed him in the ribs with her elbow. "It's just that you don't like change."

Quince smiled down at his wife. "I like you just the way you are, and my sister was all right before you cut her hair, too."

"It makes Abby look too old," Brent said, adding his assessment.

Abby bent toward him. "I am old, Brent. Frances keeps telling me that most women my age are already married."

"Not all," Crystal injected. "Melinda, the mancrazed Barton, is still single."

"Abby is just fine the way she is," Brent said with certainty, knowing his wife's barbs had been meant for him because Melinda had once had her eye on him as a potential husband.

Crystal rolled her eyes and looked at Glory. "They want to keep Abby as their baby sister forever."

Grant quietly watched the happy banter among the family, his gaze straying to Abby's face. He had often wished that he could be a part of this family. He had never had much of a family life himself, since his pa had died and his ma left him to be raised by his aunt Dora. Now his aunt was dead, and he didn't know where his ma was. For three years he had severed all ties with Diablo. He watched Abby's face light up with laughter. If she would have him for a husband, he would become a part of this family.

Glory had arranged Abby's hair on the crown of her head and allowed one long curl to hang over her right shoulder. Standing back, she nodded with satisfaction. "You are stunning!"

Abby turned her head from right to left and smiled. "I don't know—it doesn't seem like me."

Crystal lifted the canary-yellow gown off the bed while Glory adjusted Abby's stiff petticoats. "I wish I could be there tonight and see everyone's reaction when you walk into the dance."

Abby turned to face Crystal. "Why aren't you going?"

Her sister-in-law patted her stomach. "I have to be careful from now until the baby is born. Brent says no dancing."

Glory nodded. "A wise decision." Then she looked slightly dreamy-eyed. "I can't wait to have Quince's baby."

Abby was only half listening to Glory and Crystal talk about babies. "I'm grateful that bustles have fallen out of favor. I would never have worn one of those contraptions. As it is, I can hardly breathe with this corset on. Do I have to wear it?"

"Yes," Glory and Crystal said in unison.

Crystal lifted the gown over Abby's head, and it drifted down about her body. Then she fastened the hooks while Glory fluffed it out.

Abby lifted the skirt in front and glared down at the matching slippers in disgust. "I'll probably break my neck in these." She frowned. "But the heels probably aren't much higher than my boots."

The room had fallen silent, and Abby became aware that Glory and Crystal were staring at her.

"What?" She turned around and reached toward the mirror, looking at her reflection in stunned surprise. "Can that be me?"

Glory opened the door and called down the hallway, "Quince, Brent, come in here."

Moments later Quince entered the room, looking quizzically at his wife. Then he saw Abby, and his eyes shimmered. "Darlin', you're all grown-up, and so pretty."

Brent stood in the doorway for a long moment, looking for any evidence of his little sister. "You are grown-up. I suspect some man will soon come along and take you away from us." She walked into his outstretched arms. "But not yet, Abby—not for a while, I hope."

Chapter Fifteen

The road in front of the town hall was choked with the many conveyances that had transported the merrymakers to the celebration.

As Grant helped Abby out of the buggy, she watched fireworks illuminate the night sky, and she heard the music from inside the hall drift out to her.

Grant took her hand warmly in his. "Have I told you how pretty you look tonight?"

She glanced back to see Quince helping Glory out of their buggy, and she waved to her sister-in-law before she answered. "You have made mention of it at least a dozen times."

He grinned. "Too much, is it?"

"Yes. You are like a brother to me. I don't want you to think you have to flatter me."

Her words cut him deeply. "I'm like a brother to you?"

"Of course. But you already know that."

He was not going to be shy where Abby was concerned. The night was young, and he would do his best to make her see him as a man and not as a brother.

The hall had been decorated with red, white, and blue banners and streamers. There were three fiddles and a flute playing a lively tune. It looked like everyone in the county had turned out for the occasion. Those who weren't already dancing had grouped together to talk with their friends.

Jonah was standing near the door, and he saw Quince and Glory come in, but he hadn't seen Abby. He edged closer to the entrance for a better look and stopped in his tracks. Abby was a breathtaking vision in yellow as she laughed up at Grant. Gone were the trousers and boots, and he stared at the most heartbreaking, enchanting woman he had ever seen.

He watched her search the crowd, and her search stopped when she saw him. His heart was thumping inside him; he wanted to go to her and push her hand off Grant's arm and place it on his. But he did not have that right. He turned away, no longer able to watch her with the ranger.

Abby noticed that Jonah was surrounded by people who wanted a chance to speak with such an illustrious officer. He stood tall and so handsome in his dress blues, and he seemed somehow out of place among country folk who, though dressed in their best, could not compare with his regalia.

She bristled when Melinda Barton, the town flirt, paraded in front of Jonah twice before she actually got the courage to stop and speak to him. Jonah acknowledged the woman with a mere dip of his head before his gaze returned to Abby.

Abby felt Grant tug on her hand, and she smiled at him as he whirled her into a lively dance. She did not have time to wonder whether she could remember the steps her father had taught her. Grant was such a good dancer, he took her right along with him. By the time the dance ended, she was breathless and laughing.

She was having fun!

She felt Jonah beside her even before he spoke. When he was near, the atmosphere became charged around her. Her gaze went to his.

"I wonder if you might save the next waltz for me, Miss Hunter?"

Why was he being so formal? she wondered.

She had not seen him dance with anyone else. Why did he want to dance with her? Her face flushed at the thought of being held in his arms. "I . . . yes. If you like."

Being an astute man, Grant noticed Abby's reaction to Major Tremain. She was drawn to him, but he didn't yet know how deeply she was involved with the officer. And he didn't know how Jonah felt about Abby. He did know that Jonah was committed to another woman, and Abby could end up being hurt. He intended to make sure that didn't happen.

Quince took his sister onto the dance floor, and when she looked up at him she found that he was frowning. "What's wrong, Abby?"

"Who said anything's wrong?"

"We spoke about this before, darlin'. Jonah is a good friend of mine, and I know him well enough to warn you that he will always do the right thing."

"I know that."

"He will marry the woman in Philadelphia."

"I don't expect anything from him." She managed a small smile. "And I'm not foolish enough to think he would be interested in me. He would probably be more drawn to Melinda, the flirt, than to me."

Quince guided Abby into a sidestep so he could watch Jonah. His friend was definitely not watching Melinda; he was staring at Abby with a thunderous expression on his face.

"Beware, Abby. Jonah is from a different kind of world from the one you know."

She lifted her chin. "Yes. I realize that."

Quince could see she was close to tears, although she tried to hide it from him. He had said enough on the subject, and would say no more. He wanted her to enjoy this dance. "I wonder if you have noticed that you are the center of attention? Everyone seems to be watching you."

"It must be because I cut my hair."

He grinned at her naivete. "I'm sure you're right—that's probably why all the men are watching you so closely."

Abby swallowed hard, thinking everyone must be gossiping about her. "I don't care what they think." She managed a smile. "I like dancing."

*   *   *

Edmund shouldered his way through the crowd to get to the Hunter family. He had come in late and hadn't seen Abby, so when he heard her laughter and turned in her direction, he paled, feeling as though a knife had just stabbed him. It was like Beth had come back from the dead. But it wasn't his beautiful Beth, it was her daughter reborn in her mother's image.

"Abby," he said, distracting her from talking to Grant. "I believe this is my dance."

She would have liked to have refused him, but she could not think how to reject him without drawing attention to herself. She nodded and placed her hand on his arm, hoping it would be a short tune.

Edmund was a good dancer, and it was a lively polka. But the touch of his hand on her made Abby wish she had worn gloves, as some of the other ladies had.

"Temptress."

"Please don't say things like that to me. You are Papa's friend, and he wouldn't like it." She would have liked to have added that he was not her friend, but she kept that thought to herself.

"I suppose you think I'm too old for you."

She was in a quandary. Edmund was always saying suggestive things to her and touching her in a way that made her shiver with revulsion. "Why, no, Mr. Montgomery, you are not old—I believe you are my father's age, or perhaps you are a few years older, I'm not quite sure."

He gripped her hand so hard she bit her lip to keep from crying out. When she tried to jerk away from him, his grip only tightened more.

"Stop it—you are hurting me."

"Abby," he said, his voice thick with passion, "I know your family is in financial trouble, but I can help if you'll let me."

"We don't need your help, Mr. Montgomery." She glanced in the direction of her brother, wishing she could catch his attention, but Quince was dancing with Glory on the other side of the room.

"Sweet Abby, if you'll be nice to me, I'll tear up the notes I hold on the Half-Moon."

His hot breath against her neck made her feel nauseated. She took a determined stance, choosing to misunderstand his intent. "I have always been polite to you, Mr. Montgomery. As for the note, Papa signed it in good faith, and we'll pay it off in the same way."

His hand slid up her arm. "You are such an innocent. I can only imagine the delight your surrender would be for a man."

She stared at him in disbelief, stopping in midstep. "Mr. Montgomery, I don't know what gave you the notion that you could insult me this way." Anger pushed her further. "If you ever say anything like this to me again, I'll tell my brothers."

His eyes became so cold she shivered when she looked into them, and he forced her into step with him. "I will have you, Abby, one way or another, and I don't care much if you come to me willingly or I take you against your will. And when I do, neither your brothers nor that fancy officer will get in my way."

He had threatened her with the deadliness of a rattlesnake ready to strike. "You are a monster, and the last man I would ever let touch me!"

"You may feel that way now, but I can change your mind, if you will only let me."

"Never!"

"I have a way of getting what I want—and I want you. You will come to me one day because you'll have no choice."

She tried again to pull away from him, but his hand at her waist anchored her tighter to him.

"Don't make a fuss, Abby. Do you want everyone to see your distress? They already gossip about your family. Do you want to give them more to talk about? Imagine how they would react if I told them you offered yourself to me if I would tear up your father's bank debts. Who would they believe, Abby— me or you?"

"My brothers will . . ."

The hard expression on his face dared her to say more; his eyes were like dark, bottomless pits of unspeakable evil.

"If you get your brothers involved in this, one or both of them will end up dead, and that's the truth."

The music had stopped, and she was stunned as he led her off the floor. She blinked her eyes when he raised her hand and kissed it.

"Don't touch me!"

167

He smiled and bowed slightly. "I will touch every place on your body before I'm finished with you, Abby."

She stood paralyzed by fright as he walked away, and tears gathered in her eyes despite her effort not to cry. She had been touched by something vile and evil. Mr. Montgomery not only wanted to hurt her, he said he would kill her brothers if she told them what he had said to her—and she believed him.

What should she do?

She hurried in the opposite direction from Quince so he wouldn't see how distressed she was and ask questions she could not answer. As she stepped outside, the sky was glowing with silvery bursts of fireworks. She stared upward, wishing she knew what to do.

"Abby?"

She turned her head and tried to smile at Grant.

"What are you doing out here alone?" he asked, placing his hand on her arm.

"I . . . the sky is so beautiful. This is the first time I have attended this celebration."

He saw the shimmer of tears in her eyes, and he knew Edmund was responsible. "You can't fool me. I was watching you dance with the banker. He upset you, didn't he?"

She wanted to tell Grant about the foul, disgusting things Edmund had said to her, but she didn't dare. He would probably tell Brent and Quince, or face Edmund himself, and she didn't want him hurt either.

"I just don't like him very well."

His fingers lingered on her arm, conveying his feelings for her. "I have broad shoulders for you to lean on. You can trust me. Tell me what's bothering you."

Abby had so many things bothering her, she didn't know where to start. She knew only that she couldn't tell anyone about Edmund. She would have to deal with him on her own. "How long will you be staying in Diablo?"

"I see. You are telling me to mind my own business. We aren't going to talk about anything serious tonight, are we?"

"I'd rather not."

"Very well, we will talk of piddling things and not what's bothering you. I have been assigned to help Major Tremain, and I will be staying in Diablo for as long as he needs me here."

"I wonder why he came to the dance tonight?"

"I can tell you only that he's here because he needs to ask the right people the right questions without seeming obvious." He grinned down at her. "While I am here to dance with a pretty gal."

She frowned. "I didn't realize that you were working with Jonah."

"I can't really go into any of that, but yeah, I am. We are working toward the same end."

She glanced upward just as a glittering starburst spread across the sky, and the echo of it thundered into the night. "What do you know about Major Tremain?"

Grant removed his hand from her arm and stood stiffly beside her, an ache inside him. He had noticed the way Abby had tried not to look in the major's direction tonight. He also noticed that Jonah couldn't take his eyes off Abby. He hoped she wasn't falling in love with the officer.

"I know he comes from money and breeding; the men under his command respect him. He is honorable. Come on, Abby"—he lifted her chin and smiled down at her—"no long faces tonight. I hear music, and I want the prettiest gal in town to dance with me."

His laughter was infectious and almost made her forget about Edmund. They went back inside and danced around the room, and she was laughing when the music ended. If it hadn't been for Edmund's threats, the night would have been perfect.

The fiddles started to play a waltz, and Jonah appeared at her side.

"I believe this is my dance."

Abby drifted into Jonah's arms as if she had no will of her own. One of his hands went to her waist, and he clasped hers with the other. Her heart was hammering to the sound of the music, and she could hardly breathe.

Jonah took in every detail of Abby's transformation. He could feel the wires of her corset, and, knowing her, he imagined what it had taken to get her to wear one. "I like the way your hair looks tonight."

"Thank you."

He smiled slightly. "But as I told you before, I'll miss that braid bouncing around when you walk."

"I have wished it back a hundred times tonight."

Her skin had a golden glow, enhanced by the off-the-shoulder gown she wore. Her neck was long and graceful. The rosiness of her cheeks owed nothing to rouge, and her full lips were soft and tantalizing.

He touched his cheek to hers and inhaled the sweet scent of honey. "Abby, Abby, what am I going to do about you?"

She raised her head and looked into his compelling eyes, feeling as if her heart had just been clamped by an iron band. "I don't know—what?"

He laughed and whirled her around; their bodies were as one, their steps matching and harmonious. Abby thought she could go on dancing with him all night, or for the rest of her life. His chin was near her lips, and she knew all she had to do was move the merest bit to touch it with her mouth.

"I start training the mare Monday."

He was quiet so long, she thought he wasn't going to answer. "Will it take long?"

"It shouldn't take more than two or three days. I have already used the lead rope and gentled her down. Now I have only to introduce her to the side-saddle."

He closed his eyes, concentrating on the sensation of her in his arms. If he had never met her, something would be missing from his life. But since he could never have her, he would spend the rest of his life without joy in his heart. He would do the right thing and marry Patricia, and she would never guess that he didn't love her.

The music stopped, and still Jonah held Abby in his arms, because this would probably be the last time he could hold her. People were beginning to stare, and he took her hand, leading her back to her brother.

While Abby talked with Glory, Grant pulled Jonah off to the side.

"Major, something's come up, and I have to leave for a few days. I was wondering if you'd escort Abby home for me?"

Jonah was quiet for a moment. "Perhaps she would rather have Quince take her home."

"I thought of that, but since you're going to the ranch anyway, it seemed the sensible solution."

"Yes. I could do that." He didn't know whether to be glad or sorry. He shook Grant's hand. "I'll see you when you get back."

The major was unaware that Grant had manipulated the situation so Abby and Jonah would be thrown together. He didn't really have to leave town. If nothing happened between the two of them, Grant would feel free to do his own courting.

172

Chapter Sixteen

The moon was like a giant golden ball suspended in the sky when Quince lifted Abby into the carriage while Jonah tied his horse behind. "How did you enjoy the dance, darlin'?"

Other people were passing by on their way to their carriages, yawning and sleepy. Now was the time for her to tell her brother about Edmund, if she were going to tell him at all. She looked into his dear face and knew she could never put him in danger.

She forced a smile. "It was more than I could have imagined."

He placed a quick kiss on her forehead and took Glory by the arm. "Sleep late in the morning—it's expected after a big shindig like this."

She heard him mumble a good-night to Jonah and walk to his own buggy to help his wife inside. Abby was tense as Jonah climbed into the buggy beside her. She could feel the warmth of his presence, and it was both painful and comforting at the same time. She leaned her head back as the buggy moved forward. Unpleasant thoughts of Edmund Montgomery stalked through her mind like a lurking spider. She didn't want to think about that man until she had decided what she was going to do about him. So she turned her thoughts to other matters.

She almost wished Grant were beside her instead of Jonah. The ranger would tease her and make her laugh on the way home, while the man who sat beside her so silent and grave seemed incapable of either. "Do you know why Grant had to leave in such a hurry?" she asked at last.

They were just leaving the town behind when Jonah glanced at her. "No. I don't. It must be ranger business that took him away."

"I thought he was working for you."

"Not for me—with me."

The horses had just started on a downhill grade, so he moved forward to tighten the reins, brushing his thigh against her leg. Even the small contact made him turn to her with fire in his eyes. After that, it seemed to Abby he retreated into his thoughts to become cold and distant.

At last, after the silence became painful, he turned to her again. "Sleepy?" he asked, slowing the horses for a sharp turn in the road.

"A little. Are you?"

She saw his chest expand as he took a deep breath. "I haven't been sleeping very well lately."

"It's probably because you are so worried about the payroll robberies."

His lips curved slightly. "That's probably it."

She put her hand over her mouth to hide a yawn. "I'm sure my feet are going to hurt tomorrow."

"It's already tomorrow." His jaw tightened. "Not that you would notice. You were too busy charming the ranger."

She was swaying with the gentle motion of the buggy and turned her head to watch him, wondering what he had meant by that statement. He was staring into the night, and she saw his jaw tighten and his hands clench on the reins.

"What's wrong, Jonah?" She sat forward. "I am not trying to pry, but we have known each other well enough for me to sense your change of mood, and I can tell when something is bothering you, like now."

He turned to her, his eyes glistening, started to speak, and then reconsidered.

"Jonah?"

"Do you know what you just said?"

"Yes. I—"

"No, you don't know. You said you can feel my moods. Well, I know yours, too. I know in my heart when you are happy or sad; I can feel it if you are angry. I feel you in my head, my mind, my body. Why do you suppose that is, Abby?"

"I don't know why."

He stopped the carriage, and she stared at him, not knowing how to react to his behavior tonight.

"Abby, we have to talk."

"No. I don't think—"

He touched her arm, his finger sliding down to her hand. "I need to tell you about myself. I want you to understand what my life was like before I met you."

"You don't need to remind me about your fiancée."

"I don't mean her, although Patricia figures into it."

His eyes reflected a fierce light, but he seemed outwardly calm and aloof. He leaned his head back as though gathering his thoughts.

"What do you want to say?"

"My family is not like yours, Abby. The plain truth is, I wish they were. I have two sisters whom I never see because they cut themselves off from our father. The general is a hard man who insists on perfection in his offspring. He directed my mother's life, my sisters' lives, and he already had my life mapped out before I was born. That's just the way he is."

"I can't see you going along with any plan for your future if it didn't coincide with what you wanted. You are a strong-willed individual—you wouldn't be an officer if you weren't."

"It never occurred to me to challenge the general until lately—since . . . I came to Texas."

In that moment Abby realized where this conversation was headed. He was telling her good-bye. "Jonah, I understand. You don't have to say any more."

He gripped her arm and brought her resisting body toward him. "You can't possibly know how you have turned my world upside down, made me question my life, made me dissatisfied with the direction I have chosen."

Her head fell into the curve of his shoulder as his hand swept up her back to rest against her neck. "It's hard to turn my back on what I really want, but I'm trying to do what is honorable. I want to do the right thing by Patricia, and yet . . ."

Abby felt his breath on her neck, and her arms slid up his shoulders. "Jonah," she said softly. "I don't know what to say to you."

He lifted her chin and studied her face as if he were memorizing every detail. "There is nothing you can say, Abby. There is nothing either of us can say."

She felt hot tears just behind her eyes. He *was* saying good-bye.

He touched his lips to her cheek and pulled back reluctantly when he tasted her tears. "I could walk away from the army and never look back, but I can't hurt Patricia. She deserves better than that."

Abby had been sensitive all evening to their growing awareness of each other, and she sensed an aching torment growing inside him. She could also feel her own heart breaking.

What would it be like never to see him again?

"I don't know what happened between us, Abby, because it happened so fast, and I didn't see it coming. That very day, just before we met, I knew something was waiting down that road for me. But I didn't know it was going to come swinging out of a tree at me."

"I was angry with you that day."

"I know. Our relationship started off stormy, and it's only become more so."

"And now?"

"I couldn't just leave you without telling you how I felt."

She sensed that he needed her to make it easier for him to leave—and that was what she would do.

"You would be a lesser man if you could abandon the woman you are pledged to marry. And I could not respect a lesser man."

He drew her back into his arms, and she felt his intake of breath. "When you say things like that, it only makes it worse." He swallowed before he could continue. "I want to walk away from duty and honor so I can be with you. Say the word and I will, Abby." His arms tightened about her. "Say you want me to walk away, and I will."

She buried her face in his jacket. If she chose to, she could have him. All she had to do was ask him to turn his back on honor, commitment, and the kind of man he was. But if she did, the day would probably come when he would despise himself for buying passion at the expense of honor, and she didn't want that for him.

"I would never ask you to act against your principles, and I will not act against mine."

He drew in a shaky breath. "I needed to hold you in my arms this one time."

He hadn't really told her anything. He had merely left her feeling more confused than ever. "I don't understand."

"How could you?"

He traced her lower lip with his finger, and she closed her eyes against the powerful emotions that one simple gesture created inside her.

He clasped her face between his hands. "Abby, I have been trying to think of a way to tell you that I'll be leaving at dawn."

She had known this time would come, but not so soon—what would she do when she could no longer see him? "Will you be going back to Fort Fannin?"

"Not at this time. Victorio is on the warpath again. The army needs all the men we can muster to protect the settlers in that area. My troops will be joining the others that are massing near the Mexican border." He was quiet for a moment, his gaze settling on her mouth. "I want to kiss you in the worst way. I want you in every way a man can want a woman, but I'll never know the sweetness of your body."

Tears gathered in her eyes, and her head became so heavy it fell weakly against his shoulder. "You are going into battle."

"That's what I do, Abby."

She was so afraid he might be killed. She wanted to hold on to him to prevent him from leaving. But instead she had to let him go. She asked in a choked voice, "Would it be so very wrong if you kissed me good-bye?"

With an urgent groan he lowered his head, his mouth so near hers. "When I leave here I will be saying good-bye to . . . what we could have had."

His lips were soft and gentle at first, conveying sweetness and tenderness. Their need built swiftly.

Her breath became trapped in her throat, and she felt the awakening of something beyond tenderness— she felt the first unquenchable flames of desire.

Jonah ran his tongue softly across her lips, and she opened them for him. She felt him quake when her tongue tentatively touched his, and searing heat rushed through her when he deepened the kiss.

She wanted to pull him back to her when he suddenly broke off the kiss, but she closed her eyes as his mouth slid down her neck. His hand gently moved up her ribs to slide over her breast, and Abby thought she would die from the longing that shook her.

At that moment Jonah's horse stomped his hooves and whinnied, making his presence known.

Jonah drew his head back and looked into Abby's luminous eyes. The sweet honey smell of her hair, the cool smoothness of her skin beckoned to him, but he stiffened and pulled away. "I want to have you, and damn the rest of the world. Letting you go will be the hardest thing I have ever done in my life. But it is the right thing to do."

They stared at each other for a long moment, and then his hands dropped away. Silently he picked up the reins, and the buggy jerked forward.

Abby laid her head against his shoulder, knowing that one kiss was all they would ever have.

His hand found hers, and their fingers laced together. He raised her hand to his lips and placed a kiss on her wrist.

They were both silent as the horses clomped along at a steady pace. After a while Abby withdrew her hand from his and moved to the far side of the buggy. She turned her head away so he would not see how badly she was hurting.

When they reached the house, she stepped out of

the buggy as Navidad came out of the barn to un-hitch the horses.

"Did you have a fine time dancing, Señorita Abby?" he inquired, smiling at her.

"It was . . . the dancing was lively." She turned away and hurried into the house, knowing Jonah and Navidad were both staring after her.

She ran inside with her heart pounding. When she reached her bedroom, she closed the door and leaned against it so she wouldn't be tempted to open it and run into Jonah's arms.

She wanted to go to him, to beg him to love her, but she couldn't do that. They had already said good-bye, and that was the right thing to do.

But if it had been the right thing to do, why did it hurt so badly?

Abby was restless and unable to sleep. She tossed and turned, trying to find a comfortable position. Finally, in frustration, she grabbed up a blanket and wrapped it around her, not bothering to put on her dressing gown.

She moved silently out into the hallway, pausing only a moment at Jonah's bedroom door, wishing she could go to him.

She quietly opened the screen door and closed it with only the creak of hinges to betray her exit.

The barn and bunkhouse were dark; everyone had gone to bed hours ago. Her father wasn't home, and she didn't know where he was—she hoped he hadn't started drinking again.

She leaned her head against the porch post and closed her eyes, reliving the moments when Jonah had kissed her and confessed that he had feelings for her. She could almost feel the pressure of his hand as their fingers intertwined. She looked dry-eyed at the moon, wishing she could—

"You couldn't sleep either, Abby?"

She turned, startled by Jonah's voice. She could barely make out his outline because he stood in shadows at the other end of the porch; he must have been there all the time.

"I . . . no. I was restless." She took a step forward as if drawn to him like a magnet. "Why couldn't you sleep?"

He was quiet for a moment, and she heard a deep intake of breath. "I couldn't stop thinking about how you felt in my arms."

Her footsteps were measured, her actions cautious as she moved closer to him.

He advanced a step and studied her face to judge her mood. "Abby!"

There was an urgency in the way he uttered her name. It was a tormented cry from deep inside him, and her heart answered.

She dropped the blanket at her feet and flew into his open arms. He lifted her to him, and at the same time their bodies met each other, their mouths fusing together in a kiss. The fire that had been smoldering between them all evening now burst into a roaring flame.

The tight restraint he had been keeping on his emotions was released in a rush. His hands moved over her body, pressing her against him, holding her tightly to him. He could feel her lips part and soften.

She groaned a protest when he broke off the kiss

and set her on her feet, dropping his arms to his sides and tightening his hands into fists.

"You are too young and innocent, Abby. I can't do this to you."

Without hesitation, she reached for his hand and pulled him toward the door. "I'm old enough to know what I am doing. I want to give you something of myself to take away with you. Something to remember just before you go to sleep each night."

"Abby?"

"It's what I want."

He scooped her up in his arms and carried her into the house, his hunger for her so deep it tore at him. He did not even remember the short walk to his bedroom. He kicked the door shut and lowered his head, his mouth finding hers. Her lips were soft beneath his, and he had no will to resist.

Her arms wound around his neck and the passion spilled out, washing over them both.

"Jonah," she whispered, laying her cheek to his. "I want to be with you this one time. This is something I can give you of myself."

He should have resisted; he was stronger, and he knew what it could mean for her later on. But her body was like silk, and the smoothness of it jolted through him as he held her and drifted down on the bed.

Abby had very little memory of Jonah undressing, but she could see his wonderful lean body in the moonlight. She lifted her nightgown over her head, then held her arms out to him, and he came to her.

His hot flesh seared her, and she quivered when

his hand moved from her ribs to her stomach.

She was perfect, from the top of her black satin hair to the bottom of her delicately arched foot. "You are beautiful, Abby," he murmured, his hand sweeping across her skin, and his gaze taking in each soft curve.

She dug her fingers into the mattress when his mouth touched her nipple in a kiss so soft it was like velvet. She could hear his ragged breathing, and it fueled her response.

They had gone too far to stop. Her arms went around his neck, and she looked into those dynamic blue eyes that were half-closed and heavy with passion.

His mouth found and covered hers hungrily. Gently he slid his body over her, hurling her into a need so deep, she cried out to him. He opened her mind to powerful emotions that rocked her to the core of her womanhood. He guided her through a world of aching need.

Abby touched her lips to his so she could convey her willingness.

While he kissed her, he gently parted her legs. With raw passion he probed her inner folds and entered her slowly.

She gasped and closed her eyes when he filled the emptiness with such wonderment that a tear slid down her cheek.

She threw her head back to keep from crying out his name when he sank deeper into her, stirring wild, hot desire. She had dreamed of this moment, ached to be a part of him, needed his touch. His movements were gentle, and she felt he was holding back, keeping a tight restraint on his desire. But she wanted more of him, so she arched her back to take him deeper inside her.

With a soft groan his mouth came down on hers, plundering her lips, and he drove into her body with such force she gasped. He raised passion-bright eyes to her and eased some of his length out of her. "Don't tempt me like that again, Abby. This is your first time." His lips touched her breast, and he murmured, "I don't want to hurt you."

Her body throbbed and ached, but not with pain. She could feel him surround her, filling her, making her his. Love poured out of her heart and washed over her like waves on the ocean. He stared into her eyes, filling her heart even more.

"Abby," he breathed against her lips, holding her while her body shook and trembled. Moments later his arms tightened about her, and his body rocked with his own fulfillment.

He rolled over and they rested side by side, reluctant to move. Her leg was thrown over his as she rested her head on his shoulder.

Then she raised her head and touched his cheek, feeling a slight stubble where he needed to shave.

There was no false modesty in Abby, and it delighted him how readily she had thrown aside her innocence and accepted his lovemaking. She had matched his passion in every way, and now she allowed him to touch her body, sliding his hand over every curve.

"I will never forget tonight," she said, her eyes shining. "And I don't want you to either."

"How could I?" He gathered her close, touching his lips to her throat. Now that the flame of passion had been satisfied, he felt the first prickle of guilt. "But I should never have allowed it to go this far, Abby."

She raised herself up on an elbow. "You didn't have any choice. I wanted this to happen between us." She looked at him uncertainly. "Are you sorry?"

He drew her head back to his shoulder. "I am only sorry that I didn't consider what my actions might mean for you." His hand glided across her hip and up her back. "For myself, I have never felt as alive as I feel at this moment." He turned her so she fit against the length of his body. "My mind is so clear. Something happened between us that borders on the miraculous. Do you feel that too?"

"Yes."

"But what have I done to you?"

She pressed herself tightly against him and felt him swell. "It will be dawn soon, and you will be leaving . . . love me again before you go."

Her soft plea swept away the last of his willpower. He could not resist the sweet body that offered him a fulfillment he had never known. He touched her, stroked her, kissed her, and entered her.

She urged him on, and he drove deep. He was putting his brand on her—he was taking her for his own.

Abby slid off the bed, her hand lingering in his while his gaze moved over her body. She was so beautiful, with her dark hair falling tangled about her face.

"You will be leaving soon," she said, slowly and

reluctantly withdrawing her hand from his. She would have to let him go.

He was out of bed beside her, holding her tightly to him. "How can I leave you now?"

She smiled sadly. "Because you must. Nothing has changed, Jonah. You still have your duty. I offered myself to you asking nothing in return, and I still don't."

He stared into her eyes. "Abby, I can't just go away and leave it like this between us."

"I won't have you eaten up with guilt. I knew what I was doing, Jonah. You did not lure me into your bed; I went willingly."

He glanced at the window and saw the first streaks of dawn hit the ebony sky. With a feeling of frustration he traced her backbone and cupped her buttocks, lifting her to fit against his hardness. How could he tell her that he had never felt this way with a woman before, and he never would again? How could he make her understand that now that he had been with her, he would never stop wanting her? The need for possession was deep and insatiable, and it tore at him even now. But time was his enemy— he had to leave. "We will talk about this when I get back."

She nestled her head on his shoulder for a brief moment. "Be safe, and take care of yourself. Don't let anything happen to you."

Before he could say anything, she picked up her gown and slipped it over her head; then she went to him again. "I want to say good-bye to you now and not when anyone else is around."

He took her in his arms, wishing more than anything that he could take her back to bed. "Wait for me?"

She shook her head, wanting to let him know that she did not expect anything more between them. "No. We can never be together again, Jonah. As I told you last night, this is my gift to you . . . and to myself."

He brought her to him, dipped his head, and kissed her softly.

She slipped out of his arms and went out the door and down the hall to her own bedroom.

For a long time after she had gone, Jonah stared out the window, absorbing what he had done to Abby. He had always taken pride in his own self-restraint; he had never visited the prostitutes who lured other officers to their beds. He had even tried to keep Abby at a safe distance when he first began to want her. Yet he had taken Abby's virginity as if he had a right to it. He had lost control because of his own selfish need for her.

She had given him the greatest gift a woman could give a man. He knew the power of her gift would stay with him for the rest of his life. After their perfect union, he could not imagine ever finding the same joy with any other woman.

He braced his arm on the windowsill and leaned his head against it, troubled. He hadn't felt it at the time, but now he was disturbed by the way she had told him good-bye—it was as if she had closed herself off from him. What if there should be a child?

He quickly scribbled a note to her, and before he left, pushed it under her bedroom door.

Chapter Seventeen

Frances came out the back door and watched Abby hang sheets on the line with a bemused expression on her face. "You were certainly up early this morning, and doing my work, at that. You know I'da changed the bedding today and done the washing tomorrow."

Abby picked up the straw basket and walked toward the back door. "I wanted to keep busy today."

Frances noticed that Abby's eyes were red from crying. "You didn't even come out front to tell the major good-bye."

Abby paused with her hand on the screen door. She had done the washing so she could remove all traces of her lovemaking with Jonah. "I said good-bye to him in my own way."

The note Jonah had slid beneath her door had been

read and then torn to shreds. It had said simply, *Will you marry me?*

Nothing could have made her feel worse.

She hated to think he felt compelled to offer her marriage after what had happened between them. Her answer was no now, and it would be the same if he ever posed the question to her in person.

By afternoon Abby began training the mare. As she had expected, the horse took easily to the sidesaddle. With each new phase of training, a deeper pain touched her heart.

With less than a week's training, Abby concluded that even the most inexperienced rider would be able to ride the gentle mare. She would even be a good mount for a child.

She had just led the mare into a stall and shot the bolt when Quince came striding toward her.

"Is anyone using the buckboard next Friday?" he asked.

"Not that I know of. Why?"

"Jonah had asked me before he left if I'd meet his father and Patricia Van Dere if he hadn't returned by the time they arrived. From what I hear about the battles that have been going on with Victorio, he certainly won't be back in time."

Her heart stopped beating, and she leaned her back against the stall. "Do you think he'll be all right?"

"I hope so. We won't know about the casualties until it's all over."

Abby now knew what it felt like for a woman to send the man she loved into war. She was terrified something would happen to Jonah. She paced toward the front of the barn and back again. There was nothing she could do—she felt so helpless.

"Abby?"

She had to hide her distress from her brother. "Will General Tremain and Miss Van Dere be staying at Fort Fannin?"

"Jonah had made arrangements for them at the hotel in Diablo, but I thought it might be nice if we offered to let them stay here."

Abby adamantly disliked the thought of facing the woman Jonah was to marry. "Why would you think such a thing?"

"The house is large enough to accommodate them."

"But—"

"Abby, Jonah is my friend."

"I know that."

"I plan to offer them our hospitality. Will you go with me to meet them?"

"No." She walked toward the house and said to him over her shoulder, "You want them here, you bring them."

"Abby, it's not like you to be so snippy. What's gotten into you lately? Brent has even commented on your strange moods."

She stopped and turned back to him. It was one of the few times she had been angry with Quince. "There's nothing wrong with me. I just want everyone to leave me alone."

*   *   *

Abby rode out early Friday morning and stayed away from the house as long as she could. She had ridden to the cabin to see Brent and visited with Crystal.

Later Curly found her helping Brent brand several horses and informed her that the stolen mustangs had been returned. She rode out with Brent to see them safely pastured near the ranch house.

It was almost dark when she dismounted at the stable, and she was sore and tired. She was looking forward to a warm bath to soothe her aching muscles.

"Señorita Abby, the patron has been asking for you to return."

She unsaddled Sassy and tossed the saddle over the fence. "What did my father want?"

"He did not say to me what he wanted."

"Have the guests arrived?"

"Oh, *sí*. There is this man so grand, and this nice, pretty señorita who is with him."

Abby slapped her hat against her trousers and dust flew. "Feed the pinto and give her a good rubdown for me, will you, Christmas?"

"*Sí*. I will be glad to do these things for you," Navidad said. In his voice was sympathy for her obvious distress.

With a heavy heart Abby walked toward the house. As she drew near she saw the woman standing on the porch; there was no way to avoid her. She would rather have met Patricia Van Dere after she had bathed, but that was not to be.

Reluctantly she moved up the steps to face the woman she most dreaded meeting. Patricia Van Dere was more than Abby had expected. Her blond hair was swept to the top of her head in a sophisticated style. The brown traveling gown she wore was elegant and understated, a look that only the elite of society could accomplish. And, worse still, she was beautiful.

Patricia smiled and reached out her hand to Abby. "You must be Quince's sister. I have been wanting to meet you. Jonah has written me so much about your family."

Abby had not expected the woman to be nervous, but she felt her hand trembling. "I have heard about you as well, Miss Van Dere."

"My name is Patricia, and I hope you will allow me to call you Abby. I feel like I already know you."

"Of course, if you like."

"This," she said, spreading her arms wide to indicate the countryside, "is a bit overpowering and frightening for me."

"You'll have to get used to it, since you are going to be an officer's wife."

Even now, standing before the woman Jonah was to marry, Abby longed for his touch. The nights were the worst, because she had too much time to think about him. Then she would imagine him being wounded or killed, and it was torment of the worst kind.

Patricia was suddenly staring at her in an odd way, as if she were shocked. Abby realized it was her apparel that had caught Patricia's attention. She had expected nothing less.

"I have never seen a woman wearing trousers before."

"Hmm," Abby said crisply. "I would've of bet my life on that."

Patricia walked around Abby, looking her over carefully. "We are very near the same size. I would like to try on a pair of your trousers."

Now it was Abby's turn to be shocked. "I don't think the major would like it," she said.

Patricia's face fell, and she agreed with a nod. "You are probably right."

Abby frowned, wanting to hate the woman, but finding it difficult. There was something sweet and unassuming about her.

"Your life must seem so useful here. But the country is so vast. I have always been a little intimidated at the thought of the West. We hear such horror stories about gunmen and robbers."

"Well, Miss Van Dere, you heard right. We are a bit uncivilized out here. It will probably take years before we catch up with you in the North."

The Philadelphian seemed upset. "I only meant that . . ." She lowered her lashes. "I have failed miserably with you, haven't I? And I so wanted you to like me."

Abby was taken aback because Patricia seemed genuinely upset. She would have felt better if the woman were spoiled and selfish; then she could hate her without guilt.

"If you will excuse me, I'm dusty. I will see you at supper."

"Yes, of course."

Abby turned to Patricia with the screen door half-way open. "Which room have they put you in?"

"I'm told by your housekeeper that I am using your brother Quince's room."

Abby was relieved. She would not have wanted Patricia to stay in the room where Jonah had made love to her.

When she entered the house, Abby stopped at the door of the parlor, where cigar smoke wove its way to her. She heard her father's voice, warm and friendly. "General, if you are of a mind to, I'll give you a tour of the ranch tomorrow."

"I'd like that, Mr. Hunter," came a clipped Northern voice.

Jack caught a glimpse of his daughter and took her hand, leading her into the room. "General, this is my only daughter. Abby, meet General Daniel Tremain."

Abby nodded at Jonah's father and said politely, "Sir, it's a pleasure."

General Tremain had a scowl of disapproval on his face when he looked at her trousers. But his attitude did not bother Abby—she had seen that look before in his son's eyes.

"Miss Hunter, I was just telling your father that Patricia and I are grateful for your hospitality." His frown deepened. "However, I had expected my son to meet us."

If Abby had drawn a picture in her mind of Jonah's father, this man wasn't far from what she would have imagined. He was trim in appearance and had an autocratic air about him. His eyes were much the color of Jonah's, but there the resemblance ended. Jonah was several inches taller than his father. Since he was a retired general, he no longer wore a uniform but a charcoal-gray suit. General Tremain might seem to be friendly with her father, but he had not earned the rank of general without knowing how to fit in with other people. There was an astuteness in those observing eyes, and he would definitely be more at home in a lavish sitting room in Philadelphia than in the small parlor of a ranch house in Texas.

"If you will both excuse me, I need to wash before supper," she told them, happy to make her escape.

How would she get through the days ahead when she would be thrown into the company of that pair?

Jonah had ordered a cold camp, since the Apache could spot a campfire from miles away. He lay on his bedroll listening to the sounds of night all around him. A coyote howled in the distance, and an owl made its presence known by hooting in a nearby mesquite tree while locusts chirped their age-old night song.

He was bone-weary, but his mind was clear and focused. It was thoughts of Abby that robbed him of sleep rather than worry about another skirmish with Victorio, which was sure to come in the days ahead.

He watched the night sky as a cloud moved over the moon and cast the countryside into darkness. He closed his eyes, remembering the passion that had filled him when Abby had surrendered to him. He ached inside, wanting to recapture and hold on to that feeling. Without her, he would spend the rest of his life in desolation, empty inside, a man without his heart.

He heard the restless stirring of the horses. He had ordered each trooper to keep his own mount close at hand. An Apache was capable of sneaking into a camp and driving off a herd without disturbing anyone until it was too late. He thought briefly about the battle they had already fought, and the one that lay ahead of them.

His troop had joined Col. Ben Grierson's Tenth Cavalry and Company C and Company G in a skirmish with the Mescalero Apache at *Tinaja de las Palmas*. They had suffered only a few casualties and had managed to drive Victorio back across the border into Mexico.

Jonah hadn't expected Victorio to remain on the Mexican side of the border, so his troops had been patrolling the area for a week. Today they had received word from the Mexican government that the Apache chief was heading back to Texas. All the water holes and springs near the border were now fortified with troops—all except one: Rattlesnake Springs.

And that was where Victorio would be heading.

Jonah watched the sun touch the eastern sky and rolled to his feet. He allowed a small fire, since the smoke would blend with the morning shadows. His men had to have coffee to sustain them through the hard ride that lay ahead.

As the cook handed out hardtack and coffee, Jonah nodded for the bugler to sound boots and saddles.

He mounted, and Sergeant MacDougall rode to his side. "Troopers," Jonah said in a voice that could be heard by all. "We have to make a sixty-five-mile trek in less than twenty-four hours if we are going to beat Victorio to Rattlesnake Springs. We will be pushing hard—you will eat in the saddle and rest your horse only when necessary. Anyone lagging behind is likely to find himself with an Apache in his face—so keep up."

The long blue line wound its way across the arid countryside. Punishing heat beat down on them, and each trooper was aware that a fierce battle awaited them at the end of this grueling ride.

Jonah thought of Abby and the note he had shoved under her door. His hope was that she would agree to marry him, even though he knew she would refuse.

"Sergeant, let's pick up the pace," he said, nudging his mount into a heavy gallop.

Chapter Eighteen

Abby was exercising Moon Racer in the paddock when Patricia appeared at the fence to watch her. The woman looked somewhat out of place in her green-and-white-striped gown and the matching sunshade that protected her complexion against the Texas sun.

All Abby could think about was how difficult it had been to make conversation at the supper table the night before. She had to admit Patricia had tried to draw her into the conversation several times, but Abby had not been very responsive.

Her stilted replies had drawn a few disapproving glances from her father. The kinder Patricia became, the worse Abby felt.

Moon Racer flung his head back and snorted, pulling on the reins. She patted his neck and smiled. "All right, big boy, if you want to run, you're going to have to jump that fence first."

With a laugh, she dug her heels into her horse's flanks, and he easily sailed over the fence. The hot wind touched her cheeks as they raced across the meadow and up the hill. She allowed him to run until he slowed to a gallop, and then she turned him back toward the house.

When she reached the barn and dismounted, Jonah's father had joined Patricia.

The general managed a smile. "That was impressive riding, Miss Hunter, very impressive indeed."

Abby nodded her thanks. "I need to rub him down. Is there anything I can do for you?"

"No," the general said, looking about him. "I'm riding out with your father within the hour. I want to see the workings of a successful horse ranch."

With an impatient frown he took his pocket watch out and checked the time. Abby smiled to herself. She could have told him that time had no meaning on the Half-Moon Ranch. Everything was centered around the care of the stock—when they were fed, when they needed to be exercised and trained.

Jonah's father and Patricia walked beside Abby as she led Moon Racer to the barn. Patricia cautiously eyed the powerful stallion. "I wish I could ride the way you do."

"You ride sidesaddle, don't you?" Of course, Abby knew she did.

"Yes. But I don't even do that very well."

The general looked pensive for a moment. He knew his son had bought Patricia a horse as a surprise. It had been trained here on this ranch, probably by Miss Hunter; although he couldn't see her on anything but the western saddle she used.

"Miss Hunter could probably help you improve your horsemanship, if you would ask her."

"No, General Tremain," Patricia said in the most forceful voice Abby had heard her use. "I would never presume to take Abby away from her duties."

He glared at his future daughter-in-law. "Those who are too shy to ask are left out."

Abby saw the stricken look on Patricia's face, and her heart softened a bit toward her. She was in a land she didn't understand and was trying to adjust to the change in her life. It couldn't be easy for her to have to contend with a man as demanding as Daniel Tremain.

"I have the time to help you," Abby said kindly. "I would be glad to."

The woman's face brightened. "You wouldn't mind?"

"No, I wouldn't mind."

Abby was beginning to like Patricia in spite of her resolve to dislike her. And the more she liked her, the more guilt she felt about what had happened between herself and Jonah. She had never had a friend her own age, and, until now, she had never known the amusement of talking about frivolous things that would never interest a man.

Patricia told her about her life in Philadelphia. She had an older sister and a younger brother, and her home was next door to the Tremain estate. She and

Jonah were the same age, which made Abby wonder why Patricia hadn't married before now—Quince had told her that Jonah was thirty.

She and Patricia were sitting on the front porch sipping lemonade and trying to cool off in the early-evening breeze. Patricia's question came out of nowhere and took Abby completely by surprise.

"What do you think of Jonah?"

Abby stood and moved to the steps, leaning against the post. "I have heard he is a fine officer, and that he moved up fast in the ranks. Quince told me his advancements had nothing to do with his father's rank but more to do with Jonah's own abilities."

"Jonah isn't close to his father, not like I am to mine—he never has been. He resisted going to West Point as long as his mother was alive, but when she died after a long illness, he left right away." Patricia looked down at her clasped hands. "I always knew I wanted to be Jonah's wife, but I am not sure he felt the same—"

"Look, it's Quince!" Abby said, interrupting Patricia's conversation. She found it too painful when Patricia spoke about her relationship with Jonah.

And there was always the growing guilt.

After almost twenty-one hours of riding, Jonah and his troops had reached Rattlesnake Springs, where they joined a small company of cavalry men.

Jonah realized at once that the terrain would be difficult to defend, since it was located between the Sierra Diablo and the Delaware Mountains. His eyes swept the craggy land—there were just too many places a man could hide.

The troopers took up their positions to fortify the area and settled in to watch for Victorio.

They didn't have long to wait.

The first Apache appeared on the nearby hillside, soon to be joined by another, and still another. They struck with a force that staggered the weary soldiers. But the cavalry men maintained their positions and held them off.

Since Jonah's troop had traveled fast, they had lightened their loads by carrying the minimal amount of ammunition and supplies—they were now getting dangerously low on both, and each man watched for reinforcements and the supply wagons that were supposed to catch up with them.

The Apache were proving to be worthy adversaries. Victorio attacked their position again and again, but each time they managed to rebuff him.

Jonah didn't know how much time had passed since the battle had begun. He was exhausted and every move was an effort—but his men were fighting back with everything they had, and he stood with them, urging them on.

Sweat stung his eyes and burning thirst parched his throat, but there was no time to satisfy that thirst or even to wipe the sweat away. He heard a bullet whiz past his face and kick up dirt beside him. When he turned in the direction the shot had come from, he spotted a lone Indian on a ridge to his left. But it was already too late for him to defend himself. The

Apache was ready to fire again, and Jonah's pistol and rifle were both out of bullets.

When the impact hit him, Jonah staggered backward. Darkness was closing in on him, and he fell to his knees, then slid forward into blackness.

Sergeant MacDougall took up a position to stand near his fallen commander, his Springfield firing in rapid succession. With cold assessment, he glanced down and saw the blood seeping through Jonah's uniform. The wound appeared to be near his heart. It didn't look good.

Jonah didn't know when the battle ended, or that Victorio retreated back into Mexico, never again to cross the border into Texas.

Abby was training one of the mustangs to a saddle when she saw a uniformed rider heading toward the house. Her heart stopped, and she slid off the horse and tossed the reins to Curly. Without a word she hurried forward just as the man dismounted.

"Ma'am," he said, removing his cap and tucking it under his arm. "I am Sergeant MacDougall, and I have a message for you, if you're Miss Hunter."

In her anxiety, she placed her hand on his arm to steady herself. "I have heard of you, Sergeant. What is your message?"

He had certainly heard about this little gal—she would be Quince's sister. "Ma'am, the major was wounded, and he—"

There was a gasp behind Abby as Patricia came down the steps. "Tell me quickly, is he alive?" the bride-to-be asked.

"Go on, Sergeant," Abby said, her whole body trembling from dread. "Tell her."

"Begging your pardon, ma'am, the major's a stubborn man. He let the doctors bandage his shoulder when we got to the fort, but he wouldn't let them do anything else. He said to tell you he was coming to you." He settled his gaze on Miss Hunter, confused about which woman should have been given the message. "That's what he told me to say."

Abby spoke up quickly. "Thank you, Sergeant, for delivering the message to Miss Van Dere. But please tell us what his condition is."

"Well, ma'am, like I said, it's a shoulder wound. The bullet's still in him 'cause he wouldn't let the army doctor dig for it."

Abby's mind was racing ahead. "How long before he gets here?" she asked.

"He can't be more than an hour behind me. The doctors told him he shouldn't ride in his condition, but he's a contrary man." He looked from one woman to the next, his gaze finally falling on Miss Van Dere. "He is mighty partial to seeing you as soon as he can—don't seem like a bullet could stop him— it just slowed him down a bit."

"How is he making the journey?" Abby wanted to know.

"He's staying in the saddle, and it's got to hurt him like hell—" He cleared his throat. "It's got to hurt him real bad, Miss Hunter. There were times on the ride I wished that he would lose consciousness so he wouldn't feel the pain. He just won't stop till he gets here."

Patricia gasped and covered her mouth. "I cannot stand the thought of him being hurt."

Abby sprang immediately into action. "Sergeant, you will find a man in the barn—his name is Navidad—ask him to ride for Quince as quickly as possible." She ran up the steps to the house. "I'll have Frances gather everything we'll need to remove the bullet. I'll make the room ready."

Patricia looked at the tall sergeant as he led his horse toward the barn. She wished she had been able to think clearly and react as quickly as Abby had.

"Sergeant," she called, stopping him in his tracks.

"Ma'am?"

"For whom did Jonah intend his message?"

He saw trouble here, and he quickly sidestepped it. "I can't really recall his exact words, ma'am. But since you're Miss Van Dere, it was probably for you—you are his intended bride."

He walked away, still thinking the message had been meant for Quince's sister.

Chapter Nineteen

Abby had called on all her strength to step aside and not rush to Jonah when he rode up slumped in the saddle. She remained at the front door, digging her nails into the palms of her hands while Patricia rushed to him. She watched Sergeant MacDougall direct the other troopers to lift Jonah off his horse and carry him into the house.

Jonah's eyes were closed, but Abby saw him wince with pain when they carried him up the steps. She opened the door, noticing how pale he was. He must love Patricia a great deal if he was so desperate to get to her. She gathered her courage and directed the soldiers to Matt's old bedroom, where Jonah had stayed before. She turned down the covers and motioned for them to lay him on the bed.

Abby touched his forehead while Patricia huddled in the doorway, pale and shaking. "He isn't feverish, and that's a wonder, considering the bullet is still in him." Abby turned her attention to MacDougall—if she'd followed her heart, she would have gathered Jonah in her arms. "I'll give you time to take his boots off and undress him before I return."

"Yes, ma'am."

Abby took Patricia's hand and led her down the hallway to the bedroom she was occupying. "You are white as parched paper. You'd better lie down, or we will have two patients."

"I . . . never could stand the sight of suffering, especially not when it's someone I care about." She placed a delicate hand over her mouth. "And seeing blood makes me so sick."

Abby spoke more kindly. "Don't worry; just rest. I'm sure Jonah will be all right."

"Why did he push himself so hard to get here?" Tears trailed down Patricia's face. "Why didn't he allow the doctors at the fort to remove the bullet—or even one of his men?"

"I have heard horror stories about army doctors. He probably didn't want them poking around in him. As to why he pushed himself, I assume he wanted to be with you."

Patricia shook her head. "No. He would never . . . he . . ."

Abby opened a window and pulled the covers back. "Rest for a while. I'll let you know when we have removed the bullet."

Patricia looked relieved to lie down. But when Abby would have left the room, she grabbed her hand. "I wish I could be more like you. You always know what to do in every situation, and I seem to flounder at every crisis."

Abby stared at Jonah's bride-to-be. She couldn't admit to her that she would gladly trade places if she could have Jonah. "I must go. They might need me."

As Abby stepped into the hall, she wasn't feeling so steady herself. She heard Quince's voice at the front door and ran to him. "Christmas told you about Jonah?"

"Yeah. I got here as fast as I could."

"Since Dr. Gibbs left town so suddenly, Diablo doesn't have a doctor. I didn't know what to do but send for you."

He rolled up his sleeves and entered the bedroom. "You did right. But I'll need you to help me."

She nodded. "Just tell me what to do."

It was growing dark, so Sergeant MacDougall held the lamp while Abby held the washbasin for her brother.

Jonah was so pale, and his dark hair was plastered to his forehead with sweat. She gritted her teeth when Quince probed for the bullet, and a tear ran down her cheek as she watched Jonah groan in pain.

She set the basin aside and went down on her knees, taking his hand in hers. "Hold on to me, Jonah. Hold on."

His eyes opened briefly, and she stared into dark blue pools of pain.

He mouthed her name but made no sound.

"I'm here."

Quince looked at her strangely as he dropped the spent bullet into the pan. Then he dunked his hands in the basin to wash the blood off them. "You can doctor and bandage him now, Abby. I just heard riders out front. It might be Jonah's father. I'll need to tell him what happened."

She nodded, afraid to meet Quince's eyes because he already suspected what her feelings were for Jonah.

The sergeant looked on as Abby skillfully put ointment on the wound and rolled the bandage under Jonah's arm and over his shoulder. As gently as she could manage, she tied the bandage in place.

"I think he'll sleep now," she said to MacDougall. "All we can do is hope he doesn't get a fever."

"If you don't mind, I'd like to stay here until he can give me orders to go elsewhere. I can bunk down anywhere." He smiled. "Quince could tell you that."

"Of course you'll want to stay. First, go into the kitchen and tell Frances to feed you. I'll have a cot put in the parlor for you, since the bedrooms are all taken."

"Thank you, ma'am. I'm mighty obliged to you. Major Tremain is a brave man, ma'am—he was fighting at our side when he took this bullet. He's a mighty fine man."

Abby knew enough about army life to appreciate that if a hard-bitten sergeant gave a man his approval, it was certainly worth noting.

"I know he is," she said, smiling at him.

She watched him leave the room, then pulled a chair beside the bed. She should let Patricia know how Jonah was doing, but she didn't want to leave him—not just yet. She touched her lips to his hand, thinking how strong those hands had been when they had swept across her body, and how tenderly they had touched her. She tried putting a name to her feelings.

Love, that was the name of what she felt for him. The emotion Jonah admittedly did not believe existed.

She touched his cheek—he needed a shave. Patricia would probably do that for him. She had started to rise when he groaned and clamped her hand.

Patricia would have him for the rest of her life, but Abby would have him for only a few more moments. Jonah was a strong man, and this wound would not keep him down for long.

For now—for this moment in time—he belonged to her.

Brushing his dark hair out of his face, she watched the way his lashes lay against his tan cheek. She had seen his eyes blaze with desire, and it was a memory she would keep with her forever.

The hours passed slowly, with no change in Jonah's condition. Then she heard someone at the door and MacDougall appeared. "Ma'am, I can sit with him now and give you a rest."

Abby sighed when she stood to give him the chair. She was in no position to protest, although she would have liked to. She said in a whisper so she wouldn't disturb Jonah, "He's been restless but hasn't awakened. If he feels feverish during the night, no matter what time it is, knock on my door. Mine is the room next to this one."

The sergeant whispered back to her, "Yes, ma'am. I surely will."

She touched Jonah's hand once more and let her fingers drift away. "Sergeant MacDougall, whatever happened to that young private who came here looking for Jonah?"

The big man grinned. "Well, ma'am, it's like this; Davies was transferred to Fort Leavenworth, and he'll do some time in the guardhouse for actions unbecoming a soldier." He glanced up at her. "I've never seen the major as mad as he was that day—and I've seen him plenty mad before."

Jonah moaned and opened his eyes, his mind in a fog. He felt as if he were being swept along by dark waters, sinking and rising sickeningly. He closed his eyes briefly, and the world seemed to right itself a bit.

He turned his head to find Quince bending over him, pressing against his shoulder. "That hurts like hell," he mumbled.

"It's supposed to hurt; I'm tightening your bandage."

Jonah licked his dry lips. "Why am I so thirsty?"

"Because you've been dead to the world for twelve hours."

Jonah glanced around him, finding everything comforting and familiar. "I'm in your brother's bedroom."

"Your men brought you here, apparently at your insistence. You always were lucky," Quince drawled. "You never seem to get shot where it really matters. You got your leg shot up, now your shoulder—what's left, your foot?"

Jonah tried to smile, but he merely grimaced in pain. "And every time I get shot, you're there to remind me I should have ducked."

"Someone had to dig that bullet out of you this time. But I can't take all the credit; Abby and MacDougall helped." He placed the slug in Jonah's hand. "It looks like Victorio and his Mescalero didn't like you any more than Geronimo and his warriors did. You might want to avoid Apache in the future—they seem intent on killing you."

Jonah struggled to sit up and finally succeeded, lying back against the three pillows someone had provided for him. "I don't even remember arriving here."

"It's no wonder, since MacDougall told us you had been fading in and out of consciousness."

"Give me a drink, dammit!"

Quince grinned, poured him a glass of water, and handed it to him. "Are you up to a surprise?"

Jonah took a sip of water and then drank deeply. "That depends on what it is."

"Your father and Miss Van Dere are here."

Jonah knew that Quince expected him to be pleased about that bit of information—he wasn't.

"I asked you if you'd meet their stage; I didn't expect you to bring them home with you."

"It seemed the sensible thing to do at the time. And, as it turns out"—Quince watched him closely—"it was lucky. Now you can have Miss Van Dere here to nurse you back to health."

"Yes." Jonah turned his gaze to the doorway, wondering where Abby was. "Thank you for everything."

Quince moved across the room. "Just see if you can stay out of trouble for a while."

MacDougall was waiting for Quince when he came out of the house. "Thanks for what you and your family are doing for the major."

Ready to mount up, Quince thrust his boot into the stirrup and smiled at the sergeant. "When are you going to retire, MacDougall?"

"Can't. Gotta keep an eye on the major."

Quince squinted against the sun. "Yeah, I guess somebody has to."

"Can I ask you something?" MacDougall inquired. "Sure."

"Is there anything between the major and your sister? I mean, is there some reason he'd try so hard to get here to her when he was wounded?"

Quince frowned. "Why would you ask that?"

"He . . . the major asked me flat out to get him to Abby. Maybe he trusted her nursing more than the army doctor's."

Quince drew in an intolerant breath, not liking what he was thinking. "Let's just hope that's all it is."

Jonah stared at his father, who was seated near the bed, his arms folded across his chest. "It's been a while, General."

"It looks like you had one hell of a fight. I'll want to hear all the details. The talk in town is that my son is a hero."

Jonah shifted his weight and stiffened because of the pain. "I wasn't a hero. I did what was expected of me. And I don't want to talk about it with you, now or later."

His father stood up with a fixed expression on his face. "You never change. I thought when they sent you west you would learn some hard lessons, but you haven't."

"And you will never change. You still think the true measure of a man is how well he performs in battle and how many enemies he can kill."

"And it *is* the true measure, as far as I am concerned."

"Then I am your man, General. I can command troops and ride into battle with the best of them. I have a chestful of medals for deeds you would call heroic—what does that tell you about me as a man?"

"We'll discuss this later, when you are more rational. I never can talk to you when you get like this."

Jonah turned his head away. He heard the heavy footsteps as his father stomped out of the room, leaving the door open. The one thing that never changed was his father's attitude toward his only son.

He closed his eyes, knowing that when he was well enough to travel he would be leaving.

A short time later he heard Abby's laughter in the hallway, and it swept through him like a cleansing wind, leaving him without enough air to breathe.

He heard soft footsteps and watched the door, his heart pounding. A light knock on the half-open door brought hope. He pulled his shirt together, although it could not be buttoned because of the bandage. "Come in."

Patricia appeared in the doorway. She tried not to be embarrassed by the sight of the dark hair on his chest. "How are you feeling?" she asked, inching closer.

He swallowed his disappointment. "Very well." He held his hand out to her, knowing it was expected of him. "How was your journey?"

She had hoped he would show joy in seeing her, but the smile on his lips did not reach those razor-blue eyes.

"It was interesting and without incident." Her hand slid into his, and she sat in the chair beside his bed.

Patricia wore a rose-colored gown that fit her to perfection. Her hair was swept upward and held there by an onyx clasp. "You are lovely, as always."

She blinked, wishing for more from him. She withdrew her hand. "I was here earlier, but you were sleeping. Abby was sitting beside you."

There was an urgency in his tone. "Where is she now?"

The truth of her suspicions was reflected in the intensity of his eyes when he spoke of Abby. "I believe she just went into the kitchen to help Frances with the evening meal. Shall I get her?"

"No." He forced a smile. "I'm sorry for receiving you in this condition. It isn't the way I intended your arrival to be."

She touched his forehead with a soft kiss. "Your father told me that if I am to make a proper officer's wife, I must be prepared for the unexpected."

He took a deep breath, and she could tell he was in pain.

"I'll just leave you for now. Perhaps you will feel stronger tomorrow."

"Yes," he said tersely, "I should be strong enough tomorrow to get out of this bed."

"But surely that is too soon."

He smiled. "I was far worse off when I arrived, and I had come a long way to get here."

The house was dark and quiet; everyone seemed to have gone to bed. Jonah lay in the darkness, wishing he could take back the cruel words he had said to his father. It was always the same with them. They had never agreed on any given subject, and it was probably his fault as much as his father's.

He wondered what Abby was doing, and why she had not come to see him while he was conscious.

He heard someone in the doorway, and he could clearly see her slender silhouette. He could smell the soft scent of honey, so he closed his eyes, hoping she might approach him if she thought he was sleeping.

He felt her beside him and reached up and clasped her wrist. "I have been waiting for you."

She didn't try to move away. "How are you feeling?"

"I don't want to talk about that. We have a decision to make, you and I." His fingers slid between hers. "Did you read my note?"

217

His chest was bare but for the bandage, and she wanted so badly to touch his skin. "Of course I did."

"And?"

"You have no decision to make at all. I tore it up."

He pulled her down to him, and she came willingly. His lips touched and molded to hers, sending a jolt through her like an earthquake, and the tremors that followed were like aftershocks. He lightly touched her hair, and she wanted to be even closer.

With painful resolve, she eased away from him.

"Abby, don't turn away from me. I am trying to do the right thing."

"I like Patricia, and she loves you very much."

He released her arm. "Yes. I know that. Just tell me this one thing." He probed her eyes. "Are you . . ."

She already knew what he was agonizing over. He had written her the note because if she were with child, he would marry her. She wasn't, and she was glad. She would not want to marry any man under those circumstances. "I am fine. You don't have to worry."

She heard his relieved sigh. "Good night, Jonah."

He didn't answer her or try to stop her from leaving.

Chapter Twenty

The sun was just rising when Jonah got out of bed and struggled to dress himself. The most difficult part was putting on his boots, because his shoulder ached. And he couldn't button his shirt at all. He was glad when MacDougall heard him stirring and came into the room to help.

"How are you feeling, sir?"

Jonah grimaced. "Like I've been shot."

MacDougall buttoned the shirt for him. "Is there anything else I can do for you, sir?"

"I might be weak, and my shoulder hurts like hell, but I don't want you mothering me, Sergeant—save that for your new recruits, who will be arriving at the fort any day now."

MacDougall almost smiled. "Do you want me to get back to the fort?"

"Wait another day, and I'll go with you."

MacDougall would have liked to have told him that one day wouldn't be enough time to rest that shoulder, but he saved his breath, because the major would do what the major wanted to do.

The two men made their way to the kitchen, where Frances greeted them with her usual gruffness and served them a hearty breakfast. Jack and the general came in just as Jonah was having his second cup of coffee. From the looks of them, they had been up and about for some time.

Jonah couldn't help comparing the two men. They were an unlikely pair, and as different as two men could be, but they seemed to have found a common interest in horses.

Patricia came in later and was delighted to see Jonah up and dressed. She sat beside him, just needing to be near him. She politely refused the huge breakfast Frances placed before her and asked for a cup of tea.

"I have been thinking about leaving tomorrow, Mr. Hunter," Jonah said. "I have taken advantage of your hospitality long enough."

Frances glared at Jonah. "You don't need to be going off till you're better. Next week would be soon enough."

"That's what I wanted to tell him," MacDougall said.

Frances stared down at the sergeant. "He'd already be healing if you hadn't let him ride so far after being shot."

"Ma'am, you must not know how it works in the army. You see, the major here's in command, and I take his orders. Those below me in rank take my orders, but I would never—never—tell the major what to do."

Frances was still glaring at the man when she left the room, and mumbling something about "ruling the roost" under her breath.

"Now that's one scary woman, Mr. Hunter," MacDougall observed.

"You haven't seen her riled yet—this is one of her good days," Jack said, smiling.

"Admirable woman," Daniel Tremain concluded.

"Jonah," Patricia asked, "will I be staying here or leaving for the fort with you?" She wondered why he hadn't talked it over with her. She hadn't even known he was leaving until now.

He looked at a loss for a moment. His quarters at the fort were a shambles. He hadn't taken the time to move into them, and had been occupying a cot in his office. "You will have to give me a few days to make the quarters livable. There is a hotel in Diablo. I had made arrangements for you and the general to stay there. I hadn't known Quince would be bringing you here to the Half-Moon."

Patricia lowered her head. He hadn't known she would be at the ranch. It had been Abby he had wanted to see. She took a breath of air as the realization hit her: Jonah was in love with Abby.

"I won't hear of you staying in that flea trap," Jack interjected. "You will stay where you are for now.

We've got plenty of room, and Patricia has become a friend to my Abby."

Patricia wanted to return to Philadelphia that very moment, but she couldn't—not yet.

"General?" Jonah asked. "Is it all right with you to stay here?"

"Thank you, Jack. Patricia and I would like to stay. We can join my son later."

Jonah stood. "I am going to walk out to the barn. I need to get out in the fresh air."

Patricia watched him leave, wishing he had asked her to walk with him.

Abby was grooming the mare she had trained for Patricia when Jonah entered the stable. She glanced up at him and paused with the currycomb in her hand. "Should you be out of bed?" She frowned with concern. "I know you shouldn't be moving around this soon. You might reopen the wound."

Without a word he stepped close to her, took the currycomb and dropped it on the ground, then gathered her to him. "I have to come to you because you won't come to me. I want to hold you in my arms."

She muffled a sob and buried her face against his neck. "This isn't right, Jonah."

He clasped her face in both his hands and raised it to his so he could stare into the eyes that still haunted him. "I have always done the right thing, and everything that was expected of me." His finger slid across her mouth. "Until I came to Texas. Until I met you."

222

"Jonah, I know the kind of man you are, and I know you feel responsible for what happened between us. I told you then, and I'm telling you now, I was as much to blame as you were. I don't want you to have any regrets."

"Regrets . . . I'm full of them."

She turned back to the mare and picked up the currycomb, making wide strokes across the animal's back. "I feel guilty when I see how much Patricia cares for you. If I could take back what I did, I would."

He grabbed her and hauled her to him, his expression hard, his eyes glinting. "How can you say that?"

She pressed her hand against his arm, remembering his injured shoulder, but his mouth ground against hers and robbed her of all resistance. She pressed against his body, feeling the hardening of his need for her, and it awoke an answering need in her.

She felt, rather than heard, him groan. She had no substance without him, and it seemed she was even drawing her breath from him.

He broke off the kiss and stared at her. "Add that to the list of things you want to take back—I certainly can't."

She felt his warm breath on her hair, and she was weak with need. "We both know what your feelings are for me," she said, forcing the words past her trembling lips. "You have the same feelings as Moon Racer when a mare is ready for him."

She watched as he digested what she had told him, and his fierce blue eyes turned icy.

"Yes," he said at last, looking away from her. "That's what it is between us."

She stared down at the toe of her boot. She was losing parts of herself, and she was no longer sure who she was. Life had been so uncomplicated before Jonah came along. Now it was a struggle just to stay out of his arms. It was her fault that the situation had gotten out of hand—she could have put a stop to it before it got this far.

He brought his gaze back to her. "Do you really believe it's only lust between us, Abby?"

She had sensed the guilt in him, and his feeling of obligation toward her. She imagined that he would feel the same obligation toward any woman whose virginity he had taken. She ached because of what she must say to him, and she hoped she sounded convincing. "Don't look back with regret because of what happened between us, Jonah. If it hadn't happened with you, it would have been someone else."

She watched him flinch as if she'd struck him. After the initial shock of her words passed, he glared at her, and her spirits plummeted. She lowered her glance so he wouldn't see the pain she felt.

Then with controlled discipline, he stepped away from her. "I wanted to tell you that I'll be leaving tomorrow."

The coldness of that reality hit her hard. She had known he would be leaving as soon as he was able, but not this soon. "Have someone look at your wound when you get to where you are going."

She watched him struggle with whatever he was thinking. At last he spoke in a voice so cold and unfeeling that it cut her to the bone. "Your father has invited Patricia and the general to stay on for a few days. Is that all right with you?"

"Yes, of course."

"Well, then. I probably won't be seeing you again."

She concentrated on brushing the mare. "When will you give her the horse?"

"Today."

Abby nodded. "She won't have any trouble with this mare."

She could feel him behind her, and she knew he was deeply troubled, but she could be of no help to him.

After a long silence she heard him turn, and then the sound of his bootsteps faded from the barn.

Abby quickly saddled Moon Racer and rode away, allowing him to run full out—she had to get away from the ranch. She didn't want to be there when Jonah gave Patricia the mare, and she didn't want to sit down at the table with them and try to chew on food that would choke her. She found herself heading for the Diamond C and Quince. When she got there they were dipping stock, so she stayed to help them until the sun went down. Then her brother had one of his men accompany her home, because he did not want her riding alone after dark.

When she reached the barn, Navidad was waiting for her.

"Everyone has been looking for you this day, Señorita Abby. The major, he has come here to find you two, maybe three times."

"I'm tired, Christmas. I've been helping Quince today. Will you unsaddle Moon Racer for me?"

"*Sí.*" He looked at her curiously. "The major gave his señorita the mare today, and she was so happy. She hugged him plenty and was happy that you had trained the mare for her."

She walked toward the house. "I'm going to bed, Christmas."

Frances had left a lamp burning in the hallway. She blew it out and then moved quietly past Jonah's bedroom door so he would not hear her. Through the walls of her bedroom she could hear his pacing, and she wondered what could be going through his mind.

She sat back on her bed and then sank into its softness. She knew she should bathe, but she was just too weary. She had not meant to fall asleep, but sometime after midnight she awoke and undressed.

It was hot in the room, and she turned her face to catch the breeze from the open window. She thought of Jonah so close, and yet a world apart.

Was he sleeping?

If she went to him, what would he do?

He would be leaving in the morning, and that would be best for both of them.

Chapter Twenty-one

Abby was awake when Jonah left in the early-morning hours. She heard him moving about in his room, and she recognized his bootfall as he moved down the hallway. She heard him open the screen door and let himself out and then close it softly behind him.

Every nerve in her body screamed for her to run to him so she could feel his arms around her just one last time. But she lay stiffly against her pillow, willing herself not to move.

She heard Patricia's soft voice and the mumble of Jonah's deeper tones; she didn't want to hear any endearments they might exchange, so she clamped her hands over her ears.

There was no one she could go to for advice. If Iona were alive, she would empty her heart to her.

There were Glory and Crystal, but if she confided in either of them, they might urge her to talk to her brothers, and she would never do that.

She dressed and left the house, the gray, windy day doing nothing to lift her spirits. The first drops of rain fell just before she entered the barn. She stopped short when she saw her father saddling his horse, with his dog, Catfish, jumping about his feet.

"I expected you up earlier," Jack said as he took her saddle from her and placed it on her pinto. "I didn't think you would let the major leave without saying good-bye."

"I didn't want to see him."

Her father slipped the bit between her pinto's teeth and handed her the reins. "Didn't you?"

She looked up into his face. "I don't know what you mean."

"This is the first time I've ever known you to be untruthful."

"In what way?"

"Abby, Abby—it's at times like this that I wish your mother were here."

She gave him a shake of her head. She didn't want to talk about her mother with him. Their attention was drawn to the dog, who was chasing one of the barn cats. When he cornered it, he wagged his tail and bounced around as if he wanted to play. The cat would have none of it and skittered up the ladder to the hayloft.

"Don't you think I've noticed the looks that pass between you and Jonah?" her father asked. "Hell, I'd have to be blind not to see the tension between the

228

two of you." He gripped her shoulders. "I've never seen a man look at a woman the way he looks at you."

She felt a deep and sudden concern. "Did anyone else notice? I mean, Patricia or Jonah's father?"

"They may have missed it. They don't know you as well as I do, and as a father I may have been watching closer than anyone else."

"I would never want to hurt Patricia."

He leaned against the stall and looked at her. "If she loves Jonah, she's going to be hurt plenty. I saw the stiff way he said good-bye to her this morning, and I also noticed that she was crying when she went into the house."

Abby put her hand over her mouth, and her father folded her into his arms. "I don't know what to tell you, Abby. But I'd warn you to be careful where the major is concerned. He's not like you and me."

She heard the patter of rain on the roof, and she felt the comfort of her father's arms around her. "I know, Papa; he once told me that very thing."

"Then you should believe him."

"I'll never see him again. I can't."

He planted a kiss on her brow. "If only it were that easy. But you can't walk away from your feelings, Abby. You have to face them. I had plenty of time to face mine in prison."

"How did you deal with what you . . . with what you did to . . . with Mama's death?"

He breathed deeply and let it out slowly. "All I can tell you is that I miss her when I get up every morning, and when I go to bed every night. I will miss your mama until the day I draw my last breath on this earth."

"How do I face this, Papa?"

"You're a Hunter—you'll face it head-on, and not huddled in your bedroom trying to avoid the truth." He let his arm drop. "I have a meeting with Edmund at the bank. Then I'll be gone for a few days."

She was on the verge of telling him about the threats Edmund had made to her, but the banker was capable of hurting her father just as he might hurt her brothers. "Why do you like Mr. Montgomery?"

Her father drew on his rain poncho and studied her for a moment. If he thought her question odd, he didn't say so. "I don't know for sure. Maybe it's because he reminds me of a time gone by—a time that can never be again. You may not know this, but he loved your mama, too. He thought she would marry him, but she loved me—you might say I took her away from him. Anyway, I'm grateful to him because he was the only person in all of Diablo who welcomed me home when I returned."

No—she could not tell her father about the indecent things Edmund Montgomery had said to her.

"You aren't going to borrow money from him again, are you?"

"That's nothing for you to be concerned about, Abby. Look after that mangy dog while I'm away."

She nodded as he swung into the saddle and rode out of the barn.

Later Abby rode out herself, the rain mingling with her tears.

* * *

Abby sat on the porch step talking to Patricia and General Tremain. She noticed that every gesture Patricia made was feminine. She walked like a lady; she spoke like a lady. No wonder Jonah had chosen her to be his wife.

Abby suddenly had the urge get rid of all her trousers. She wanted to be poised; she wanted to be ladylike—she wanted to be more like Patricia.

Abby was deep in thought, and it took her a moment to realize General Tremain had been speaking to her.

"Since your father said he'd be away for a long stretch, I wonder if you would consider taking us to the ranch."

She blinked in confusion. "What ranch would that be?"

"Why, my son's ranch—surely you know about it. I don't know what he was thinking when he bought land here in Texas. I always supposed he would return home when he retired. If you ask me, I believe someone took advantage of him and sold him a parcel of worthless land. I want to find out for myself."

"I don't know what you are referring to."

He sat down on the steps beside Abby and unfolded a piece of paper on his lap. "This is a map Jack drew up for me." He stabbed his finger against the markings. "And this would be the land my son bought. Have you any notion where it is?"

She frowned and took the paper, identifying the location by tracing creeks and rivers. "If I am not mistaken, this is the Taylor ranch." She looked up at him. "But why would Mr. Taylor sell his ranch?"

"Because he found someone with money who was unsuspecting enough to buy his worthless property."

"Your son is not a person anyone could take advantage of, General."

"I'll decide that for myself when I see the land."

Abby remembered Jonah telling her he would like to try ranching; she hadn't taken him seriously at the time. "General Tremain, this property isn't worthless. After the Half-Moon Ranch, the Taylor ranch is one of the most prized properties in this part of Texas."

He looked doubtful. "Will you take me there?"

"Yes, of course. I'll have Christmas hook up the buckboard." She looked at Patricia. "You might want to change into something more practical. It's a dusty ride."

"I wasn't thinking of going. I'd rather Jonah be the one who showed it to me." Patricia backed toward the door with something like terror in her eyes. "I didn't know he would want to settle here in Texas."

"I think it might be best if you wait," the general stated. "My son probably bought it for you as a wedding present."

Abby nodded in agreement. "If Patricia isn't going, perhaps you would prefer to ride horseback."

"I'd relish a good ride in open country, Miss Hunter."

"Then we'll start first thing in the morning."

It promised to be a beautiful day. The bloodred sun touched the eastern sky, dappling the land with an ethereal beauty.

Abby rode up to the house on her pinto, leading a sorrel for the general. He had just come out on the porch while she was checking her rifle to make sure it was loaded. After she was satisfied it was, she shoved it into her saddle holster.

He lifted an eyebrow at her after he was mounted. "Are you a good shot, Miss Hunter?"

She smiled. "Good enough."

He laughed, looking forward to the day ahead. "I just bet you are."

The ride was uneventful and they traveled in companionable ease. Abby found Jonah's father inquisitive and intelligent, and to her surprise she was actually enjoying herself.

"Tell me what you know about this ranch."

"I've never actually been to the ranch house, but I've heard it is very grand. At one time Mr. Taylor was a wealthy man."

They forded several creeks, and at last they came to the Guadalupe. "This river actually runs through the Taylor ranch, giving it a constant source of water."

He nodded, glancing down at the clear water that rushed by. "Is it ever dry?"

"It's low in years of drought, but to my knowledge it's never been dry."

He took out the map and studied it intently. "I think I can find the place from here. Let's see if I can."

She watched him turn his mount and ride down river rather than in the direction of the ranch house. "We have to head west, General."

"Not according to this map." He reined in and looked at the map again. "Look. Right here is the house, and here's the river."

"Yes, but you just forded the river, and you are holding the map upside down."

His brow furrowed in a frown. "You said you hadn't been there, and yet you question my judgment."

"It isn't your judgment I question, General, it's your sense of direction. Out here distance is deceptive because of the many hills and woods. It's easy to become disoriented by the sheer size of the wilderness."

She pointed to the west. "That is the direction of the Taylor ranch."

"I don't agree."

"You will be lost if you go downstream."

He clamped his jaw. "I certainly know how to read a map!" he said imperiously, reminding her of his son.

"You can come with me, or you can go by yourself—it's entirely up to you. But when you get lost, don't blame me."

No one had ever spoken to him in that tone before. He felt his anger flare, and then he considered for a moment. "We'll try it your way, but if you are wrong, I want an apology."

She smiled. "Agreed. And if I'm right, I'll never speak of it to anyone."

Abigail Hunter was like no woman he'd ever known. She was damned pretty, and she had a head on her shoulders as well. She had spirit and spunk, and he liked the stubborn streak in her—it reminded him of himself.

Why hadn't some man snapped her up and married her?

Jonah walked into the trading post with Sergeant MacDougall on one side of him and Grant on the other side. He now had enough evidence to take the Indian agent into custody.

The place was permeated with the smell of rotten meat, and Jonah's boots crunched against the filthy floor littered with broken glass. The shelves were spilling over with salt pork and range beef, no doubt meant for the Indians but denied them by Williamson's unscrupulous greed.

Norman Williamson was standing behind a counter of sorts; it was honed out of logs that still had the bark on them. A pile of wolf pelts lay on top.

"To what do I owe this honor, Major?" he asked, folding his arms over his chest and leaning against the wall. "You don't often come down to my level, so there must be a reason you're here now."

"I can't reach far enough down to touch your level, Williamson."

The man's dull brown hair was worn long, and it looked unkempt and unwashed. He wore a fringed buckskin shirt and trousers and fringed boots laced up to his knees. He was a large man and muscular, with a wide chest.

"Don't go too far, Major. I've been tolerant of you so far." His amber-colored eyes looked almost wolfish. "But even I have my limits."

"You have already reached your limit. I'm here to arrest you in the name of the government of the United States of America. You will be transported to Fort Worth, where you will be brought up on charges of cheating the Indians and robbing army payrolls."

Norman Williamson's face whitened, and he sank down onto a chair. "You can't do that—you don't have the authority to arrest me, and you don't have anything to arrest me for."

"Ah, but I do. We have traced the stolen payrolls to you and three other men. They were glad to tell us all they knew and to return their portion of the money." Jonah nodded at MacDougall. "I don't think he is foolish enough to hide the money here, but search anyway."

MacDougall saluted. "Yes, sir. With the greatest of pleasure, sir."

Williamson looked at the ranger with uncertainty and fear. "He can't do this, can he?"

"Yeah, he certainly can," Grant said. "You should have looked ahead to this when you started working outside the law and cheating the very people you were hired to help. You got careless, Williamson; you left too many trails that led back to you."

Jonah saw the fright in Williamson's eyes. "Put the cuffs on him, Grant."

"Sure thing, Major. It's always a pleasure to do a service for the United States government." He grinned. "This is the part of my job I like best. Looks like you aren't going to have to worry where your next meal is coming from, Williamson. The government, being kindly and all, will probably agree to feed you for the rest of your natural life."

The man's face went even whiter as Grant handcuffed him. The ranger was enjoying himself too much.

"It might go easier for you," Jonah said, propping his booted foot on a chair, "if you agreed to tell us who your accomplices are."

"You said you already arrested them."

"Those men were nothing more than saddle bums. I want the man, or men, who gave you the information on when our shipments would be leaving Diablo."

Williamson shook his head. "I'd rather be locked up for the rest of my life than be dead."

Jonah moved forward and got in the Indian agent's face. "I'm going to throw out some names to you, and you tell me if I am looking in the right direction."

"I ain't saying nothing more."

"Edmund Montgomery?"

Williamson flinched. "I don't know him."

"Yes, you do. He was with you when you tried to buy the Taylor ranch not too long ago. I have witnesses to that fact."

"He's just a friend of mine. He was going to loan me the money to buy the place, and that's all I'm saying."

"If you won't tell me about Montgomery, tell me the name of his man who rustles horses from the Half-Moon Ranch."

"I ain't saying nothing more. I don't care what you do to me; it wouldn't be as bad as . . ." He shook his head, his color turning grayish. "I ain't saying nothing more."

"He's all yours, Grant. Thank you for your help."

"Don't mention it. I'm always ready to lend the army a hand." He grinned. "We're all better off now that this one is headed for prison."

Jonah started to leave, and then he halted in midstride. "Williamson isn't the head man."

"No," Grant agreed. "He's not smart enough for that."

Chapter Twenty-two

Abby pointed along the tree line. "That will be the Taylor place just ahead. I don't know Mr. Taylor very well, but my brothers have told me he is a decent man." She made certain not to mention the fact that she had been correct about the direction, and the general wrong.

As they rode up to the ranch house, the place was astir with a beehive of activity. Some men were carrying lumber into the house, probably doing repairs. The barn was getting a new coat of paint, and there were even men landscaping the yard.

When Abby dismounted, Lester Taylor came out of the barn to greet them. "Why, it's Abby Hunter, isn't it?"

"Yes, sir. And this," she said, indicating Jonah's father, "is General Tremain."

Lester's eyes twinkled with friendliness. "Well, now, this is a real pleasure. I'm happy to meet Jonah's pa."

Tremain was looking about him, clearly impressed by what he saw. "My son bought this place from you?"

"He surely did, and became a friend to me for life. He saved me from sure ruin."

Abby was looking around as well. She didn't know how to interpret the feelings that rocked her. "There seems to be a lot of repair going on, Mr. Taylor."

"The major wanted everything done to fix the place up. I have to tell you, General, your son is the finest man I've ever known."

Abby realized that the two men needed to talk, and she didn't want to see the inside of the house. This was the place Jonah would bring Patricia after they were married.

She excused herself. "General, I'll be waiting for you at the river crossing when you're ready to return. If we are going to make it home before dark, we need to leave within the next two hours."

He was so deep in conversation with Lester, he merely nodded at her.

Abby sat on the bank of the river watching the clear water of the Guadalupe rush by. She had tried not to think of Jonah, but it was impossible to forget him.

She looked around at the beauty of the place. This was good land—Jonah would make a go of it, because he was not a man to settle for anything less than success.

She had changed drastically since he had come into her life, and she would never again be the girl she had been before she met him.

She plucked at her trousers and frowned. She still had the money Matt had recently sent her, and it was a substantial amount. She had tried to give it to Brent to pay some of their father's debts, but he had insisted that she spend the money on herself.

That was just what she was going to do.

She heard a rider approach, and she slid off the rock, watching General Tremain dismount. He was smiling as he came toward her.

"I tell you, Abigail, I'm seeing my son clearly for the first time. He has done his old father proud, although I hadn't noticed his worth until others told me about him." He rested his back against a huge boulder and spread his hand on the warmth of it.

"What do you think of my son, Abigail?"

"I think you should have seen the kind of man he was without someone else having to convince you."

"Dammit, gal, you do have a sharp tongue!"

"So I have been told."

He looked at the sky and gauged the hour. "Why do you suppose Patricia didn't come with us? She's been acting strange lately. It might be that she is just homesick."

She was about to answer when she glanced down at his hand resting against the rock. There had been no warning rattle from the large diamondback rattlesnake that was coiled at his fingertips. The reptile was actually smelling the general's hand with its forked tongue!

"General, if you trust me, do not move a muscle—stay exactly as you are. Don't move!"

He froze. Something in her tone told him she meant just what she'd said. He watched her race to her horse, grab her rifle out of the holster, and cock it. He took a deep gulp when she seemed to be aiming at him.

"Trust me, General. Do not move your hand!"

He slowly glanced down, and when he saw the rattler every instinct in him screamed for him to run. But he trusted Abby, so he froze in place. He watched as the forked tongue touched his hand and retracted several times.

He glanced back at her as she aimed the rifle and fired. He whitened when he saw the impact of the bullet jerk the snake upward and slam it to the ground. His legs went weak, and he crumpled to his knees.

"You were marvelous," Abby said, going down beside him and holding her canteen to his lips. "You looked death in the face and didn't blink. I don't know many men who could have done that."

He smiled weakly. "I don't want to *ever* do it again."

"Take small sips of the water."

"I'd rather have a shot of whiskey at the moment." He raised the canteen to his lips. "Damn, Abigail! That scared the hell out of me!"

She helped him stand. "Are you all right?"

"I think so." He saw the concern on her face and managed to smile. "Lucky for me you're the best damned shot I ever saw."

A smile curved her lips, and a teasing light came into her eyes. "I was lucky this time. I usually miss."

When they reached the house, it was long after dark. Frances had left food warming on the back of the stove, and the general and Abby sat down to eat. Over the day they had formed a bond and now felt easy in each other's company.

Patricia heard the laughter coming from the kitchen, and she went to investigate. Abby was pointing her finger at the general, and he was smiling.

"It's lucky for me that you trusted me when I told you not to move. I didn't relish the thought of cutting into your hand and sucking the poison out of you."

"And I wasn't sure you weren't going to miss that damned snake and hit me!"

She wiggled her nose. "You're just lucky I like you, or I might have missed on purpose."

He laughed and motioned for a confused Patricia to join them.

"What happened today?" Patricia asked curiously.

"Abigail saved my life. She shot a snake not half an inch from my hand."

Patricia paled. "I would have fainted dead away."

The general looked from one woman to the other, comparing them. They were both beautiful, Patricia in a refined way—Abby, mysterious, almost exotic with her cat-green eyes. Patricia would be an ornament for her husband; she would never cause him a moment's concern. She would be adored and paraded for all to see. His gaze went back to Abby. She would be a companion to her husband; someone to stand as his equal, to walk beside him to face whatever life threw her way. Both women would make admirable wives, but some men would soon tire of Patricia's sweetness. Abby would plant her scuffed boots and dig in if she thought she was right about something. Yet she was fragile and delicate—very definitely a woman.

A man would never tire of Abigail Hunter's exuberance for life.

"I was just thinking what a wonderful wife you would make for some lucky man, Abigail."

Abby arched an eyebrow. "Are you proposing?"

"If I were younger, you would be the woman for me. But I'm almost certain I couldn't handle you at my age. I probably couldn't even have handled you when I was younger."

"Did you just pay me a compliment?"

He grinned. "Yes. Yes, I did."

They both burst out laughing while Patricia looked on, aghast.

Abby wandered through the general store, looking at different fabrics. She disregarded the pinks and other pastel colors and finally settled on a bolt of deep maroon broadcloth, a green-striped lawn, and a deep blue serge. She was still undecided about the deep green silk taffeta, but she quickly added it to her purchases before she changed her mind. After some agonizing, she chose three leather split skirts, a brown, a black, and a light tan one.

With her arms loaded she walked the short distance to the Herbert house, where the local seamstress lived.

Her knock was answered immediately by Mary Herbert. "Abby Hunter," the sweet-faced woman said, smiling, "please come in."

Abby struggled with her packages until Mary took them from her and placed them on an empty chair.

"Mrs. Herbert, will you help me pick out patterns, and make several gowns for me?"

The woman smiled warmly. "Abby, after what you did for my Rob, I will make you the most beautiful gowns this town has ever seen."

"How is Rob?"

"He's feeling good about himself. He always tells me he can't turn into a bully like Johnny Brisco or his friend Miss Abby won't like it."

Abby was suffering from conflict as she gathered all her trousers and carried them out of her room. She now wore one of the split skirts and found it surprisingly comfortable.

She walked out of the house to the back of the barn, where she deposited the trousers in the barrel where trash was burned.

Navidad appeared at her side, looking amazed at the way she was dressed. "What is it you are going to do, Señorita Abby?"

"Burning the past. Light the fire before I change my mind, Christmas."

He nodded. "It will be as you say."

He watched her walk back to the house, thinking there was something very different about her. And what did she mean, she was burning the past?

He shook his head. With Señorita Abby there was always mystery.

Jack had returned home in the early afternoon. Again, Abby was glad to see that he was sober, and she was genuinely happy to see him.

As they sat around the table eating supper, no one commented on Abby's changed appearance until Frances came into the room.

"I see you finally took my advice," the housekeeper said, pushing a plate of chicken and dumplings in front of Abby.

"Yes. It was time."

Patricia touched Abby's hand. "I would like to have a skirt like yours."

Abby took a bite of dumpling before she answered. "That's easy. We just have to ride to town. They have it in three different colors at the general store."

"If the two of you are finished talking about fripperies, I would like to tell you about the letter I got from my son today," the general announced. "He says the other officers' wives at the fort want to give you a grand party, Patricia." His gaze moved to Abby. "He asked that you come as well as a companion to Patricia."

"I got a letter from him too, saying much the same thing," Patricia said. "Abby, you must come with me.

I would be terrified of so many strangers."

"Of course she'll go," the general blustered.

Jack saw the torment in his daughter's eyes before she lowered her head. "You will go, won't you, Abby?"

"I would rather not."

"You *should* go, Abby," her father pressed.

"Please say you will," Patricia pleaded.

She didn't want to go, and yet she was afraid of never seeing Jonah again. The fact that he would even want to see her after what she had said to him was a wonder.

"If you would like me to, I will," she said finally, knowing she was making a mistake. But she couldn't help it. This would be her last time to see Jonah.

Chapter Twenty-three

Fort Fannin, one of the more picturesque forts of Texas, had been constructed of limestone because the stone littered the area and was easily accessible. The entire outer wall of the fort was stone and virtually impregnable when manned by guards. The officer's quarters were actually a two-bedroom house set apart from the other dwellings.

Abby was seated in the back of the buckboard beside Patricia when the guard on duty waved them through the gate. As they drove in, she entered a world she could never have imagined. Soldiers were marching on parade, and they stopped and turned in the general's direction, standing at attention.

The general smiled because he knew the tribute was for him. He saluted, and the sergeant at arms had the men stand at parade rest.

The ladies had been helped out of the buckboard by two eager troopers, so the general could turn his full attention to the honor his son's troops were offering him.

"Sir," the sergeant said respectfully, "would you care to inspect the troops?"

Abby wondered where Jonah was. She had expected him to be there to greet Patricia upon her arrival.

After the general had done his duty by inspecting the troops, they were escorted to Jonah's quarters.

The main room was spacious, with spears, lances, and other Indian artifacts adorning the rustic walls. A colorful woven Indian rug covered the middle of polished wooden floor.

Sergeant MacDougall appeared at the door and greeted them with a smile. "The major sends his regrets, sir, and begs to be excused until tomorrow. He said I was to explain to you that he had been called to Fort Worth on army business." He waved forward the men who were carrying the trunks. "I was asked to put the ladies in the back bedroom, and you can have the major's room, sir. He's been bunking in his office since he took command here, and never actually used the room."

Abby didn't have long to consider whether she had done the right thing in coming, because Grant appeared at the door and she was happy to see him. She smiled and clasped his outstretched hands.

"Look at you, all dressed up," he said, kissing her cheek.

Remembering her manners, she introduced Jonah's father and Patricia to the ranger.

"The fort's been buzzing with word of your arrival, sir," Grant said, shaking the officer's hand. "Most of the soldiers have never seen a real general before."

"Sergeant MacDougall, Mr. Zachary, suppose the two of you show this general around the post. I have been looking forward to seeing the fort my son commands."

Grant looked at Abby as he walked to the door. "I'll want to see you tonight."

She nodded. "You can tell me all the news."

Grant had been escorting Abby around the fort, and they had just come out of the infirmary. He steered her toward the stables, where they saw several Half-Moon–trained mustangs. She saw the U.S.A. brand on a brown filly she had trained herself and felt great satisfaction.

"What are you doing here, Grant?" she asked, turning to the tall ranger. "Did you find the men who had robbed the payrolls?"

"I didn't, but Jonah did. He's one smart man, Abby."

"Yes," she said, looking down at the toe of her slipper, "he is."

He tilted her chin upward. "What's wrong, Abby?"

"Everything and nothing."

"That's not an answer."

She looked into his earnest eyes and wished with all her heart that she loved him instead of Jonah. He was safe and familiar, and he didn't stir passion in her like Jonah did. "Grant, there is really no one I can talk to about what I am feeling."

"You can talk to me."

She walked into his arms. "I have never been ashamed of my actions before now. I feel like I have betrayed Patricia, and I don't know if the feeling will ever go away."

"Do you mean because you are in love with Jonah?"

"I . . . yes."

"Abby, none of us can help who we love. You don't need to feel guilty about that."

"I shouldn't have come here."

He held her away from him, studying her expression when he asked, "Why did you come?"

"Jonah asked his father to bring me. I could have refused, and at first I did." She looked at him pleadingly. "What am I to do?"

He watched her face closely when he said, "You could always fall in love with me."

She smiled at his teasing. "I wish I could."

He tugged at a stray curl. "I was almost in love with you, but not so deep that I couldn't climb out." He grinned. "Course, if you were to give me the least encouragement, I could be hopelessly lost in those green eyes."

"I don't want you to love me, Grant. And I don't want to love anyone."

"Well," he said, steering her out of the barn with his hand at her waist, "now that we've settled that, you can go riding with me tomorrow."

She laughed up at him. "I would love to."

Patricia was waiting for Abby when she returned from her walk with Grant. "Mr. Zachary seems a very nice sort of man."

"He is. Some woman is going to be very fortunate to have him for a husband."

"But not you?"

"No. We're just friends. I like him too much to marry him without loving him."

"Yes. That would be a tragedy for anyone."

Abby settled on the bed. "Show me what you are going to wear tomorrow night."

Patricia opened her trunk and spread a pale yellow creation across the foot of the bed. Abby touched the delicate fabric and smiled. "You are going to be so pretty in this."

Patricia folded her gown and laid it back in the trunk. "Let me see your gown."

Abby had to think for a moment. She had hurriedly collected her gowns from Mary Herbert the day before they left town, and she hadn't looked at any of them except the wine-colored traveling dress she now wore. "I don't know what it looks like. I remember the material was green."

Abby placed the box on the bed and opened the lid to find a note lying on top of the gown, and her curiosity was piqued. Unpinning the note, she read aloud: " 'Abby, I don't usually do this much work on anyone's gown, not even my own. But this is my way of saying thank-you for what you did for my son, Rob. I know his gift to you was one of Clover's litter—mine is this gown and the gloves. I only wish I could see you in them. You have a true and loving nature, and you are my son's friend for life.' "

There were tears in Abby's eyes as she lifted out the gown. It was made from the pattern Mary had helped her select, but it didn't quite look the same. There was a soft fabric drape down the back that swept to the floor. The neck was low, and the sleeves were tiny and puffed. Around the hem and around the band at the sleeves, Mary had embroidered tiny pink rosebuds. A pair of elbow-length gloves were at the bottom of the box.

"It's so lovely," Patricia said. "Whatever did you do for her son?"

Patricia looked shocked when Abby laughed and said, "I taught him to fight."

Abby and Grant had been riding for several hours and had just returned to the fort when she saw the line of cavalrymen in the distance. Grant motioned for her to follow him, and they galloped into the fort.

There was a sudden stirring of excitement as the soldiers became more alert and watchful and came to attention. "That would be Jonah," Grant observed as the blue line of cavalrymen entered the fort.

This was a Jonah Abby had never seen. He dismounted and two men ran forward to take his horse. Sergeant MacDougall stepped forward, saluted, and stiffly reported on all that had happened while Jonah was away. There was something he handed Jonah to sign, and everyone was quiet as he read it over, scribbled his name, then handed it back to MacDougall.

"Sergeant, dismiss the troops," Jonah said. Behind his order was a tone of undeniable authority.

Troopers suddenly seemed to relax and went about their usual activities. That was when Jonah turned to Abby. He walked toward her and Grant, but his gaze was on her. His uniform was dusty, and he looked weary, she thought.

"You have been riding?" were his first words to her. "You are wearing a skirt."

She nodded, raising her gaze to his. "Yes."

For a long moment he stared at her with those sky-blue eyes. He almost seemed nervous, and Abby wondered why. "You came. I wasn't sure you would."

She tried to smile but couldn't. "You invited me." Her gaze went to his shoulder. "How is your wound?"

He flexed his arm. "All but well."

"I'm glad."

He took a breath and turned to Grant. "I would like to see you in my office on the matter involving Williamson."

"How did the trial go?"

"He will spend the rest of his natural life in prison." He glanced at Abby. "If you will excuse us?"

"Yes, of course."

He turned and walked stiffly away, and immediately two soldiers fell in behind him to do his slightest bidding.

"Now, that's a strange situation," Grant remarked to Jonah as he followed him.

"What?"

Grant noticed that Jonah had come straight to Abby, and had not gone to the officer's quarters to see Miss Van Dere. "It's nothing, I'm sure. I was just thinking aloud and deciding I was going to back up a bit and watch how things go."

"I don't always understand what you are talking about."

"I know you don't. But I understand you, though. You're so mad at me at the moment you could bite the head off a penny nail."

Jonah didn't deny it as he gazed coldly at the ranger. "I wish I could tell you to leave her alone, but I don't have that right."

"No. You don't."

Jonah entered his office and moved to his desk. "We will speak of the Williamson matter."

Patricia had arranged Abby's hair, and then Abby helped Patricia with her hooks and laces.

"You look wonderful," Abby said, standing back. "Jonah will love you in that gown."

"I'm nervous. I know he's waiting for me in the other room, but I don't want to see him just now."

Abby frowned. "Why ever not?"

She shook her head. "If you were ready, you could come with me."

"I still have to get into that gown. He will want to introduce you and his father to everyone. You don't need me for that."

Patricia reluctantly left the room, and that puzzled Abby. She could hear their voices, and she turned to the window. She would like to go back home and not attend the dance at all tonight.

Why had she put herself in a situation that could only be torture for her?

Chapter Twenty-four

Abby stepped up to the door of the reception hall, her heart drumming in her ears. She stopped twice before she entered, knowing that Jonah, his father, and Patricia would be in a receiving line. This was such a formal affair, and she was afraid she would do something to disgrace herself. She wished Grant were with her. She could use his strong presence tonight.

Finally she drew a deep breath and stepped inside. Of course, Jonah was the first person she saw. He was wearing his dress blues with a scarlet sash and a silver-handled saber at his waist. She was barely aware of her footsteps as she approached him. His head was bent as he listened to what the lady in front of her was telling him.

When the woman moved on, Jonah turned to Abby.

Time had no meaning; there was no one else in the room as his gaze swept over her. She saw a muscle in his jaw tighten, and a vein in his neck throbbed. He reached out his gloved hand to her and held her hand for a moment longer than he should have.

"Abby, you are looking . . . beautiful. You take my breath away."

"You are more than kind."

She quickly moved to Patricia and kissed her cheek, and then to the general, who kissed her on both cheeks. He looked handsome and distinguished in his uniform, and it made her smile that he wore no medals or adornment on his chest—the Tremains of Philadelphia would not do anything so tasteless as to clutter their uniforms with decorations.

Unlike Diablo, where few people ever spoke to Abby, here she was readily accepted. She exchanged greetings with the wives of officers, while several young officers lined up to sign the dance card that Patricia had insisted on giving her.

She tried not to think about Jonah, but his presence seemed to fill the room. It seemed that she had danced with almost every officer there, even the general himself. But the evening was almost over before Jonah finally approached her. He stopped in front of her, standing still and rigid, his eyes holding a hard expression. She wondered what she had done to make him so angry. If she had acted improperly, she wasn't aware of it.

To those who didn't know him, his voice might have sounded tranquil, but he was anything but calm. His blue eyes were sharp and stabbing.

"Is this dance taken?"

Her next dance partner, a lieutenant, had just walked up to her and stood waiting. "I . . . yes, it is."

His gaze went to the young officer. "You will not mind forgoing this dance, will you, Harrison?"

"No, sir. I mean, not if you—"

"That will be all," Jonah said in a dismissive tone.

When he turned back to Abby, his eyes dared her to reject his offer to dance.

She stepped into his arms, and she had the feeling it was where she belonged. As his gloved hand slid around her waist, and the other one gripped her hand, she closed her eyes, wondering why she felt like crying, and at the same time felt like a wilted rose that could not hold itself upright.

Her head drifted toward his shoulder, where she wanted to lay it. What would his reaction be if she committed such an outrageous act? she wondered. As sanity returned, she jerked herself stiffly upright, thinking she must be losing her mind.

"I watched all night as other men held you, made you laugh. I watched them line up, hoping for a chance to dance with you. Did you enjoy torturing me?"

"I didn't . . . they weren't—"

"Didn't you? Weren't they?"

His words wound their way through her mind and through her body, forging a path of warmth and torment. She had to fight against the power he was exuding over her. When she attempted to wrest her hand free of his grasp, he held it fast.

"You should not be saying such things to me," she whispered, so stunned by what was happening between them that she could not find her full voice. "Please don't say any more."

His voice was gentle but commanding. Abby could feel the tension in him. "I can't seem to help myself."

All the fight went out of her. She could smell the wonderful spicy scent of him when his chin touched her forehead.

He whispered against her ear, and the sound of his voice seemed to fill her whole being. "Since I first looked into your eyes, Abby, I have been caught in your spell."

Abby struggled to find her voice, and when she spoke it was breathless, as if she had been running a great distance. "Please, no."

Jonah's gaze fell on Abby's mouth and stayed there for so long that she felt as if he had physically kissed her. He took a deep breath and let it out slowly, and it seemed to Abby that she could hear his heart hammering against his chest.

Her throat choked tight when he touched his cheek to hers. "I want to touch your spirit and make it mine. I'm jealous of every look you get from other men."

She swallowed twice before she could answer. "Please don't hold me so close." She swallowed again. "And think of Patricia."

"Don't you think I know I'm hurting her?" he whispered, his breath stirring against her ear. "Do you want to hear how my heart is so filled with you that I can't see other women, not even the one I'm supposed to marry?"

Heat burned through her, and the uneasiness receded, just like the ebbing of a frothy wave. She raised her head and met his gaze, then quickly lowered it when she saw the fierceness in his eyes. His words whispered through her mind, and he didn't miss a step as he released her hand and tilted her chin up to him.

"I can never have you again—you can never be mine."

She glanced across the room at Patricia, who seemed to be deep in conversation with one of the officers' wives.

"Don't worry, Abby," he said, when he saw where her attention was directed. "I will marry Patricia and make sure she never has reason to regret it, but tonight I am saying good-bye to you."

She had never felt such pain. "Yes."

"I'll never forget how it felt to make love to you, Abby. God help me, I have had visions of a daughter with your green eyes and your wild spirit." He lowered his voice to whisper against her ear, "I want to fill you with strong sons, and when they grow older, let them decide for themselves if they want a military career."

She tried to hold her head up, but it was so heavy. She refused to cry, but she wanted to. "No, Jonah. I can't stand any more."

"What you said to me in the barn that day wasn't right. Tell me you don't believe that."

"It wasn't true."

The dance ended, and Abby became aware of other voices around her. She forced her steps to match Jonah's as he led her across the dance floor.

He whispered near her ear, "I beg you to forgive my actions tonight. I did no honor to you or Patricia." He squeezed her hand. "I just can't seem to find the way to say good-bye to you."

Patricia had watched Jonah and Abby dancing together, and she knew they loved each other. She knew them both well enough to see they were denying their own hearts because they didn't want to hurt her.

She had to do something about the situation, and she had to do it that very night!

"Miss Van Dere," Grant said, coming up to her. "Is this dance taken?"

She was grateful for the tall ranger's appearance. "No, it isn't."

He held his arms out to her. "Then I'm a lucky man."

He was a good dancer and easy to follow. She was silent for a moment, as if she were judging him, and then she asked, "How well do you know Abby?"

"I've known her since she was small."

"She is in love with Jonah."

He was quiet for a moment, and then he said, "I know. But you don't need to worry. Jonah will marry you."

She looked up at him. "That would be the problem. You see, Jonah loves her, too."

He smiled sadly, feeling pity for her. She was a breathtaking woman, and yet she was losing Jonah, and she knew it. "What are you going to do about it?"

"Let him go."

He nodded. "It won't be easy. I know—I had to step aside, too."

"You love Abby?"

"Almost." He smiled down at her. "But I could probably love a beautiful woman with the brightest, bluest eyes I have ever seen."

She stared at the handsome ranger, whose teasing had already made her feel better. And he was easy to talk to. "I believe I love the thought of being married to Jonah more than I love Jonah."

"What would you do if I should show up on your doorstep in Philadelphia one day?"

She blushed when he stared into her eyes, and she felt positively giddy. "I would invite you in and then have to fight off all the females who would vie for a place at your side," she answered, a little breathless. She had never thought of any man except Jonah. But this ranger had made her see that she could feel emotions with another man. She could certainly feel the pull of this ranger's charm.

Chapter Twenty-five

Jonah played his part as host as his guests began to take their leave. Dutifully Patricia stood beside him, grave and pale. He felt a sudden rush of pity for her—she deserved so much better than he had given her so far. But he would make it up to her after they were married.

"The general is having a jovial time speaking to everyone in the room."

"Yes, it would seem so." But Patricia was watching Abby, who was surrounded by people and charming them into laughter.

Patricia touched his shoulder. "I wonder if I might have a moment alone with you when the guests have all gone?"

He nodded. "Of course."

*   *   *

Jonah had escorted Patricia to his office, and she now stood in front of the window that looked out on the parade ground. He watched her for a moment and went to her, placing his hands on her shoulders.

"Do you want to tell me what's bothering you? Although I think I have already guessed."

She turned to him with a serious expression on her pretty face. "I don't imagine you know what I'm about to say."

He led her to a chair and sat down beside her. "Suppose you tell me."

"Is there anything you wish to say to me before I begin?"

"No, Patricia. Unless you have something to discuss about the wedding."

"Jonah," she said, staring at him, "there will be no wedding, at least not between you and me."

He lowered his head for a moment, hating the fact that he had hurt her. "I don't blame you for being angry. I've behaved abominably."

She placed her small hand on his. "Jonah, it's my fault for allowing this farce to go on as long as it has. In all the time we have known each other, you have never once told me you loved me."

He was not going to lie to her now . . . he never had. "I certainly liked you better than any woman I knew when I asked you to marry me."

She smiled slightly. "How noble of you to remember it that way, but you didn't ask me to marry you—the real truth is, I forced a proposal out of you."

"What do you mean?"

"The night just before you were to leave for Arizona, you found me crying in the garden."

"Yes, I remember."

"I threw myself at you, professing my love for you and exclaiming that my life would be desolate without you." She stood up and walked back to the window. "Jonah, being the kind of man you are, you felt compelled to ask me to marry you. I knew that then; I know it now."

"You don't want to marry me?"

She turned to him, her eyes sparkling with tears. "No, I don't. I deserve better than what I would have as your wife. I deserve a man who will love me and look at me the way you looked at Abby Hunter tonight. I want that kind of love from the man I marry."

He stood and started pacing the room, ashamed of his ungracious conduct. "Patricia, I don't know what love means. If you can find it in your heart to forgive me for tonight, I will be a good husband to you."

"It's no good, Jonah. I have a feeling love is eating away at your insides right now. I don't want to stand in the way of your happiness and condemn you to a life without love, or me to a husband who doesn't love me."

He wished he could tell her that it had all been a mistake, but he couldn't. "What do you want me to do?"

She touched his hand and slid her arms around his waist, laying her head on his shoulder. "Tell me good-bye."

"I never meant to hurt you."

"I know that. You deserve to be happy, and so do I."

He held her away from him. "I am sorry this happened. Forgive me."

"You are forgiven. Abby is the right woman for you. She is so full of life—she is gentle and kind, spunky and stubborn. I wish I could be like her, but I never could be." She took a step away from him. "I have seen a change in you since you came to Texas—you came alive here, but the vastness of this place scares me. I want to go home, where my life will be ordered and each day will be much like the one before."

His eyes reflected a deep, piercing pain. "I don't even know how Abby feels about me, Patricia."

She was startled by that admission. All the women of their social circle in Philadelphia had been in love with Jonah. He could have had any woman he wanted. She had never seen him this uncertain about any woman. "Neither of you has confessed your love?"

"Of course not. Not love, exactly."

She realized something deep and meaningful had happened between Jonah and Abby, but they had pulled away from whatever it was because of her. "In trying to do the noble thing, you both turned your back on love. I will never settle for anything less than the deepest love, and neither should you."

He managed a smile. "I can think of half a dozen men in Philadelphia who have already lost their hearts to you."

She laughed softly. "I believe you might be right. In any case, I will be leaving as soon as it can be arranged. I suppose, for the sake of gossip, I should reject you publicly before I leave."

"Are you sure, Patricia?"

"Yes, I am, and so are you."

"The man who wins you for his wife will be fortunate indeed."

She moved to the door, and he walked beside her to escort her back to his quarters. "Yes, he will." She said with a glimmer of humor. "I'm quite a catch."

Patricia had expected to feel completely destroyed when she gave Jonah his freedom, but she didn't. She would miss him—what woman wouldn't?—but she was glad she had come to her senses. Perhaps it was as she'd told Grant; she hadn't loved Jonah so much as she loved the idea of being his wife.

They stopped at the door just as the guard on duty called out the hour. "Do you want me to get Abby for you?"

He hesitated, wishing he could have Abby in his arms at that moment. Then he shook his head.

"No. It's late, and I still have paperwork waiting for me."

She stood on her tiptoes and brushed a kiss on his forehead. "I'll see you tomorrow."

Abby heard Patricia enter the room, but she pretended to be asleep. She had been crying, something she had rarely done until she met Jonah—now it seemed to be second nature for her to cry at the slightest provocation.

"Are you asleep, Abby?"

She could not ignore Patricia. "No."

"I need to talk to you, if you aren't too sleepy."

Abby knew what was coming—she had expected it. She deserved everything Patricia had to say to her. "I'm not sleepy."

Patricia lit a lamp and sat down on the foot of the bed. "I will be going back to Philadelphia."

Abby sat up quickly and grabbed Patricia's hand. "No. You mustn't do that! Don't blame Jonah for my bad behavior. I threw myself at him. He's such a gentleman he didn't want to hurt my feelings. You have to believe me; it was all my fault tonight."

"Yes, in a way it is your fault. It's your fault because you are exactly the kind of woman Jonah needs and wants—it's your fault that he is so deeply in love with you, he's miserable."

"He told you that?"

"No. As you say, he is a gentleman. I am the one who did most of the talking tonight. When Jonah was at your ranch he hardly touched me, and when you were in the room his eyes followed you with such . . . hunger, I could see his pain."

"You are mistaken, Patricia. It's you he wants. After all, he asked you to marry him."

"I almost begged him to propose to me—it wasn't his idea. Until that night I don't think he had even considered marrying me. There were so many women in love with him, Abby. I was just one of them."

"If you love him enough, you could make him happy."

"He would never be happy with me, but he would have gone through with the wedding because that's the kind of man he is."

Abby said nothing, so Patricia continued. "I think I first realized his feelings for you when he insisted on being brought to you when he was wounded. You see, Abby, he didn't even know I was staying at your ranch at the time."

Abby buried her face in her hands. "He doesn't love me. He only . . . he only . . ."

Even though she couldn't say the words, Patricia understood what Abby meant. She went to her and hugged her. "My poor little friend, he could have what you are implying with anyone—don't you know that?"

Abby clasped Patricia's hand. "Don't leave him. Don't do this to him. He will be so miserable if you go."

Patricia moved away and blew out the lamp. "He will be more miserable if I stay."

Abby had been unable to sleep. She buried her face in her pillow so Patricia would not hear her crying. She had destroyed any hopes Jonah might have had for happiness—and Patricia, too. She waited for the sun to light the darkened corners of the room before she quietly dressed and left Patricia sleeping.

She hurried outside, frantically seeking Sergeant MacDougall. He had been putting young recruits through their daily drill, so she waited until he had finished and dismissed them.

"Miss Hunter, you're up mighty early after such a late night."

"Sergeant, do you know where Grant Zachary is?"

He heard the desperation in her voice. "Why, yes. He's quartered next to me."

"Would you please tell him I need to see him at once? And please hurry."

"Yes, ma'am, I surely will."

MacDougall watched her hurry away. Everyone was talking about the major and Miss Hunter—about how the major kept staring at one woman while he was engaged to another. But he had known for some time that his commander loved the Hunter gal. Otherwise why would he have been so frantic to see her when he wasn't sure he was going to live?

As far as MacDougall was concerned, Quince's sister was the right woman for his commander.

The young corporal skidded to a stop before Jonah and issued a quick salute. "I'm sorry to interrupt you, sir, but Miss Van Dere told me to tell you that Miss Hunter left the fort this morning with Ranger Grant Zachary."

"She went riding?"

"No, sir—she left."

"Dismissed, soldier."

Jonah blamed himself for hurting Abby with his little display the night before. He could only imagine how she must have felt, and how difficult it would be for her to face Patricia. If there was one thing Abby tried to avoid, it was gossip, and he had certainly brought that down on her head.

Jonah frowned and moved to the window in time to see his father striding across the parade ground. It was obvious from his stiff motions that he was mad about something. And Jonah knew what it was.

The general burst through the door and faced his son. "What in the hell do you mean, Jonah, by what you have done?"

He had been expecting this; he just wondered why it had taken his father so long to seek him out. "I'm in no mood for your accusations, General. Just say what is on your mind, and let me get on with my work."

"What do you mean by allowing Abigail to get away? Don't you know you could lose her?"

Jonah was struck silent. He had certainly not expected those words from his father.

"I have known for some time that Abigail was the wife for you. I just wondered how long it would take you to realize it. I was certainly concerned with what your stalling was doing to Patricia. It would have been just like you to marry her, knowing you wanted Abigail. I guess Patricia took care of that herself—she has a real elegance of mind, like a true Philadelphian."

Jonah could hardly believe his father's glowing approval of Abby. "So you have already decided which woman I am to marry—just like you decided everything else in my life?"

"Hell, Jonah, you couldn't keep your hands off Abigail last night. Son, you didn't buy that ranch with Patricia in mind, and you know it."

"No. I don't suppose I did." He looked up at the ceiling to gather his thoughts. "I don't even know how she feels about me. After last night she probably despises me."

"Then it's about time you found out, isn't it?"

"I can't leave just now." He shook his head. "Duty first."

"Well, I'm going to be leaving tomorrow to escort Patricia back to Philadelphia, where she belongs. When I return in the spring, I expect there to be a wedding—if you can wait that long—and from what I saw last night, you'd better waste no time in getting Abigail to the altar."

Edmund read Kane's letter for the third time, trying to figure out its meaning; there were so many misspelled words it was hard to tell. He shook his head and stuffed it in his pocket. Kane couldn't write worth a damn, but for him to even make the attempt meant something had happened.

He mounted his horse and rode out of town. Sometime later he arrived at Kane's cabin to find him sitting on the doorstep whittling a piece of wood.

"You sure took your time getting here."

Edmund dismounted. "I had bank business to tend to before I could leave town."

"Yeah. I just bet you did. Foreclosed on any orphans or widows lately?"

Edmund scowled. "It's too hot to play your little games. Just tell me what you want so I can get back to town before dark."

Kane sliced his knife down the wood and sent a chip flying. "I don't know where to start." He aimed his knife, and it went whizzing past Edmund's ear and stuck in the trunk of a tree just behind the banker.

"Dammit!" Edmund said, flinching. "You could have hit me with that knife."

"You were in no danger—I always hit what I aim at."

"Just tell me why you dragged me all the way out here."

"For one thing, your friend Williamson has been arrested and sent up to Fort Worth."

"Are you sure?"

"Yeah. I have ways of finding out things."

"What was he charged with?"

"Several crimes. All you need to worry about is that he's charged with robbing the army payroll." He smiled, showing a flash of white teeth. "Can you imagine anyone doing such a thing?"

"You can't get to him to shut him up at Fort Worth. Will he talk?"

"Can't say. But he's a coward, and his kind will always look after their own skin."

Edmund looked disgusted. "You called me all the way out here just to tell me that?"

"There's more. The word is that the Hunter gal has been with Tremain at Fort Fannin, and they was looking into each other's eyes and heating up the place. It seems the woman from back east has left for home—you know which one I mean, the one Tremain was supposed to marry. Guess you can draw your own conclusions from that."

Edmund felt a rush of rage so thick and hot he wanted to hurt someone. "Has that bastard had her?"

Kane shrugged his shoulders. "I'm not hired to peek into people's bedrooms." He smiled, his black eyes going even darker—he was enjoying himself. "There's more still."

Edmund jammed his hands in his pockets. "You have cheered me up quite enough for one day."

"I saved the best for last."

Irritation tinged the banker's words. "What is it?"

He stood up and stretched his arms over his head. "Your major went shopping for a wedding present. And guess what he bought?"

"I don't care, Kane."

"Oh, but you will when I tell you what it is. He bought the Taylor ranch. I bet you can guess who he bought that for."

Edmund went perfectly still.

He tried to swallow the red hot rage that coiled inside him. He knew he had been distracted lately, but how could he have missed the fact that the lien had been paid off on the Taylor ranch? He almost choked on his fury. Grabbing his chest, he sank to his knees. "I'll kill him for this—I swear I will. I'll kill them both!"

Kane's walk was almost a slither as he went to the tree, retrieved his knife, and slid it into his scabbard. "It don't seem like the major's easy to kill. The way I hear, the Apache have already tried twice. But I bet he's going to have himself a good time when he takes that pretty Hunter gal to bed."

Edmund stood up on shaky legs and braced himself against a tree. After he caught his breath, he walked to his horse and climbed into the saddle. Someone was going to be sorry for this.

Abby would be sorry before he was finished with her!

Chapter Twenty-six

Frances eyed Abby speculatively. "You've been moping around like a cat that's lost its tail. What happened at that fort that made you come home acting like you lost your best friend?"

Abby picked up her hat, slammed it on her head, and walked to the door. "I have lost my only friend."

When she left the house, she let the screen door slam behind her. Frances was right about one thing—she had been moping. It was time for her to help out around the ranch.

Brent had said he wanted the black mustang cut away from the herd because the horse was too aggressive with the others. That would get her away from the house for most of the day.

It was peaceful at the pasture where the new herd of mustangs were being held. There was only an occasional whinny from the horses to break the silence. She had only to show Sassy which horse she wanted to cut out, and the pinto would do the rest. Her little mare was an excellent cutting horse.

It took her the better part of an hour to drive the mustang to a fenced area. She dismounted and watched the black horse run free, then let her mind take her where she didn't want to go. Patricia would be back in Philadelphia by now, and Abby was sure it was all her fault. She had ruined Patricia's life, and she had also ruined Jonah's hope for happiness.

She glanced down at her split skirt. At least knowing Jonah had improved her taste in clothing. She wondered why she hadn't thrown those old trousers away long ago.

She glanced upward and marveled at the beauty of the white fluffy clouds; it looked like someone had taken a basket of cotton and scattered it across the blue sky. She shaded her eyes when she looked westward—someone was approaching. She waited until the rider was closer, thinking it might be Brent. But when she recognized the man, her breath hissed out in irritation, and then she felt a prickle of fear along the base of her spine.

What was Edmund Montgomery doing there?

Abby's first instinct was to get on her horse and ride away as fast as she could. She sure didn't want to be out here alone with him.

She was terrified of him!

Her pinto had wandered several hundred yards away in search of shade—she would never be able to get to the mare before Edmund reached her.

"Abby," he said, dismounting smoothly. "What a surprise to find you out here alone."

"Frances wouldn't have told you where to find me—how did you know I was here?"

He stopped close to her and looked over the land. "I have my ways of knowing. I have had you watched," he admitted.

She took a few paces away from him. "I have to go now."

"Not yet. I just want to talk to you."

"You said quite enough that night at the dance. I don't ever want you anywhere near me, and you can get off our land."

"Now, Abby, you don't mean that." He reached out to her, and she backed farther away.

"Don't touch me!"

He moved fast, grabbing her arms and taking her by surprise. He was strong, and his hands were like vises as he pinned her arms behind her.

"I'll touch you, all right. And I'll take my time about it. There is no one here to help you, and if someone did come, we would hear them from a distance."

he struggled and pushed against him, but his hold only tightened. She felt a scream rise in her throat when he jerked her forward to press his mouth over hers. She tried to twist away, but his hands went up to hold her head in place.

Queasiness churned through her stomach, and she thought she was going to be sick. His lips were wet and hot, and when he raised his head she gagged.

"Has Tremain had you, Abby—has he?"

She pushed against his chest, but he shook her until her head snapped back. She would not have thought him capable of such violence, but there was a glint in his eyes that suggested he might be capable of anything.

"Let me go!"

"So," he said, gripping her arms, "you won't answer—that means the bastard has been at you! If he hadn't, you would have denied it."

His eyes were suddenly like swirling tides of madness. He threw his leg against the back of hers and flipped her to the ground. She landed so hard it knocked the breath out of her. Before she knew what was happening, he was on top of her, ripping her blouse open and exposing her breasts.

She struggled and pushed against him as hard as she could, but he was a hard mass of unmovable and unspeakable evil. "I don't want your hands on me. Let me up!"

The more she fought him, the darker his eyes became. He breathed in her ear with lustful laughter. "My hands are going to be on you, Abby. Everywhere. Now be still!"

She arched her back and pushed against him, then tried to roll sideways, but it was no use.

She tried to dodge when he raised his fist, but it came down hard against her jaw, and her face exploded with pain. Swirls of darkness floated toward her, and she struggled to stay conscious. Her scream was muffled when he hit her again, and she felt the black tide widening to capture her in its depths.

At that moment Abby's pinto whinnied right at her head, bending its sleek neck to touch her face.

"What the hell!" Edmund said, swatting at the horse.

The momentary distraction gave Abby the time she needed to roll out from under him and scramble to her feet.

She hurt everywhere, but she couldn't let that stop her. She dove for her saddle and ripped the rifle free of the holster. Cocking it, she laid her cheek against the stock, aiming at Edmund's heart. "If I pull this trigger, you will be dead before you hit the ground."

He took a step toward her, anger making him rash. "Give me the gun, Abby."

She dipped the gun and fired, barely missing his foot. "You have my word, the next shot will draw blood. Get on your horse and ride away from here right now!"

His blue eyes were almost eaten away by the reptilian black irises, and she shivered in spite of the fact that she had the advantage of the rifle. "I'll do it—you know I will if you don't leave."

"We aren't finished, Abby. This isn't the end."

"If you come near me again, I will shoot you stone-cold dead."

His face was red, and his breathing was shallow as he gathered the reins and mounted his horse. "You'll plead with me many times before I've finished with you. It could have been nice between us, but you had to be like—"

She aimed the rifle at his face, her finger pressing harder against the trigger; she wanted him to come toward her so she could fire. It was with the greatest effort that she resisted that urge. "You are on Hunter land—don't trespass again, or I will shoot you!"

He turned his horse and rode away. She was trembling so hard, she fell to her knees sobbing. She watched him until he was out of sight, making sure he rode toward town and didn't double back.

She couldn't stop shaking, and she was so bruised and hurt, it took her three tries before she could mount the pinto. She took in a shuddering breath and tried to calm her racing heart. Already her face was beginning to swell, and when she touched her head, her fingers came away bloody. She couldn't think clearly, and she was still dizzy. It was a long way to the ranch house, but Brent's place was less than two miles away—she could make it there before she passed out.

She slumped in the saddle and cried so hard her body shook from the intensity of her sobs.

Frances had directed Jonah to Brent's cabin. He dismounted and looked about him at the tranquil scene. He could live like this if Abby were with him.

The door of the cabin swung open, and Brent came out.

"Jonah, this is a surprise! I thought you would still be at the fort."

"I'd like to talk to you, if you don't mind."

He nodded. "Sure. Would you like to come into the house? Crystal is inside. Are you hungry?"

He certainly wouldn't be able to swallow food at the moment. "I would rather talk to you privately, if you don't mind."

"Of course." He was puzzled by Jonah's strange behavior. Something was definitely bothering him.

Jonah paced a few steps and turned back to him. "It's about Abby. I would have gone to your father with this, but I know how close she is to you."

He frowned, feeling protective of his sister. "Yes, we are close."

Jonah decided the best way to handle the situation was head-on. "I want to marry Abby, and I'm asking for your permission before I propose to her."

Brent walked down the path toward the stream and motioned for Jonah to follow him. He stopped at the paddock where he and Crystal kept their horses and braced his foot on the bottom rung.

"The last time I looked, you already had someone you were going to marry, and it wasn't my sister."

"Patricia has returned to Pennsylvania."

"I'm not sure I like the sound of this—why Abby?"

"Because I can't imagine life without her. I want her to be the mother of my children. I want to wake up beside her every morning and grow old with her." He glanced at Brent. "Does this make any sense to you?"

"Hell, no."

Jonah shook his head. "It doesn't make any sense to me either. I only know that I'm not happy when she isn't with me."

"Well, that's just not good enough for me. I'm more interested in my sister's happiness."

They both heard the rider coming, and the horse was galloping at a fast clip.

"It's Abby," Brent said, spotting her pinto as she crossed the stream, riding so fast the water sprayed around her. "She would never ride her horse into a lather—something's wrong!"

When Abby saw Jonah and her brother, she slid off her horse and ran toward them. She must have realized she was still holding the rifle, because she threw it down and kept running.

"My God," Brent said, "something has happened to her!"

Abby didn't have time to wonder why Jonah was there. She only knew she had to be in his arms so she could forget about the things Edmund had done to her.

Brent took a step forward, expecting to catch her in his arms, but she ran past him and threw herself into Jonah's embrace, sobbing uncontrollably.

"Sweetheart," Jonah murmured, holding her against him as if he could absorb the quaking of her small body. "What happened?" He brushed the hair out of her face and saw the bruises and the blood. Anger coiled inside him like a snake. "Who hurt you?"

She felt so safe being held in his arms. She pressed her face against his jacket and tried to control her tears. "He touched me," she said, fresh tears moistening her eyes. "He put his hands on me."

Jonah went down on one knee and held her on the other, rage thrumming through him. He examined the bruise and gently rubbed at the dirt on her face with his handkerchief. That was when he noticed her blouse was ripped—he met Brent's eyes and pulled the blouse together, turning her against his chest. His voice was icy cold. "Who did this to you, sweetheart?"

Brent crouched down beside her. "Who, Abby?"

She looked into the eyes of her brother and hesitated. Edmund was dangerous, and if he threatened to kill someone, he'd do it.

"Brent," she cried, reaching toward him. "It was so awful. He . . . he . . . kissed me. I fought him, I did, Brent."

Brent's eyes were burning with anger. "What did he do?"

Jonah closed his eyes, imagining the worst. His hand moved up and down Abby's back, trying to soothe her. "Tell us, sweetheart."

"He kissed me and tore my blouse."

"Who?" Brent demanded. "Dammit, Abby, who did this?"

"Edmund Montgomery," she said, laying her head back against Jonah's shoulder. "I hated the feel of his mouth on mine!"

"Did he do anything else to you, Abby?" Brent asked the question that was tearing at Jonah.

"He would have, but I managed to get away from him before he could. I ran for my rifle." She buried her face back in Jonah's jacket. "I wanted to pull the trigger—I wanted to see him dead!"

By now Crystal had heard the commotion and joined them. She took Abby by the hand and pulled her up, assessing her injuries. "Isn't it just like a man to keep a woman talking when she needs doctoring."

She smiled gently at Abby. "Come with me, honey. I'll clean your scrapes."

"I'll kill him for this," Brent said, striding toward the cabin to get his rifle.

"No, you won't," Jonah said, standing slowly. "It's my place to take care of him. Abby is mine."

Brent watched his wife lead Abby into their cabin and turned back to Jonah. "I guess she is. She decided that today, didn't she?"

Jonah was trying to deal with his anger. "I want to kill him for what he did to her—but it would be far better if we work on this through the law. I can't tell you any more than that."

"He isn't going to get away that easily."

"No," Jonah said, stalking toward his horse. "He isn't. I'm going to ride into town and find the bastard."

Abby was still shaking when Crystal seated her in a chair. "Where did he hurt you?" she asked, reaching for a clean cloth and water.

"He threw me down on the ground, hit me with his fist, and tore my blouse."

Crystal looked at her sister-in-law carefully. "Is that all?"

Abby gulped back a hiccup. "Yes, thank God. He was strong, Crystal. I couldn't have fought him off if he hadn't been distracted."

"It's all right," her sister-in-law told her. "He will get what's been coming to him for a long time."

Chapter Twenty-seven

Jonah went directly to the banker's house, but the housekeeper informed him that Edmund wasn't at home. The woman told him she hadn't seen her employer since early that morning.

It was getting late, and the bank was closed, but he peered in the window, seeing nothing but the dark interior. He entered the general store to ask if anyone there had seen the banker, but the owner was just closing, and he hadn't seen Edmund all day.

The saloon was the only other place left to look. He shoved the doors open and went inside. It was noisy in the smoked-filled saloon as Jonah scanned each face to see if one of them was Edmund.

He walked up to the bartender. "Have you seen Edmund Montgomery today or tonight?"

O'Malley was drying a shot glass as he watched the major's face. "It's possible. Why?"

Jonah's voice was forceful. "Just tell me."

O'Malley didn't like the banker; he had seen him plenty of times sneaking off to visit a woman who lived just outside of town, even while his wife was dying. The town praised him as a virtuous man, but the bartender knew better. "Is it going to bode well or ill for Montgomery if you find him?"

"Very ill."

The bartender smiled. "Then you will find him at a house just outside town." He lowered his voice and leaned across the bar as he gave Jonah directions.

Crystal had taken Abby home in the buggy. She helped her into a nightgown and pulled the covers back for her to get into bed. She saw the angry red scrapes on Abby's back, and the sight made her furious.

"Edmund Montgomery is going to be sorry he ever laid a hand on a Hunter," she assured Abby.

"Where is Jonah? I want to see him."

"He left. I believe he intends to find Mr. Montgomery."

Abby moved to her knees as fear tore at her mind. "Did Brent go with him? He can't have gone alone!"

"Brent went to get Quince, and they will both be going into town. Even if Mr. Montgomery is hiding, he can't escape all three of them."

Abby slid out of bed. "I have to go to Jonah. Someone has to help him. He doesn't know how evil that man is!"

"Get back in bed, Abby. Brent and Quince will help him. You have to rest for now."

Abby was so exhausted, she nodded while Crystal pulled the sheet up and tucked it about her chin.

"I don't think you have anything to worry about. I believe your major can take care of the banker."

Abby turned her face into her pillow. "I want to know the moment Jonah comes back. I don't care what time it is, Crystal."

Crystal blew out the lamp and sat down in the chair beside Abby's bed. "Are you sure he'll come here?"

"I'm sure. Promise me."

"I promise. I'll just sit here beside you until you fall asleep."

"It can't be comfortable for you. You must think of the baby."

"Me and this baby are just fine. It's you we are worried about for now. You need to sleep."

Abby closed her eyes. There didn't seem to be a place on her body that didn't ache. She wanted Jonah, and then she could sleep.

Jonah didn't bother knocking on the door, but shoved it open with such force it vibrated against the wall. He walked through the three rooms until he came to the bedroom, where a woman was huddled in the bed, looking at him with frightened eyes.

"Where is Edmund Montgomery? And don't tell me he isn't here, because I saw his horse out front."

The woman's dark eyes darted to the door just behind Jonah as if she were trying to signal him—he saw the fear reflected there and dodged just as Edmund swung a chair at his head.

Jonah sidestepped the older man and faced him with fists tight. "You might want to ask the lady to leave. She might not like what I'm going to do to you."

"Arrogant pig!"

"I'm not a woman, Montgomery. How brave are you when you are facing someone stronger than you?"

Jonah grabbed Edmund by the shirtfront and slammed him against the wall. He didn't give him time to recover before he slammed his fist into his stomach, and the man doubled over. As Edmund slumped to the floor, his mouth hanging open, Jonah lifted him up and drove his fist into his face with all his strength.

He hit him again and again, anger and rage driving him.

Someone caught his arm and held it. Jonah was ready to hit whomever it was when Quince spoke. "He's had enough for now. I sure wish you'd saved a piece of him for me, though."

Brent bent down to examine the banker. "He's out cold. It'll be a long time before he can show that battered face in Diablo. Looks like you broke his nose."

Jonah reached into his pocket and tossed money to the woman still huddled in bed. "That's just in case he hasn't paid you, ma'am. And you did warn me that he was behind that door."

The three men walked out of the house, mounted their horses, and rode silently into the night.

They didn't see Kane slither behind a tree with a smile curving his thin lips. Seeing Edmund get beaten by the major was just too good to pass up.

When Jonah dismounted, he hurried toward the house.

"We need to talk," Brent told him.

"Later."

Brent caught Jonah's arm. "Now."

Jonah shook his hand off. "I am going into that house, and I'm going to see Abby. When I am satisfied she is all right, then we'll talk."

Quince smiled as he leaned against the porch post watching Jonah push past his brother. "You heard the man, Brent—he said later."

Abby saw Jonah's silhouette in the doorway, and she slid out of bed and threw herself into his arms. "I had to see you before I could go to sleep."

He nodded at Crystal, and she vacated the chair. "I'll take care of her now, ma'am." He sat down with Abby on his lap and pulled the cover off the bed to wrap it around her.

"I'm here now." He pushed her hair aside and touched her cheek tenderly with his lips. "I won't leave you tonight. Go to sleep, sweetheart."

Brent and Quince had come into the hall and were standing at the doorway. "He can't stay in there with her," Brent told his brother.

Crystal took her husband's hand. "Honestly, Brent, do you think she's going to come to any harm from him?"

"No," he conceded as he heard Jonah talking in

whispers to his sister. "But we'll be staying the night here just the same."

Quince squared his hat on his head. "Well, I'm going home. I'll be back in the morning."

Abby curled up against Jonah and burrowed her face against his throat. The strength of his arms sheltered her while the heat of his body brought her comfort and held her fear at bay. He helped her forget Edmund Montgomery, and the smothering evil that had touched her. "Don't leave me, Jonah. Stay with me."

"I'm not going anywhere." His lips touched her brow. "Close your eyes and sleep. I'll be here."

When Brent came back to check on his sister an hour later, he found both her and Jonah asleep in the chair. The major's booted feet were propped on the bed, and he held Abby snugly against his body as if he would never let her go.

Brent tiptoed out of the room.

If he had to let Abby go, he couldn't be giving her to a better man.

Jonah awoke and tried to move his cramped body, but Abby moaned in protest. He touched his lips against her cheek, and her arms slid around his neck.

His lips slid to her ear and then to her neck. "Marry me, Abby," he said softly, not really sure she was awake. "You are already mine. You have been since our first meeting. Say you will be my wife."

"Yes," she murmured, her head falling against his chest, her tangled hair spilling over his arm. He dipped his head, touching his lips ever so softly to hers. She groaned and snuggled closer to him and fell asleep once more.

Jonah sat there in wonder. Had she just agreed to marry him?

He touched his lips to each bruise, wishing he could hit Montgomery again.

He doubted the cowardly banker would come anywhere near Abby now, but he wanted to make sure—he wanted her where he could protect her.

The sun had barely touched the horizon when Jonah stood and placed Abby on the bed. She curled against her pillow and sighed in her sleep. He stretched his cramped muscles and made his way to the kitchen.

Frances had her hands in dough, making the morning biscuits, and she glanced up at him with a twist to her mouth. "Well, I hear there was quite a to-do last night." She nodded toward the coffeepot, indicating he could pour his own coffee. "I suppose you are going to marry Abby, since you spent the night in her room."

He poured a cup of the steaming brew and sat down at the table. "Yes, I am going to marry her."

She rolled out the dough and slapped it with the palm of her hand. "I suppose you asked her?"

His lips curved into a smile. "Yes." He frowned. "And I think she said yes, but I'm not sure she was fully awake at the time."

"I wondered when you'd realize you wanted her."

He took a sip of coffee. "I'm not sure when the notion struck me. It could very well have been the day she knocked me off my horse."

Frances paused as she pinched off bits of dough. "She did what?"

Jonah grinned. "If she didn't tell you about it, I'll let it remain a mystery."

Frances dipped the biscuits in hot bacon grease, arranged them in a pan, and shoved them in the oven. She then stood back and gave him her full attention. She had never seen him with his hair mussed, and she kind of liked the idea that he could be just like any other man.

"You slept in the chair all night."

"Yes, I did."

She glanced at his hands and saw the knuckles were red and raw. "I heard you got in a fight. I'll doctor your hands."

Jonah smiled. Frances never asked; she ordered. "Yes, ma'am."

She filled a washbasin with hot water she had boiling on the stove, cooled it down a bit, and nodded for him to dunk his hands. After she was satisfied the blood was washed away, she dried them and applied ointment.

"They are going to be sore for a few days." She looked down at him. "But I'd wager they aren't half as painful as Edmund Montgomery's wounds are."

"Nothing gets past you, does it?"

"Hardly ever."

Frances sighed inwardly, knowing Abby was going to be taken care of. She had known almost from the beginning that these two were right for each other— it had just taken them a little longer to find out.

Chapter Twenty-eight

The ranch was stirring to life when Jonah returned to the house after talking to Navidad. He'd already had coffee; now he was ready for breakfast. Quince rode up just as Jonah reached the porch, and the two men went in together.

"I asked your sister to marry me."

"I figured you would after last night."

Frances had heard them coming and placed two full plates of eggs and bacon on the table in front of them. Jonah was eyeing the golden-brown biscuits the housekeeper had just removed from the oven.

Quince buttered a hot biscuit. "I've already eaten, but I never can resist your cooking, Frances." He took a bite and swallowed before he asked Jonah, "Is it true you bought the Taylor ranch?"

"I knew when I saw that ranch that it was where I wanted to live. I think I bought it with Abby in mind, and perhaps to thwart Montgomery."

"It's a mighty fine spread. One of the best. I heard you were tearing most of the old house down and building a new one."

"No. I'm just adding on. The old structure is sound."

"What about your army career?"

"I still have two years to serve, and then I plan to retire. Abby and I will spend as much time at the ranch as we can until then, assuming they don't assign me to another fort miles from here or in another state."

Quince didn't like the notion of Abby being too far away from the family. "Is that a possibility?"

"I shouldn't think so. There's a lot of work to do at Fort Fannin."

Frances was humming as she went about her work, and Quince turned his attention back to Jonah. "I wanted to talk to you about my sister last night, but it didn't seem like a good time. How is she?"

"She slept fretfully. She was badly shaken by what happened."

"I'd like to kill that son of a—"

"Quince!" Frances warned him. "There'll be no such talk in my kitchen."

He nodded and smiled at Jonah. "You see how she orders us all around. And we all do exactly what she says because she puts the fear of God in us."

"Humph," Frances said, leaving the room with a laundry basket on her hip. "As if anyone listens to me."

Quince took a drink of coffee and set the mug back on the table. "I guess this is the part where I ask you what your intentions are concerning my sister?"

Jonah looked straight into his friend's eyes. "I'm going to keep her safe and see that she's never unhappy."

"After last night I don't think there's any doubt of my sister's feelings for you, and it seems to me you care for her. Do you?"

"I want her so much I hurt inside when I'm not with her. I want to spend my life with her. If you hadn't stopped me last night, I would have killed Montgomery for what he did to her. Does that qualify as love?"

Quince grinned and clapped Jonah on the back. "You'll probably bring an air of respectability to our family. When's the wedding?"

"I hope as soon as possible. I wanted to ask Abby if she would consider having the wedding at our ranch. I could have Chaplin Moody from the fort perform the ceremony."

Quince frowned, watching him closely. "Is there any need to rush into this?"

"No reason other than that I miss her every day she isn't with me. But I will leave it up to Abby to decide the date."

"My father won't be back from New Orleans for several weeks."

"Is it necessary to wait for him?"

"Not to me. Probably not to Abby, but you'll have to ask her." Quince stuck out his hand, and Jonah shook it. "You are never going to know a dull day with my sister as your wife."

"Don't I know it!"

"Welcome to the family."

Abby had slept late. She sat up slowly, her body aching with each movement she made.

In the vague recesses of her mind, she seemed to remember sleeping in Jonah's arms and his asking her to marry him.

Had she only dreamed it?

She filled the basin with water and bathed, scrubbing vigorously everywhere Edmund had touched her.

She glanced in her mirror and was horrified by the blue-and-purple bruise on her chin and the swelling of her left cheek. She touched her face and winced. Her hair was tangled, and she brushed it until it crackled. She dressed in one of her split skirts and pulled on her boots.

On her way to the kitchen she discovered the house was empty. The coffeepot was still warming on the back of the stove, so she poured a cup and sat down at the table, still feeling a bit shaky.

She buried her face in her hands, wishing she could forget about what Edmund had done to her. When she heard Jonah's voice, she stood up, not wanting him to see her with bruises on her face.

But he was there, standing in the doorway, his blue eyes soft, his hand held out to her.

Without hesitation she went to him and felt his arms close around her. He touched his lips to her forehead. "Are you sore this morning?"

She nodded, too choked up to speak.

He lifted her chin. "Do you remember agreeing to marry me last night?"

"I thought I might have only dreamed it."

"It wasn't a dream. Do you still want me for your husband?"

"Are you sure?"

Laughter rumbled deep inside him. "I have never been more sure of anything in my life." He gently touched her bruised cheek. "Will you be my wife?"

"Yes." Her arms went around his waist and joy sang in her heart. "Yes, I will."

He kissed her gently, then put her away, not trusting himself to touch her; just being near her was enough to make his body tighten. "Abby, I have to leave you for now. But I have already spoken to Quince, and he's agreed to bring you to the ranch. I want you to see it, since it will be our home when we are not at Fort Fannin."

She remembered refusing to enter the house when she thought Patricia would be living there with Jonah. "I want to see it very much."

He pulled her back to him and smiled against her cheek. "If you were my wife right now, I could take you into that bedroom—"

"We're not married yet, and I want to wait," she said seriously. "When we made love before, I was afraid you might not come back alive."

He touched her hair. "Now we have the rest of our lives."

Her laughter was the most beautiful sound he had ever heard, and it seemed to set his heart free of the shackles that had bound him for so long.

He held her away from him. "Abby, there are so many things I want to show you on the ranch. I had the whole inside of the house gutted and two more rooms added on. I want you to choose furniture and make it into the kind of home you would like to live in."

She snuggled her head against his chest, her heart so full she could hardly speak. She loved him so much, and it seemed he loved her, too, although neither of them had said the words.

He kissed her softly, and when he raised his head his eyes were gentle with a calmness she had never seen in them before.

He didn't have to say he loved her—she saw it in his eyes, she heard it in the tenderness of his voice, felt it in the touch of his hand.

Jonah walked toward Abby with long strides, and her heart took wing. Then she blinked her eyes, realizing she had never seen him dressed other than in his uniform. He wore trousers and western boots, and she could tell by the scuffed toes that the boots weren't new. His green shirt was open at the throat, and she could see a muscle working there. Smiling, he lifted her off her horse, planting only a quick kiss on her mouth, since Brent and Quince were watching.

Big brothers, when they were as tall and fierce as the Hunter brothers, could be a bit intimidating.

Brent was already assessing the white-faced cattle in the stock pen, while Quince was looking at all the building going on around them.

"Come, I want to show you the house first," he said, anxious for her to like what he had done so far and wanting her approval. He was also hoping he could get her alone.

Brent started to follow them, but Quince put his hand on his brother's shoulder. "Guess we'll be looking the stock over."

Brent caught his brother's look and his meaning. "Yeah—that's what we'll be doing, all right—looking at cattle."

Quince watched Abby's hand slide into Jonah's and smiled. "I already told him he's going to have his hands full with her as his wife."

Brent frowned. "We won't get to see her much after she's married."

"But we'll know she's happy, loved, and taken care of."

"Yeah, I guess so," Brent mumbled. He had looked after Abby for so many years, he sometimes forgot she would one day grow up and leave him.

As soon as they were inside the house, Jonah pulled Abby into his arms. "Going three whole weeks without seeing you has been hell."

She raised her face to him and smiled. "Hadn't you better kiss me then?"

He gripped her about the waist, drawing her tightly against him, his gaze moving over her face, satisfied the bruises had mostly faded. He dipped his head, his mouth shaping itself to hers while he smoothly unbuttoned her blouse. He slid his hand over her breast, lifting, caressing, touching, knowing it was his right, or it soon would be.

"Ohhh," she breathed as her knees went weak under his masterful manipulation.

"In three days," he whispered against her mouth, "you will be mine."

She pressed herself against him, feeling the proof of his need for her. "Yes. If you are going to run, it had better be now."

"I am not going anywhere until I can take you with me." He straightened her blouse and with a grin buttoned it. "I think I should show you the house."

She spread her hand across his chest, noticing that his heart was pounding in rhythm with her own. "I think that might be a good idea."

"The men are working in the kitchen, so you can see that later."

She stepped across polished wooden floors and looked at a dining room that was twice as large as the one at the Half-Moon.

"We will put a crystal chandelier in here," he told her. "But you can decide on what you want. I know nothing about furnishings. The only furniture I have here is the bed." He smiled wickedly. "A must."

She blushed and lowered her head, and he laughed. "Come; I'll show you the bed."

When he led her into the bedroom, she saw that it was an enormous room. "I had the back wall knocked out so it could be enlarged. I like the thought of a sitting room in the bedroom so I can watch you sleep while I work."

The bed was of dark wood and huge.

Her mouth opened in surprise. "You must have a great deal of money."

"Yes, a great deal. Does it matter to you?"

She locked her arms around his neck. "I would live with you in a cave if you had nothing at all."

He pulled her down on the bed and molded her against his body. His mouth was warm and seeking, his touch gentle because he remembered her bruises. "Abby, the truth is, for the next two years we won't be spending that much time here. Will you mind living with me at Fort Fannin?"

She ran her fingers over the frown lines on his brow. "Wherever you are is my home. I don't care where we live, as long as we are together."

He smiled. "We will have two weeks here before I have to report for duty."

Quince's voice was loud at the front door, as if warning them of his and Brent's presence. Jonah got up, grinning, and helped Abby to her feet. "Our first guests. Come with me. I have a surprise for you—I hope you will like it."

They met her two brothers in the entry, and Jonah led them to the parlor. "This was the first room the workers finished. I had two walls knocked out in here." He waited for Abby to notice the surprise.

She saw the four framed drawings that hung on the far wall. On closer inspection she realized they were her own sketches of Moon Racer. "These are

not good enough to hang so everyone can see them,"
she protested.

"Yes, they are," Brent said, looking over her shoulder.

Quince nodded in agreement.

"There is a reason I hung the drawings, Abby."

She turned to him. "Why?"

"I had the brand of a rearing horse struck last
week. The name of the ranch is Moon Racer."

He laughed at the funny expression on her brothers' faces and the astonishment on Abby's. "Do you
like it?"

"Yes. But how did you come to name it after my
horse?"

"I thought about a name, and nothing came to me.
Obviously I couldn't go on calling the place the Taylor ranch. Then I thought of Moon Racer, the only
other love of your life, and it just seemed right."

Chapter Twenty-nine

Abby came out of the general store, her arms full of purchases. Tomorrow was her wedding day, and her heart was not large enough to hold her happiness. She hadn't seen Jonah since the day he had shown her around the ranch. She smiled to herself—the Moon Racer Ranch.

Her skin tingled when she thought of spending the rest of her life with Jonah. She felt safe knowing she would be under his protection. She still marveled that such a magnificent man wanted her for his wife. But he did.

She frowned. Her father was still in New Orleans and wouldn't be attending the wedding. Brent had sent Jack a telegram informing him about the wedding, and he had wired back that he wished Abby happiness. The general would not be attending either, but he promised to come for a visit in the spring.

Her brothers had been angry with their father because he was buying more horses, and he was probably incurring more debt for them to pay off.

But that was her father—he would never change.

She refused to allow anything to keep her from feeling happy today. She passed the bank without fear. The word had spread that Edmund was away on an extended vacation. Only her family knew that he didn't want to show his face in Diablo until it had healed.

Quince had been almost sure Jonah had broken Edmund's nose. She could not help smiling at that thought—a broken nose would surely mar the good looks Edmund was so proud of.

She stepped into the street on her way to the livery stable, where Navidad was waiting for her with the buckboard.

"Miss Hunter, could you wait a moment? I have been watching for you because I need to ask you about something."

Abby nodded as she waited for Hilda, Edmund's housekeeper, to tell her what was on her mind. She certainly did not want to hear anything about the woman's employer.

The woman was out of breath from running. "I have been watching for you to come to town for days."

"What is it, Hilda?"

"It's about Mrs. Montgomery. Some time back I was cleaning out her drawers, like Mr. Montgomery told me to, and I came across a letter. I stewed and stewed, not knowing what to do about it."

"Who is the letter intended for?"

"Mrs. Montgomery's daughter, Juliana."

"Why didn't you just send it on to her?"

"At first I thought about giving this to Mr. Montgomery, but . . . well, I don't like the way he treated . . ." She shook her head. "He's out of town. I don't know where. He just up and went away in the middle of the night without telling me he was going. He left a note saying he didn't know how long he'd be gone."

Abby gained a great deal of satisfaction from that bit of information. He would not want to answer awkward questions about his battered appearance.

"The way I see it," Hilda continued, "I don't think Mrs. Montgomery wanted him to know about the letter, or she wouldn't have hidden it among her unmentionables."

Abby wondered if Iona had discovered Edmund's true evil before she died. Her heart hurt for the woman who had been like a mother to her. "You are probably right, Hilda."

"Could I give you the letter, and let you decide what's to be done about it?"

Abby nodded. "Yes. I'll see that it gets in the mail today."

The housekeeper thrust the letter into Abby's hand, looked about her as if she were afraid Edmund would see her, and then hurried away.

Abby watched the woman dash across the street

before she glanced at the letter. Although the hand-writing was shaky and smeared, Abby recognized it as Iona's. She didn't like the thought of doing any-thing for Juliana because of the way the woman had neglected her mother when she needed her most.

Still, Iona had intended the letter for her daughter, so she would honor her wish. With determined steps, Abby made her way to the post office.

She was doing this for Iona, not Juliana.

The house was dark except for the soft lamplight in the parlor, where Abby sat holding the same pearl hair clasps her mother wore in the portrait. Abby, wanting to wear something that had belonged to her mother, had chosen to wear them at her wedding.

She heard a soft knock on the door and went to answer it. Navidad stood on the porch, his hat in his hand.

"Señorita Abby, Brent told me to take Moon Racer to your new house."

"I hadn't thought of that. Thank you, Christmas."

"Señorita, I have looked after that horse. He needs knowledgeable hands to see to his care."

"I know."

He looked down and then back up at her. "I asked Señor Major Jonah if I could . . . if there would be a place for me on his ranch. He said there would be. He also told me to give you this letter from him."

She smiled at him affectionately and kissed his cheek, bringing a shine to his dark eyes. "I'm glad

you are going with me. You were one of the people
I would have missed the most."

He nodded and backed away. "Have a happy,
good night's sleep, little señorita."

When Navidad left, Abby went back into the parlor and unfolded the letter, held it under the lamp,
and began to read.

My dearest Abby,
I sit here in the ranch house alone, but I am not
lonely because I know you will be with me to-
morrow night, and for the rest of our lives. Your
gowns have been hung in the wardrobe beside
my uniforms, your shoes are arranged beside
mine, and I admit I go to the bedroom to look
at them several times a day. Good night, my
dearest love. Sleep well, knowing I love you.

She held the letter to her breast and bit her lip to
keep from crying. "He loves me," she said softly. "He
loves me!"

Abby went to the portrait of her mother, wishing
she could have her wisdom tonight. She was going
into a life with the man she loved, and she would
have liked to share this moment with her mother.

She reached upward to the portrait, placing her
hand on her mother's hand. "I'm happy, Mama. I
wish you could know Jonah. I love him so much—
and he loves me."

The day of the wedding dawned bright and clear,
without a cloud anywhere in sight.

The guests filled the parlor and watched the bride join the groom. She was dressed in a simple white gown, her hair pulled away from her face with her mother's pearl clasps.

Jonah's hand was warm as the army chaplain stood gravely before them, reciting the words that would bind them together.

Jonah's eyes were on Abby's face, and he heard her voice quaver as she promised to "love, honor and obey."

As instructed, he slipped the ring on her finger. Then he startled her and the wedding guests as he pulled her to him and kissed her reverently.

The chaplain laughed softly. "Sir, I haven't finished yet." To those gathered he said, "Course, he outranks me, so I can't insist too much."

Jonah raised his head. "Go ahead, I just wanted to kiss her while she was still single. That way I can have another kiss later."

Everyone laughed. It was an unceremonious event despite the high rank of the groom. Joy and kinship filled the room, and everyone felt it.

The chaplain spoke loudly, and the laugh lines at his eyes flared. "I *now* pronounce you man and wife! You may *now* kiss the bride."

Jonah drew Abby into his arms. "Mrs. Tremain, may I be the first man to kiss you since you changed your name?"

Her arms went around him, and their lips molded together. After a moment Abby would have pulled away, aware of the others looking on, but Jonah held her to him.

"I'm next in line," Brent said, pulling his sister away from Jonah and putting his arms around her. "Be happy, Abby—that's what I want for you."

She nestled against him, feeling almost sad that she would no longer be under his care. "I am." She met his gaze. "So very happy."

Next she went to Quince, and he hugged her tightly. "I couldn't have let you go to a better man, darlin'."

The family circle closed in on the newlyweds. There were officers and their wives from Jonah's command mingling with the cowhands from the Half-Moon and Moon Racer ranches. The Fort Fannin military band played softly for the reception, and food and wine were plentiful.

Jonah was talking to Quince, and Abby looked about her, thinking what a different turn her life had taken. The people she loved most were in this room, except for her father and Matt. But Jack Hunter would always do what Jack Hunter wanted to do. And Matt . . . she wished with all her heart that he could be with her on this day of all days. An ache touched her heart, and she wondered if she would ever see him again.

"I am going to take my wife to bed," Jonah told Quince. "I'm leaving you here as host. I assume you can move all these people out of my house."

Quince grinned. "Yeah, I can do that. I don't have to tell you to be good to my sister. I know the kind of man you are, so I'm not worried about her. But Abby is different from most women; sometimes you have to—"

"Treat her like a blooded mare and gentle her down?"

"Yeah. Something like that," Quince answered, looking relieved that Jonah understood Abby so well.

Abby was talking to Glory and a very pregnant Crystal. "You are going into a new life, Abby," Crystal told her. "I want you to be as happy with Jonah as I am with Brent."

She kissed Crystal's cheek. "I'm sure I will be."

Glory hugged her. "If ever I saw a man in love, it's your major. Take care of him. I know he is going to take care of you."

"Sisters-in-law," Jonah said, sliding his arms around both of them, "if you will excuse my wife and me, we are leaving this party. As family members, I hope you will help Quince get everyone out of here."

His eyes were dancing with humor until he looked at Abby, and then they gleamed with something akin to worship.

Abby did not object as Jonah waved good-night to everyone and led her out of the room, down the long hallway, and into their bedroom.

She turned to him as soon as the door closed behind them. "Jonah."

"You are mine now." His gaze went over her slowly, sensuously. She was so beautiful he could only stare at her. He had watched her emerge like a butterfly from a cocoon. She was delicate, her skin soft like satin, and she was his.

"I love you," she whispered, hardly able to breathe because of the way he was looking at her.

"I have been waiting a long time to hear you say that." He unbuckled the ceremonial sword at his waist, tossed it on a chair, untied the red sash at his waist, and let it drop to the floor, all the while watching her.

She stepped forward and unbuttoned the brass buttons on his jacket, and his arms eased around her.

"I want you," he told her. "All the while I was being polite to our guests tonight, all I wanted was to have you naked in my arms."

She shivered as his breath stirred the curls at her neck. "That's what I wanted too."

"Did you now?" He smiled enigmatically, unfastening and unhooking her garments until they had all been stripped away. "If I recall, you once told me you would never let a man order your life."

She stared into his eyes, suddenly serious. "I have just promised that I will allow you to order my life."

"Yes. You did." He grinned. "But the Abby I know has a mind of her own. I think that is what I first fell in love with."

She gave him a look of pretend shock. "You fell in love with my mind?"

"Well," he said, arching his brow, "there were other considerations, too."

His hand went to her neck, and he brought her head forward, his lips touching hers, probing for entrance into her mouth, which she granted, the feel reminding her of another invasion to a different part of her body. She went weak against him, and he lifted her in his arms.

"Since the first time I had you, I knew I would never be whole until I had you again."

His eyes were deep, deep blue, the bluest she had ever seen them.

"Make me whole, Abby."

The breath was trapped in her throat as he placed her on the bed and stood over her while he removed his clothing, his heated gaze touching on every part of her nakedness.

He was magnificent! He was lean and tall, his body beautiful. She reached forward, her hand sliding across the black hair on his chest. When she saw the swell of him, she pulled him down to her. His body pressed her into the mattress.

This was her husband, to love, to walk beside, to hold and to take into her body. Her heart was too full and beating too fast for her to speak when he touched his lips to her breasts.

"Ohhh," she moaned. "Mmmm." He was doing such wonderful things—his mouth moved over her, creating sensations that surprised her.

She arched her body flirtatiously, invitingly, and it was enough to draw him to her to give her what she ached for.

He glided slowly inside her, staring into her eyes, watching her lashes drift downward. She closed around him, soft and warm, and his body caught and held her trembling.

Soft words were spoken as the night shadows crept into the room. Heated passions were satisfied, only to rise again and provide the same joy and fulfillment.

Abby quaked in his arms, and he held her, thrusting deep until tremors shook him.

Afterward, when they were lying in each other's arms, her hand drifted over his chest.

"It is so good between us, Abby."

"Yes."

She traced his nose and then his lips and suddenly pulled back and giggled. "I wonder if our guests have gone?"

"I trust Quince got them out the door."

He gently stroked her breasts. She offered him her mouth, and he took it—she offered him her body, and he took it. She rolled on top of him, and his hands slid down her back.

He suddenly frowned. "There is one thing I want you to obey me in, Abby."

"What is that?"

"Promise me you will never attempt to break a wild horse again."

She traced the frown lines on his forehead with a delicate finger. Then she smiled and saluted. "Yes, sir, Major, sir. I promise."

He seemed to relax. Abby was like a whirlwind or a tornado, and he never knew what she would do next. But he didn't want to change her; it was her difference from other women that had won his heart.

"Am I in the cavalry now that I'm the commander's wife?" she asked innocently.

He slid into her warmth and smiled tantalizingly as he watched her eyes drift shut. "No, sweet Abby—the cavalry is in you."

Later they lay intertwined with an occasional kiss or a soft stroke of a hand, a murmured endearment.

"Frances once told me," she said, "that I would one day meet the man I would want to change for, and she was right."

He tucked her into his arms and rested his chin on the top of her head. "What else did Frances say in her wisdom?"

"She compared men to horses. It went something like, if I fed and watered a man and gave him a rubdown, he would give me his affection."

"Mmm." His fingers slid downward across her stomach and into her warmth, bringing a gasp from her. "I like Frances's reasoning—she is a wise woman."

Sometime just before dawn the lovers had fallen asleep. They had made love and found out little things about each other. They had talked about the future and put the past to rest.

The sun had been up for some hours when there was a loud banging on the bedroom door.

Jonah stirred, and Abby sat up. Sleepily, she exchanged a puzzled glance with him.

Frances's voice boomed through the door. "It's after the noon hour. If you want to eat, food's on the table."

Abby got out of bed and slipped into her robe. "I didn't know she was going to be here."

"Neither did I," he said, pulling the sheet over his naked body and following her to the door.

Abby opened the door and came face-to-face with the housekeeper. "Frances, what are you doing here?"

"I moved into the room next to the kitchen, 'cause I decided you're gonna need me. And if the two of you have a daughter—and lord help us all if she's anything like you—you'll be needing me to use a firm hand with her."

Abby could hear Jonah's laughter behind her. "Frances," he said smoothly, "you are right about that."

Abby took the housekeeper's hand in hers. "I would have been lost without you. I'm glad you are going to live with us."

Jonah poked his head around the door. "We need someone to run things around here."

"Humph." Frances stalked off, but Abby saw the smile on her face.

She closed the door and leaned against it. "Do you mind her moving in?"

"Not if it makes you happy. Besides, I like Frances." He pulled Abby to him and pushed the robe off her shoulders. "But she must learn to keep the food warm when I want you in my bed."

She laughed and leaped into his arms. "If you are able to handle Frances, you are better than I am."

"Not me," he said. "She scares the hell out of me." He was tantalized by the rosy nipple that drew his attention. "I should have known the day you took that dog home with you that you attracted strays. It seems everyone wants to be where you are. Sergeant MacDougall indicated he would like to join us here

321

when his stint is over." He covered her breast with his hand and smiled. "Can you imagine what Mac-Dougall and Frances will do to our lives?"

"I'm more interested in what you are going to do to me right now."

"Sweet Abby, am I one of your strays, too?"

"No." Her green gaze mesmerized him. "You are my love."

He eased down onto the bed with her in his lap and kissed her. They both sank backward into the softness of the mattress.

Epilogue

Fort Fannin

The sun was just going down when Jonah made his way across the compound to his quarters. His footsteps were hurried because he could not wait to get home to Abby. His life was so full and happy he sometimes wondered how he had survived before he met her.

Abby had the kind of personality that drew people to her, and the ladies at the fort had readily taken her into their group, not altogether because she was the commander's wife, but because they liked to be with her. The children seemed to flock to her. They knew that if they found themselves at her door, they were likely to get a sweet treat and a hug. She often played games with them, and they jealously vied for a place at her side. He wanted the laughter of children in their home. He could not wait to become a father.

He was welcomed home by the soft glow of lamplight and delicious smells coming from the kitchen.

When Jonah appeared at the kitchen door, Abby was just taking a loaf of bread out of the oven. She wore a green gingham gown with her hair drawn back in a matching ribbon. She came readily into his arms, nestling her cheek against his shoulder.

Abby still could not believe that this wonderful man loved her. He had changed her life in so many ways. With him she felt alive and happy; there were no longer any dark clouds hanging over her—he had swept them all away.

She pulled back and looked at him. That afternoon the fort had been visited by dignitaries from Fort Worth, and Jonah was still dressed in his formal regalia, and looked so handsome.

His arms tightened about her and he rested his chin against her forehead. "Something smells good." He laughed softly, cupping her face in his hands. "A wife who is beautiful, delightful, and can cook as well—I'm a most fortunate husband."

"Frances was determined that if I ever did get married—which she doubted—I would know how to cook. It's lucky she taught me, since she insisted on remaining at Moon Racer Ranch. Someone has to feed you."

He caressed her cheek with his thumb. "Can the meal wait?"

She sensed the urgency in him. Moving out of his arms, she set the bubbling pot on the back of the stove, then took the hand he offered.

She laughed when he lifted her into his arms and carried her toward their bedroom. Once inside, he slid her down the length of his body, his mouth covering hers in a kiss that made her insides melt.

She suddenly pulled away from him, her eyes gleaming, her dark hair swirling about her face. Her tongue darted out to wet her lips, and she became the perfect seductress. He watched, fascinated, as she unbuckled his gun belt and placed it carefully on a chair. He was spellbound when she removed his saber, then stood back and tapped the point against his brass buttons.

"Take it off," she said.

He stared into the eyes of a temptress, arched his brow, and unbuttoned his jacket to let it slide to the floor.

"The shirt as well."

His shirt soon lay at his feet.

She tapped the saber against his boots. "Remove them."

He did as she said, a slight smile curving his lips.

Next she pointed the saber at his trousers. "Take them off."

He readily obeyed and soon stood before her in all his masculine glory.

She laid the saber across her bent arm, offering it in surrender.

He ignored her gesture. Grabbing her to him, he allowed the saber to clatter to the floor. He lifted her in his arms, need tearing at him. "Abby, Abby, do you know what you do to me?"

"I think so—if it's anything like what you do to me." Her fingers laced through his thick black hair. "I know I love you so much it hurts."

His gaze softened. "I can hardly get through a day without wanting to be with you. I never knew love could be like this."

He slowly removed her garments, kissing her as he went and setting her heart on fire.

As Jonah gathered her close, the cooling meal was all but forgotten. They made love, slowly and lingeringly, and then fast and hungrily.

Abby threw her head back and bit her lip as he filled her with his velvet hardness.

His blue gaze captured and held hers while he murmured words of love—the emotion he had once denied existed.

As she lay with her head against his shoulder and his fingertips slowly caressing her skin, she trembled with a powerful need.

Later, she would tell him that she was going to have his baby.

Diablo

Edmund Montgomery stood just inside the door of Sam Larkin's office, impatiently watching the lawyer finish his business with Spindle, the owner of the general store.

"It's always good to get these unpleasant transactions over with," Larkin said, standing and shaking Spindle's hand. "I'll have your will drawn up so you can sign it next week. Just come by anytime."

Montgomery ground his teeth together but managed to smile at Spindle as he nodded and walked out the door. He waited until the storekeeper had disappeared down the street before he spoke.

"I told you I wanted to see you earlier, and that means you come to me—I shouldn't have to wait around while you do mundane tasks like Ed Spindle's will."

The lawyer stared at Edmund with a funny expression. "I hadn't noticed before, but there is something different about your face since you got back from your trip. Where did you go, anyway?"

"I'm not here to talk about my face, and where I was is of no importance to you."

"I know what it is," Larkin continued doggedly. "Your nose is different, wider at the bridge. Has it been broken?"

Edmund glared at the rail-thin lawyer, realizing he was going to have to come up with some kind of story, because everyone was commenting on his nose. His anger toward Jonah Tremain was limitless. But he would have to wait for another day to exact his revenge.

"It's nothing. Just a simple carriage accident." He eased himself down in a chair because his ribs were still bothering him. "Now can we get down to business?"

Sam Larkin had not missed the edge to Montgomery's voice. He was more afraid of the banker than of any man he had ever known. Edmund was always in control and controlled everyone. If the people of this town knew just how much they had been manipulated by him, they would be shocked and more than angry.

Larkin sat down at his desk, his hands nervously drumming the surface. "I heard Abby Hunter, er . . . I guess I should say, Abby Tremain, is living at Fort Fannin with her husband."

Fury had control of Edmund, and he grabbed the lawyer's hands to still them by slamming them down on the desk. "Stop that thumping, and don't ever, as long as you live, mention Abby to me again!"

Larkin's usually florid complexion paled, and he ran his hand through his thinning brown hair. He had never seen Edmund in such a state—his eyes were hard and frightening. "I . . . what did you want to speak to me about?"

Edmund closed his eyes, trying to empty his mind of Abby. "I was wondering if you have heard anything from my stepdaughter, Juliana?"

"Not lately."

Edmund smiled. "So it doesn't look like she will be returning to Texas. Not surprising, since she has no family here and nothing to come back to. She never liked me, so she won't be coming back to see me."

"I hope she never comes back."

Edmund laughed, and it wasn't a pretty sound. "I just bet you do. I don't like her any more than she likes me, but she's smart. If she comes back, you may be in for real trouble."

The lawyer stood and started pacing. "You have to help me here, Edmund. I invested her trust fund—that's all."

"You spent it. And you lost it."

"She'll probably look at it that way," he said bitterly.

"When the news gets out, so will everyone else."

"I don't know what I'm going to do."

Edmund cast him a hostile glare. "Will you sit down and stop pacing?" he gritted through his teeth. "Your fidgeting is getting on my nerves."

Larkin did as he was told and clamped his hands in his lap so Edmund couldn't see them trembling. He wished he had a drink—he had a bottle in his drawer, but he couldn't take it out until Edmund left. "I'm scared, Edmund."

"You should be. But I may be able to help you."

"You would help me?"

"For a price."

"I . . . A price?"

"I need legal work done from time to time. It's no secret to you that I want to get my hands on the Half-Moon Ranch, and I may need your help to do it. I know you will be discreet, since you don't want anyone to find out you are a thief." Edmund leaned in closer, his gaze fixed on the sweating lawyer. "You keep my secrets, and I keep yours."

Larkin knew he was making a deal with the devil, but what choice did he have? "I can do that."

"Good."

"If you hear from your stepdaughter that she's coming back, will you let me know?"

Edmund stood and straightened his coat, his cordial smile sliding into place. "If Juliana does come back, I'll be the last person to know."

"You have to keep her away."

"I don't need her here stirring things up any more than you do. I need a clear mind for what I'm about to do." His eyes flashed and he swiveled to face the lawyer. "If it's the last thing I ever do, I will bring down every one of those Hunters!"

Matt saw the bastard as soon as the buckboard entered the main street of Diablo. A hypocrite and a liar, a banker and deacon of the church, Edmund Montgomery gave a bad name to both money and religion.

Standing in front of the bank, oblivious to the people passing behind him, Montgomery waved him down.

His butt sore, Matt shifted on the hard seat. Once he got to the Half-Moon, he would stand for a week. In the meantime, he'd deal with another pain in the same part of his anatomy. With the horse trailer rattling behind the wagon, he reined his team of mules to a halt at the side of the deeply rutted street and stared down at the man who had tried to bring the Hunter ranch to ruin.

Even on the dingy wooden walkway, the banker presented a dignified appearance, tall and stately in his dark suit and paisley vest, lean and tightly muscled despite his age, his blond hair barely streaked with gray.

But looks could be deceiving. Matt was not impressed.

Montgomery glanced curiously at the trailer, but smiled at Matt.

"Is that you, Matt Hunter?" he asked. "I do believe it is. Seems all our chickens are coming home to roost." He chuckled. "You were no more than a raw-boned youngster, last time you were in town. I hardly recognized you."

"I recognized you," Matt said flatly.

Uncertainty darkened Montgomery's pale eyes. But his smile stayed in place.

"Well you should. I've been a friend to your father and your mother, may she rest in peace, since long before you were born."

A bad subject to bring up. The man wasn't as smart as he tried to appear.

"You wanted something?" Matt asked.

Like maybe to apologize for threatening to foreclose on the Half-Moon mortgage the week Jack Hunter went to jail. The years should have blurred his memory, but there were some things a Hunter did not forget.

Maybe the banker didn't know Matt knew. Maybe he thought the youngest Hunter brother, the wild one, hadn't cared.

But Matt cared, all right. He just didn't let it show.

"You'd best mind your manners," Montgomery said. With a crowd gathering around them, he kept his voice low.

It was advice Matt had heard before, advice he usually ignored, but the banker gave him no chance to respond. Nodding toward the back of the wagon, he said, "You wouldn't be pulling a racehorse in that contraption, would you?"

As if he understood the question, Dark Champion whinnied and moved restlessly in the narrow confines of his wooden trailer.

Matt shrugged, letting the horse speak for him.

Montgomery shook his head. "So you really made it to England and back. The betting money around Diablo went against your return."

Matt glanced at the dozen men and women stirring around behind the banker, some trying to look like they weren't listening in, the more honest ones staring outright at him and the trailer. A few he recognized, but there was no one he cared to acknowledge. He shifted the seat, thinking he should have kept riding through town.

Montgomery's eyes narrowed. "Mind if I take a peek inside? Those slats don't allow much of a view."

"Yep," Matt said, adding, lest the banker misunderstand, "I mind."

"Now, now, son, I mean no harm."

"Then look at his tail. It's hanging out the rear. But I ought to warn you, he tends to kick. When he's not dropping horseshit on whoever's nearby."

Someone in the crowd snickered.

"That's considerate of you to warn me," Montgomery said through clenched teeth.

Matt half heard him. The long journey was weighing on him, the ocean sailing, the cross-country train ride, the switch to buckboard at the San Antonio depot. And he hadn't lied. Dark Champion did tend to kick, and to anoint anyone who got too close. He might not be much good at stud service, but he could sling his droppings in a way that raised admiration in onlookers standing out of range.

"If you've got anything to say, Montgomery, then say it. I've still got a few hours to ride."

Montgomery looked as if he were about to speak, but he fell silent for a moment. Matt could see the rage in his eyes. But the banker was a cool one. He got the rage under control.

"I've got lots to say, Matt, but I'll wait until you're more in a mood to listen. Things have changed at the Half-Moon. You'll have to find them out for yourself."

With a sharp nod, he pushed his way through the gathering of townspeople and entered the bank. A lion returning to its den, Matt thought, then changed the comparison. A snake slithering back to its pit.

Turning his attention to the muddy, rutted street, he slapped the reins and left the onlookers without so much as a nod. There wasn't anyone in the town he felt particularly friendly toward. After the shooting, folks hadn't treated the Hunters well, as if the sins of the father were visited upon his offspring.

He had deserved their scorn, more than they knew. But not his brothers. And not Abby.

Only one person had been truly kind to her. Iona Montgomery. If he saw her, he would give her a far warmer greeting than he'd shown her husband.

He made the journey through town as fast as the mule team would allow, ignoring the passing riders and carriages. After England, with its streetlights and tree-lined parks, everything looked drab and poor. Even the new hotel had a thrown-together look to it, not like the centuries-old buildings he'd seen in London.

But Diablo was home, or as close to it as he was likely to get. If it weren't for the people in it, he would have felt nostalgic about his return.

It wasn't until he was out on the road that he felt really good about where he was. Even this close to town, the landscape had a wild look to it, with sharp drops and rocky soil, distant hills, clusters of oak and mesquite and the thick, dark shrubbery of juniper growing close to the road.

A half mile out of town, the road lost some of its sharp dips and curves. When the wagon topped a rise, he could get a view of the rolling, broken country that was in his blood. He took a deep breath. The smell of open air was a fine perfume. He was trying to concentrate on the land and the sky and the air, trying not to speculate about the changes he might find at the end of the journey, changes Montgomery had darkly hinted at, when he heard a high, loud neigh from the horse trailer. It was like nothing he'd heard from Dark Champion before.

By the time he had reined to a halt and jumped to the ground, the trailer was rocking from side to side and the neigh was close to a scream. Slashing hooves kept him at a distance, but he needn't have worried about freeing the stallion. Dark Champion managed that on his own, kicking out the slats and, eyes wild, bounding onto the roadway. With the rope that had secured him trailing on the uneven ground, he took off cross country.

Yelling every obscenity he'd ever heard, Matt cut loose the remains of the trailer from the back of the buckboard, then scrambled onto the seat and took off in pursuit. The weary mules did their best to set a fast pace, but he might as well have been on foot. By the time he got really underway, the racehorse was already out of sight beyond a ridge.

A crushing sense of guilt overcame Juliana. It hit her hard and fast, like a fist squeezing her heart. Dizzy, unable to breathe, she abandoned her unpacking and hurried to the bedroom window. Resting her forehead against the sash, she waited for the attack to pass. These things usually did, after a minute or two.

This one was no exception. Slowly her ragged gasps eased and she returned to sanity. But not total comfort. An ache lingered in her breast, a sense of loss and hurt she doubted would ever go away.

"Mama," she whispered, but of course there was no response. Mama had died months ago, without her only child at her bedside.

"Damn you, Edmund Montgomery," she cried,

wanting to place blame on her stepfather. But it was a shared blame. She should have been aware of her mother's health. Others must have known about Iona Montgomery's illness. They could have let her know. Even in far away Saratoga, Juliana was not unreachable.

But she'd been kept in ignorance. Until the letters, the first informing her of her mother's death, and then weeks later, the second one, the strange communication that had brought on the attacks.

Juliana had been more than grieved. She'd been devastated, and she'd had to leave, to get away from the cocoon of her wealthy widowhood, and the solicitude of her late husband's family. Over their objections, she'd returned to Texas. With her back to the musty upstairs bedroom, she breathed in the fresh air and studied the land that was part of her inheritance. Small by Texas standards, half the size of the neighboring ranch where she'd been born, the Lazy Q had been bought by Harlan on a whim. But after their marriage, they had never lived on it.

For her, the reason had a name: Edmund Montgomery. Her widowed mother's ill-chosen second husband had made her eager to leave the state. Almost a decade later, her memory of him, and a heartbreaking letter, had impelled her return.

Sighing, she stared down at the fenced corral that lay behind the ranch house. Like the rest of the Lazy Q, it showed signs of neglect—too many weeds, too little grass, stretches of barren, hard-packed dirt. But the grass was enough to satisfy the lone horse in its confines, the beloved blood bay mare she had brought with her from the East. Most of her husband's possessions she had been able to sell to her in-laws, including some prime racing stock, but not Pepper. The mare was her pet, her only family, in a way taking the place of the child she'd never had.

Suddenly Pepper's head raised. Even from a distance, Juliana could see the laid-back ears and flared nostrils of the mare. From beyond the corral came the wild neigh of a second horse. In a high whinny Pepper answered the call.

Juliana had been around horses all her life. She knew what was going on. It was impossible. Yet the whinny rang in her ears.

She ran from the room, racing swiftly down the stairs and through the empty house. She burst through the kitchen door into the backyard in time to see a magnificent black stallion soar effortlessly over the corral fence.

"No," she screamed. Lifting her skirts, she darted toward the enclosure. Pepper was too young, too small. The stallion, lathered with sweat, was a monster.

He was also a beauty, but if she'd had a gun, she would have shot him.

Stepping on a middle board of the fence, she bounded over the top, then grabbed at the ground for rocks, dirt, anything to throw, knowing as she did so, her efforts would be futile. But she could not stop. Something primal was burning within her, a ferocious desire to protect what was hers.

She hurled her feeble weapons at the horse, thrusting herself dangerously close to his massive, heaving bulk, aiming for his eyes, but he veered around too quickly for her. The rocks bounced unnoticed off his rippling hide and the dirt did little but stick to the sweat.

"Pepper," she cried, but the mare was too busy whinnying, rolling her head, and stepping sideways, tail shamelessly lifted, to pay her mistress any mind.

The stallion snorted, teeth bared, and shifted his hind quarters about as he pranced toward his destination.

Juliana circled the pair, giving them as narrow a berth as she dared, screaming, flapping her skirt, her heart pounding so loudly in her ears, she could scarcely hear the noises of the lustful horses. Pepper ignored her. The stallion, irritated, lashed out with a vicious hoof, coming close to her head. She stumbled backward and sat hard on the ground.

"Kick him," she cried out, but to her own ears the order was half spirited. A well-placed hoof in the stallion's distended penis would disable him, even render him permanently impotent, but the mare showed no inclination to discourage him.

Instead, more than a ton of horse flesh, male and female, pranced and flexed muscles, keening in a language anyone, rancher or not, would understand. The ground beneath her trembled from their zeal.

With the air full of neighs and snorts and whinnies, dirt from the long-neglected corral stirred into choking gray clouds, she watched in horror as the stallion mounted her precious virginal Pepper, landing against her spread haunches with a force that should have collapsed her.

But the mare held strong, eager as he, eyes equally wild. With his powerful forelegs hanging limply against the mare's flanks, he rutted, again and again, a thousand times, his massive body shuddering in the throes of lust.

Juliana watched in horror. She could not look away.

Suddenly, shockingly, he stopped the rutting and collapsed backward, spent, his head low, a groan replacing the high-pitched whinnies of moments past. And then came silence, as deafening as the wild lust sounds, the air heavy with the scent of horse and sex.

Turning his backside to Pepper, the stallion walked desultorily to the fence and stopped, his attention focused on the rolling land beyond the corral, no thought given to the mare, not so much as a bob of the head in her direction.

In a way he reminded Juliana of her late husband, with one exception. Harlan Rains had never shown so much fervor when he mounted his wife. But he had shown nonchalance in the aftermath.

It was a stupid thought. She had no idea where it came from. With a sigh, she pulled herself to her feet, brushing the loosened hair from her face, smudging a cheek in the process. Her once fine silk dress, a shade of amber that Harlan had said brought out the color of her eyes, was soiled beyond repair. In bounding over the fence, she had caught the hem on a loose nail. The tear could not be mended.

The damage was of little note; she had a wardrobe full of similar dresses. And what use did she have for such finery in the life she was determined to live?

She shook off a fleeting moment of self-pity, an emotion far less welcome than the burden of guilt that had brought her back to Texas. When she walked over to Pepper, the mare had the grace to bow her head low, not in the nonchalant weariness of the stallion, but as if in contrition. Or was her mistress visiting upon her pet a wished-for regret?

She fingered the mare's dark mane, grateful that the stallion hadn't bitten her neck as was often the case at the moment of ejaculation. Indeed, Pepper looked remarkably unchanged. There was not even a smear of blood where she had been penetrated for the first time. A quick glance as Juliana walked to the mare had revealed the flesh swollen and red, but from friction, not broken skin.

"He really did it."

Startled, Juliana looked beyond the mare to the man standing at the outside edge of the corral. Tall and lean, yet projecting a sense of powerful muscle, his collar-length black hair unkempt, his face bristled, he presented a picture of male determination rather like that of the stallion.

Not that he was equally beautiful. But he almost was.

What if he bounded over the fence? A tingle not totally akin to fear whispered through her. If she had a gun . . . well, she didn't know exactly what she would do, but, isolated as she was, she would feel more secure.

His words registered.

"If you're speaking of the stallion, he most definitely assaulted my mare."

His thick-lashed eyes flicked to the mare. "By invitation."

"Pepper couldn't be in season. She's too young, barely past two. Besides, it's already fall, much too late in the year for breeding."

"Not in Texas. And she looks ripe enough."

He might have been speaking of the horse, but his eyes were on her. Easing out of his leather jacket, he laid it over the top of the fence and rested his booted foot on the bottom rail. He was wearing a black shirt and dark trousers; they fit him like a glove.

Juliana's stomach knotted. Her trigger finger wasn't the only part of her that itched.

She kept a sigh to herself. What was done was done. Her task now was to deal with it as best she could.

Which meant showing no sign of weakness. If Harlan Rains had taught her anything, it was that. Not that he gave her much opportunity to exhibit strength. But he was no longer around.

"If there's a foal, it's mine," she said.

"For the usual stud fee, of course," he threw back as coolly as she.

"You're crazy."

His expression remained mild, noncommittal, and she caught the hint of a twitch in his lips.

"I've been called worse," he said.

He was not a man easy to insult. She would have to try harder.

"I don't know who you are, but you and your horse are not welcome at the Lazy Q."

"Tell that to Dark Champion here."

"I'm speaking to the one who's supposed to control him."

"Not after he got a whiff of your mare. We must have been close to two miles away." From halfway across the corral she could see the gleam in his eye. "Nothing like the call of flesh to flesh."

"Horse flesh."

"What else?" he asked, all innocence. "By the way, he was wearing a rope. Have you seen it? No matter. I'll add it to your bill."

"You really are crazy."

"Then there's the trailer he kicked to hell and gone. And the wear and tear on the mules and wagon. After your mare perfumed the air, I had to take off after him cross country. Broke a wheel, too, and exhausted the mules. They're at the front of the house, in case you're thinking I dropped out of the sky. I've some supplies in the wagon, and a valise. I'm hoping they'll be safe enough unattended. It'll take me a while to get them off your land."

"You're enjoying this, aren't you?"

"More than you know."

"Do you get a vicarious thrill when your beast here performs?"

"The beast, as you call him, wasn't supposed to—" He shook his head. "Never mind. You should be the one who was thrilled, catching the action up close the way you did."

Juliana's cheeks flushed. "I beg your pardon!"

He had the decency to shake his head. "Sorry. That wasn't gentlemanly of me."

"Whoever you are, I doubt you've ever been regarded as a gentleman."

His eyes narrowed. "You don't know who I am, do you?"

Difficult though it was—he had a maddening habit of studying her as if he could see through any pretense—she studied him in much the same way. He was as lean and muscled and rough-edged as she had first thought, but another quality lurked behind his hazel eyes and sharply honed face, a hint of danger similar to heat, as if anyone who got too close to him would get burned.

Which was no problem for her. If she ever saw him again, she would remember to keep her distance.

"No, I don't know you. Should I?"

With consummate grace he leaped over the fence and started walking toward her. Instinctively she took a step backward. The horses drifted deeper into the corral, as if determined to remain separate from the humans as well as each other.

He stopped an arm's length away. "It's been a long time, Juliana."

Her name was soft on his lips, almost lilting. She swallowed and continued to study him. Something about the set of his mouth stole her attention. A name occurred. Impossible, but it wouldn't go away.

She closed her eyes and pictured a lanky youth, mostly gangling arms and legs, hair longer than he was wearing it now, peach fuzz on a rounder face where now dark bristles grew. There was a hardness around his eyes she did not remember, and fine lines that testified to the passing of ten years.

"Matt Hunter," she said in almost a whisper. The wild Hunter boy, only a year older than she, the drinker and carouser at far too young an age. "You filled out," she added in what had to be the understatement of the year.

His gaze drifted down the length of her, from the loosened fair hair to her dust-covered shoes, lingering at places on her soiled gown she would rather he not notice.

"So did you," he said.

The dry autumn air crackled between them.

"I was sixteen the last time I saw you. It was—" she began, then broke off.

"It was at my mother's funeral," he said, finishing for her.

Dangerous ground, far too delicate for her to trod. At least he had been at the service. Her absence at her own mother's burial was part of her crushing guilt.

"You were the wild one, weren't you? If anyone had asked, I would have predicted an early death for you. That, or prison."

"Prison was my father's fate."

She smoothed back her hair. "I'm sorry," she said, genuinely contrite. "I'm not handling this very well."

"No one does."

He wasn't making this any easier for her. But why should he? He was a Hunter. For years, from half a continent away, she had believed them her friends and, more importantly, the friends of her mother.

She had reason to think differently now.

And what had gotten into her that led to this almost civilized exchange? It was as if Matt Hunter had willed it, from the moment he said her name. He was manipulating her, as easily as his stallion had manipulated her mare.

A small voice reminded her Pepper had been a willing participant. It only showed the trouble a female could get into when cooperating with a male.

She thrust a hand into the pocket of her gown and felt the letter, the devastating one, the last communication she had received from her mother, the last words, as far as Juliana knew, Iona Montgomery had written before she died.

The feel of the wrinkled paper against her fingertips reminded her of why she was here. Back straight, she hurried to the corral gate and opened it. Much to her relief, when she whistled, Pepper trotted to her side.

"Please leave," she said to Matt. "I'm sorry about the broken wheel, but you used to be good at getting yourself out of difficult situations. I don't imagine that has changed."

Without waiting for a reply, she hurried toward the barn, stopping halfway across the weed-choked yard at the back of the house. She could feel his eyes on her back. Something she did not entirely understand made her turn.

"Care for the mules as you see fit. The water trough's full and there's hay in the barn. Take what you need."

He nodded, but she wasn't done.

"Until you can get the wheel repaired, I will, of course, have to charge rent for the space your wagon is occupying, if, as you said, it's on my land."

He registered no surprise.

"How much?"

"I want to be fair. The stud fee and cost of the rope should even things out. And, as I said, I keep the foal."

She waited for an argument.

Instead he eyed her carefully, as if trying to figure her out. "I heard your husband died. How long ago?"

The question startled her. She answered without thinking.

"Close to two years."

"An older man, right?"

By thirty years, she could have told him, but the detail was no one's business but her own.

"No new fiancé?" he asked. "No one waiting to take his place?"

"I hardly see how that has anything to do with anything," she said, puzzled.

"Just trying to understand why you're so prickly."

Her puzzlement did not last long. Matt Hunter assumed abstinence was the cause of her attitude, making her prickly, as he put it. Did he really think she needed to feel once again the arms of a man?

He was crazy. And he couldn't be more wrong.

How long have you been without a woman?

She almost put the question to him. But this very day he'd probably stopped by the saloon in Diablo. He could even have spent last night in one of the upstairs rooms. On her ride through town yesterday, she'd noticed the Lone Star open and doing a lively business.

Staring at him, imagining a repressed smirk on his ruggedly handsome face, she didn't pretend innocence.

"You were insufferable as a young man, Matt Hunter. You haven't changed."

Without waiting for a reply, she hurried into the barn, Pepper following, once again subdued and obedient.

Inside the darkened interior, a figure moved from the shadows. She stifled a gasp, recognizing the hired hand arranged by Sam Larkin, Diablo's lone attorney, after she wrote him concerning her return.

It took a minute to remember his name.

"Kane," she said, using the only identity he had given her. "I thought you were out on the range."

"I just got here. You were busy. I figured you didn't want me to interfere. You'll find, Miz Rains, I know my place."

He sounded docile enough, a lowly work hand trying to do his job. But he had a dark, grizzled look about him that didn't go with the voice. When Larkin brought him out late yesterday, he assured her Kane would do what was needed at the Lazy Q. Besides, he said, the man was the best he could come up with on short notice. She needed to reserve judgment.

She could not be so generous with Matt Hunter. Once a scoundrel, always a scoundrel, she reminded herself. It was a truth she had bitterly learned for herself.

Half-Moon Ranch

Somewhere in the lush grasslands of the Texas hill country is a place where the sun once shone on love and prosperity, while the night hid murder and mistrust. There, three brothers and a sister fight to hold their family together, struggle to keep their ranch solvent, while they await the return of the one person who can shed light on the secrets of the past.

From the bestselling authors
who brought you the *Secret Fires* series comes . . .

The Agreement

SECRET FIRES

Constance O'Banyon

In the midst of the vast, windswept Texas plains stands a ranch wrested from the wilderness with blood, sweat and tears. It is the shining legacy of Thomas McBride to his five living heirs. But along with the fertile acres and herds of cattle, each will inherit a history of scandal, lies and hidden lust that threatens to burn out of control.

Lauren McBride left the Circle M as a confused, lonely girl of fifteen. She returns a woman—beautiful, confident, certain of her own mind. And the last thing she will tolerate is a marriage of convenience, arranged by her pa to right past wrongs. Garret Lassiter broke her heart once before. Now only a declaration of everlasting love will convince her to become his bride.

___4878-7 $5.99 US/$6.99 CAN

TEXAS PROUD

CONSTANCE O'BANYON

Rachel Rutledge has her gun trained on Noble Vincente. With one shot, she will have her revenge on the man who killed her father. So what is stopping her from pulling the trigger? Perhaps it is the memory of Noble's teasing voice, his soft smile, or the way one glance from his dark Spanish eyes once stirred her foolish heart to longing. Yes, she loved him then . . . as much as she hates him now. One way or another, she will wound him to the heart—if not with bullets, then with her own feminine wiles. But as Rachel discovers, sometimes the line between love and hate is too thinly drawn.

___4492-7 $5.99 US/$6.99 CAN

San Antonio Rose

Constance O'Banyon

Sam Houston knows he needs all the help he can get to defeat Santa Anna's seasoned fighting men. But who is the mysterious San Antonio Rose, who emerges from the mist like a ghostly figure to offer her aid? Fluent in Spanish, Ian McCain is the one man who can ferret out the truth about the flamboyant dancer. Working under Santa Anna's very nose, he observes how the dark-haired beauty inflames her audience, how she captivates El Presidente himself. But as she disappears with a single yellow rose, he knows that despite the tangled web of loyalties that ensnare them, he will taste those tempting lips, know every secret of that alluring body. And before she proves just how effective she can be, he will pluck for himself the San Antonio Rose.

___4563-X $5.99 US/$6.99 CAN

TYKOTA'S WOMAN

CONSTANCE O'BANYON

Tykota Silverhorn has lived among the white man long enough. It is time to return to his people. Time to fulfill his destiny as the legendary tribal chieftain he was born to become. So what need has he for the pretty white woman riding beside him in the stagecoach, trembling beneath his dark gaze? Yet when Apaches attack the travelers, when one of his own betrays him, Tykota has to rescue soft, innocent Makinna Hillyard, teach her to survive the savage wilderness . . . and his own savage heart. For, shorn of the veneer of civilization, raw emotions rock Tykota. And suddenly, against his will, blue-eyed Makinna is his woman to protect, to command . . . to possess.

___4715-2 $5.99 US/$6.99 CAN

Dorchester Publishing Co., Inc.
P.O. Box 6640
Wayne, PA 19087-8640

Please add $1.75 for shipping and handling for the first book and $.50 for each book thereafter. NY, NYC, and PA residents, please add appropriate sales tax. No cash, stamps, or C.O.D.s. All orders shipped within 6 weeks via postal service book rate. Canadian orders require $2.00 extra postage and must be paid in U.S. dollars through a U.S. banking facility.

Name_____
Address_____
City_____State_____Zip_____
I have enclosed $_____ in payment for the checked book(s).
Payment <u>must</u> accompany all orders. ❑ Please send a free catalog.

LOVE'S FIERY JEWEL
ELAINE BARBIERI

When Damien Straith, captain of the *Sally*, first meets Amethyst, named for the rare color of her bewitching eyes, she is no more than a thin child with a tongue sharper than the icy winter wind cutting through Charleston Harbor.

Upon their chance meeting eight years later, Damien can see she's a child no more, but a raven-curled, intoxicating woman, fiery-tempered and ripe for love.

Amethyst tries not to be affected by Damien's piercing gray gaze and muscular body, but her passion burns fiercely. Delirious with longing, yet afraid of the consequences, Amethyst hates the power Damien holds over her body—a power which will lay bare her passions and let the mysterious captain turn pirate and plunder her heart.

___52391-4 $5.99 US/$6.99 CAN